THE GENERAL OF CARACAS

A SPY NOVEL

OLIVER JARDINE SERIES
BOOK 2

LACHLAN PAGE

WJ PRESS

Published by WJ Press in 2022.

Author Website — www.LachlanPageAuthor.com

eISBN (ebook): 978-0-6489669-3-7
ISBN (Print-Paperback): 978-0-6489669-4-4
ISBN (Print-Hardback): 978-0-6489669-5-1

"America is ungovernable; those who have served the revolution have plowed the sea."

— *Simón Bolívar*, Venezuelan military and political leader, and liberator of Colombia, Venezuela, Ecuador, Panama, Peru, and Bolivia.

PROLOGUE

THE BLUE POLICE HELICOPTER CIRCLED LOW IN THE sky, gliding across the Caracas skyline. It fleeted past the skyscrapers of now-nationalised corporations, fluttered over the twin towers of the decaying national oil company on Veracruz Avenue, and hovered amongst the empty apartment buildings of the five million Venezuelans who had fled. Below, confused onlookers filmed the spectacle with their mobile phones from the Bolívar-statued parks, on cement balconies, through office windows and while idling down the humid streets, where the sweet scents of mango and freshly baked bread had been replaced by rotting garbage and tear gas. There had been months of unrelenting protests on the streets of Caracas and chaos still reigned.

At first the helicopter appeared to be a regular police operation to monitor the protests, until two men in military fatigues slung open its side door to reveal a banner reading, '*350 Libertad*'—a reference to Article 350 of the Constitution, the so-called Magna Carta of Venezuela which called on

1

the Venezuelan people to not recognise a regime that went against the republic's democratic values and diminished their human rights.

As the blue banner fluttered in the breeze, residents poured into the streets, waving Venezuelan flags as if watching Miguel Cabrera hit a home run in the Major Leagues. Jubilant cheers rang out throughout the city. It became increasingly apparent this was not a regular police or military operation against *el pueblo*—the people. This was not the *Policia Nacional Bolivariana* nor the *Guardia Nacional* aiming to quell dissidence on behalf of the government and the president.

There was a hint of rebellion in the air, seeping its way through the tear gas.

The helicopter continued to cut through the sky, the chopping hum of its blades echoing through the valley, pulsing like a *cumbia* beat as it headed for Venezuela's Supreme Court. The courts were an institutional ally of the dictatorial Madera regime and had recently stripped the now-exiled Prosecutor General of her authority, handing it to a key Madera crony. Hovering above the courts, the helicopter released four grenades, creating a lingering rumble. Later, it would be revealed they were flash grenades. It was attention the instigators wanted, not destruction.

As the smoke from the flash grenades cleared, the helicopter banked sideways, the verdant mountains of El Ávila National Park floating in the background, as it turned its mission towards the Ministry of the Interior—the key security apparatus of the state, directly under the command of the president. Here, one of the men in the helicopter unleashed fifteen shots—blanks—from high-powered rifles. Each shot rang out in a steady, rhythmic flow. The perpetrators were sending a clear message to the increasingly tyrannical regime of the current president and his corrupt institutional allies. A warning to the corrupt Supreme Court for uprooting the democratically elected, opposition-held National Assembly— the nation's Parliament. And a threat to the Ministry of the Interior whose repressive security forces did the president's bidding. It was an explicit forewarning that the Bolivarian revolution had come and gone, spawning a tropical tyranny masquerading as a socialist utopia. And *el pueblo* wouldn't take it anymore.

Almost simultaneously, in a recorded *Instagram* videocast, a man dressed in a forensic police investigator's uniform appeared online, flanked by four men in black balaclavas holding AK-47 assault rifles. After identifying himself as the pilot of the helicopter now flying through the sky, he reiterated his aerial actions in words. Reading from notes held in front of him, his piercing blue eyes threw a penetrating gaze down the barrel of the camera lens. "Venezuelans, we speak to you as representatives of the state; we are a coalition of military officers, police officers and civilians. We are fighting for harmony and against this provisional criminal government. We are not against the military or state forces; we are against the tyranny of the current government."

The message, in action and words, was now complete, not only to the *Caraqueños*—as residents of Caracas are known— and Venezuelans, but to the entire world who watched via social media. The operation hadn't just been televised; it had been tweeted, live-streamed, reeled, TikToked and filtered in sepia.

As the helicopter continued to circle, eventually fleeing into the mountains, government troops from the Venezuelan National Guard surrounded the opposition-controlled National Assembly. The Leader of the Opposition, Frankie Guerra, appeared in the car park, shouting into a mobile phone which was live-streaming on *Facebook*, "The world is watching; please allow us to do what we were elected to do."

Briefly looking over his shoulder in fear, he continued, "One of our deputies was hit by a National Guard member. We are the elected members of the National Assembly and we will stay here and stand against this tyranny created by Presidente Madera and the Ministry of the Interior. We call on *las fuerzas armadas* to stand with us as representatives of the Venezuelan people. If you choose not to, know that you will pay for your crimes if you are accomplices to this dictator."

Online, a *Twitter* storm ensued, creating a flourishing rumour mill which ground the truth down until the public would only believe what they wanted to believe: confirmation bias at its worst. Tweets from opposition politicians spread rapidly like bullets before being deflected with posts by government supporters claiming CIA and foreign powers' involvement in a murky operation to overthrow the president's regime. Cutting through the noise, a video of President Madera speaking solemnly to the camera was shared online. "If Venezuela is plunged into chaos and violence and the Bolivarian revolution destroyed, we will go to combat. We will never give up. What can't be done with votes, we will do with arms. We will liberate the fatherland with arms."

The sliver of hope the helicopter represented was extinguished as quickly as it had begun, with the president's message clear that he would continue with the decision by the government-backed Supreme Court to dissolve the opposition-held National Assembly, assume extraordinary powers, and then convene a handpicked constituent assembly to rewrite the constitution. To many it was straight out of the Dictator's Playbook: stack the courts with your supporters, lock up your opponents, dissolve Parliament and change the constitution. A self-coup, or *autogolpe*, as people would say in the streets.

In the aftermath, the protests continued. But this time the government crackdown was even more brutal and repressive.

Opposition leaders, ex-mayors, governors, dissenting military personnel and instigators of the protests were rounded up. Some were simply warned and threatened; others were beaten. Some were condemned to the notorious *Helicoide* prison where they were tortured and held by agents of the feared *Servicio Bolivariano de Inteligencia Nacional*, the SEBIN, as they attempted to glean information from the so-called saboteurs. Among the prisoners was a retired general who had watched as his fatherland, his *patria*, slowly slipped into chaos and disorder and was now deteriorating into a dictatorship. As he was dragged from his home, he vowed one day to escape and to find a way to end the regime of Tomás Madera Toros and to save Venezuela from the failed state it had become.

CHAPTER 1

San Antonio de Táchira (Venezuela/Colombia Border)

I YEAR LATER

THE DOG'S BARK WAFTED THROUGH THE NIGHT AIR, the only other sound the soft crunch of rocks and dirt below the man's shuffling feet. His limbs felt heavy like his hands and feet were made of lead, pulling down at his extremities. His calves burnt and his Achilles tendons felt like tight rubber bands. *Being locked up will do that to you*, he thought. He stopped for a moment and sucked in a few gulps of fresh air, appreciating the glowing full moon among the clouds. It shone down on the riverbed of smooth rocks scattered amongst the sandy, reedy riverbed below him. After a year in the *Ramo Verde* military prison outside of Caracas, he'd developed a new-found appreciation for things most people take for granted—clean air and to look at the sky. His gaze shifted downwards to the path ahead. *Ya casi*, he said to himself. Almost there.

Pushing forward, he could hear the slow flow of waist-high water in the *Rio Táchira*—the border between San Antonio de Táchira in Venezuela and Cúcuta in Colombia. The river rarely raged and was easy to cross, more like the memory of a river than a real river, although in the wet season, it could be dicey. As he descended an embankment, darkness swept across the land. Clouds drifted through the sky, covering the moon like a blanket. The fresh night air turned ashy as smoke from nearby campfires became trapped under the layer of clouds. The man's throat began to itch and he stopped momentarily to sip water from a metal container which he took from his backpack. The water sloshed as he raised the container to his lips and drank in large gulps. As he screwed the lid back on, he strained his eyes to see how far it was to the other side of the river, then heard a sound behind him. He crouched, remaining still in the darkness amongst a clump of reeds. He heard a rustling sound and muffled voices floating in the air. His breathing slowed as he felt a few large raindrops land on his head; they splattered on the rocks and sand of the surrounding path. An empty tin can rattled across the rocky ground, instantly reminding him of the metal bowl scraping across the floor of his prison cell. The memory triggered an acrid metallic taste on his tongue from the stale black beans and crunchy rice he was served in a metal dish while locked up.

Was he compromised? Was a border patrol nearby? The National Guard? SEBIN?

He heard the voices more clearly now and lifted his head above a bush, looking to the right. With the cloud cover, the night was black. Figures moved nearby. A low rumble sounded, followed by a flash of lightning which illuminated his surroundings. In that moment he saw the source of the voices: a young father and mother, each carrying a suitcase. They were followed by two young children, a boy and a girl, each with little backpacks. The girl carried a small plush toy rabbit nestled in her left arm. Its floppy ears bounced as she walked, its black plastic eyes shining briefly as if alive.

He rose to his feet, relieved. *Migrants, not unlike myself*, he thought. But not wanted fugitives. It was not an uncommon sight. In the past years millions of migrants had crossed the same border, hoping for better lives in Colombia or onwards to Peru, Chile, the USA, and Spain—anywhere but Venezuela. Unlike other borders around the world, the Colombian authorities allowed Venezuelans to freely cross, taking in millions of their neighbours.

With the coast clear, the man stood and looked left towards the *Simon Bolívar* International Bridge—the official international border crossing between Venezuela and Colombia. Families wheeled suitcases from Venezuela to Colombia as touts offered accommodation and taxis. The only people going the other way carried large plastic tubs and empty two-litre Coca-Cola bottles to fill with dirt-cheap petroleum. Soldiers from both countries stood around, some looking down at their mobile phones, others chatting with each other or fielding questions from the stream of people. On the Colombian side, a police tent was illuminated, the officers equally as bored as the soldiers. A Colombian coat of arms was printed on the tent as if welcoming him. It wasn't the Colombian authorities that he was worried about; it was the Venezuelans he feared—his own *patriotas*. In particular the *Servicio Bolivariano de Inteligencia Nacional* or SEBIN, Venezuela's Bolivarian National Intelligence Service. They'd become the attack dogs for the government, first with the ex-president, the now-deceased *Comandante* Sánchez, a messianic, former paratrooper who led the socialist Bolivarian Revolution, and then with the current president, Tomás Madera Toros, Sánchez's handpicked successor. The Madera regime had only strengthened its grip on the country and dissent of the ruling party was not tolerated, nor anything that would damage the cult of personality of the late President Sánchez. As the banner now floating above the Venezuelan customs post said: *En esta Aduana NO se habla mal de Sánchez. At this customs checkpoint, you don't talk badly about Comandante Sánchez.* That is why he was here in *las trochas*—the name given to the labyrinthine of pathways that criss-crossed the border, smuggling petrol and people to Colombia, and everything else towards Venezuela.

He was a wanted man. A dissident. Someone who *had* spoken badly of the former president, the current president, and anyone who he thought was betraying *la patria*.

He peered right now along the open expanse of the river, away from the border bridge. He could vaguely see the small fires of people camped on the riverbank among the reeds. Another flash of lightning revealed the migrant family continuing their dash across the riverbed, moving swiftly as if they already knew the way. He turned his head now, looking straight ahead towards the Colombian side.

Where are they? he thought, his eyes squinting to see through the darkness. He spent several seconds scanning for a sign, a light, a beacon, anything. Then he clicked his tongue in annoyance and moved forward. He needed to move more rapidly, if he was spotted; then *se acabó la vaina*. It would be over.

Another large flash ripped through the night, revealing a dark swirling mass of clouds accumulating in the sky. A low rumble shook the ground followed by another crack of thunder as the large raindrops increased their descent, coming down larger and wetter in soft thuds on the ground around him. Then, as if the thunder had summoned them, a pair of headlights flashed twice from the Colombian side. He stayed still, watching. After a few moments, they flashed again and then there were three flashes in quick succession. It was the signal he'd been waiting for. *They've arrived, and the heavens are about to open. Time to move.*

The man moved quickly over the dry part of the riverbed, through the reeds and the sand, his backpack rocking from side to side as he ran. He could feel the manila folder in his backpack moving as he ran: a cache of government documents he had managed to hide before being arrested. Another flash in the sky, then a crack of thunder erupted across the night. He heard loud voices but didn't stop. He glanced back as he ran, seeing torches waving through the trees and bushes lining the river. He heard the dog bark louder as the voices also increased in volume. This time the voices were not those of a family, fleeing a corrupt nation, nor the murmurs of vulnerable migrants. These voices were deeper, shouts of authority. He'd passed the midway point of the river and was almost in Colombian territory now, he thought. Another flash of lightning lit up the sky, illuminating all around as the voices converted into shouts, echoing through the night air and pricking his ears as loud as the thunder.

"*Alli esta! Cruzando el rio,*" they said. There he is! Crossing the river.

They had spotted him.

He felt his feet submerge in water but continued onward without hesitation, swiftly plunging into the river. The icy water reached his mid-thighs, numbing his legs. The stones underneath were slippery but manageable with his boots. He pushed through as if moving in slow motion, forcing his body against the resistance of the water. Eventually, he felt the water give way to dirt and sand, and he scrambled up the bank on the Colombian side of the river.

Sano y salvo, he thought. Safe and sound. Those cowards will know better than to enter Colombian territory. Tensions were already high enough between the two countries without inflaming them with an incursion into *la tierra querida*—the Promised Land—as Colombia was known.

A small spotlight swivelled around from the bridge now, scanning the river but not finding him as he scrambled up the riverbank. Looking back and with the residual light from the spotlight, he could make out several figures standing on the Venezuelan embankment. Thunder erupted again, emanating through the night with a low crack, and with it, he heard four crisp gunshots ring out. Rocks around his feet exploded, bursting up into the air.

Hijueputa, he said to himself. I *may be safe from capture, but that still doesn't mean they can't pick me off like a little metal duck at a fair.* The four shots had been perfectly masked by the thunder; the soldiers on the nearby bridge stood as usual, glancing down at their phones, occasionally inspecting a passing car. Another crack of thunder and three more shots were fired in quick bursts, tickling the ground near his feet. Tiny rocks ricocheted, brushing his ankles.

On flat ground now, he sprinted towards the headlights, the loose rocks under his feet causing him to slip and slide along. It didn't matter; he propelled his burning legs forward —as long as it was forward, he didn't care. His breathing increased as he sucked in air in dramatic gasps. The large drops had increased and were now coming down in a steady downpour, the slippery loose rocks merging with the mud sticking to his boots. He saw the headlights ahead become larger and larger until he saw the outline of a vehicle. He ran towards it; a large SUV came into view. He arrived at the side of the vehicle and skidded to a halt as the back passenger door swung open. He launched himself inside as the vehicle revved and backed up, throwing a U-turn and speeding off down the dusty side road.

The man's breath came in hard and fast as he lay across the

back seats of the SUV in darkness. He turned his head to the front of the SUV. A man wearing a baseball cap in the front passenger seat switched on the internal light and turned around to greet him. "General Angel Pereira?"

"*Quien más*?" Who else?

The man smiled warmly and nodded. "Welcome to the Republic of Colombia."

CHAPTER 2

Villa de Leyva, Colombia

THEY WERE ON EDGE, EVERY ONE OF THEM. SOME paced back and forth, some jostled for position. Others stood still, appreciating the calm before the impending onslaught.

A short, plump, elderly woman wearing a woollen poncho, known as a *ruana*, held a small string of rosary beads in her hand. Her rough thumb pushed the beads downwards, one by one, through her closed fist. Two teenage boys with backpacks looked ahead along the road, their eyes full of a patient wisdom that only befalls those that must take up responsibilities at a young age, perhaps to support a husbandless mother they love dearly or a young family. Around them the sky was a soft orange with streaks of pink as the sun set. Tiny yellow lights appeared in the valley below, like hovering fireflies. Silky grey streams of smoke began their journey skyward from small chimneys poked into terracotta tiled roofs atop whitewashed stone cottages. A slight chill made its presence felt as light faded to dark.

Despite the tranquil setting, the air had a feeling of impending unease. Something was coming.

In the distance, two round yellow spheres appeared, gradually becoming bigger and bigger. A soft murmur began amongst the crowd, "*Allí viene, allí viene.*" Here it comes, here it comes. A tall man with light brown hair cast his eyes sideways towards the woman beside him, a wry smile on his face. The woman looked up at him through glassy eyes, her wavy hair bouncing gently in the wind.

It was almost time.

The yellow spheres abruptly morphed into headlights as the bus screeched to a halt near the small group mingling on the side of the road. The formerly patient mob pushed, heaved and spilled forward towards the door. Bony elbows flew in the air as short, thick-set bodies pushed and nudged, jostling for position. It would have seemed like an unruly crowd were it not for the polite, old-fashioned utterances from the residents of *Boyacá*, a verdant, mountainous region north of Bogotá. A flurry of *permisos* (excuse me) and *que pena con sumerced* (sorry, your mercy) floated through the air as polite chaos reigned at the small bus stop.

The tall man and his partner sat back and watched the mayhem. Normally it would annoy them, but they were relaxed and on holiday, so they waited patiently. After a few minutes they managed to find a seat together towards the back of the bus.

Slumping into his seat, Oliver Jardine asked: "Are you sure the car will be alright there?"

"I hope so," replied Veronica Velasco as she slid in next to him, glancing out of the window at the hire car they were leaving at the small repair shop on the side of the road.

"Can't believe it just gave out on us like that," said Jardine shaking his head.

Veronica shrugged. "At least we'll still make the wedding."

The bus rumbled along towards *Villa de Leyva*, a small colonial town of whitewashed buildings and cobblestone streets. It had once been a retreat for military officers but now it was a retreat for well-heeled Bogotanos to spend the weekend and a popular wedding spot. Sitting at the back of the bus, the green hills of the Boyacá department flashed by as they rolled past the *Puente Boyacá*, a small bridge and memorial park commemorating victory at a key battle in the independence wars: The Battle of Boyacá. Mist spread around the large statue of Simon Bolivar surrounded by five angels depicting the countries he liberated: Colombia, Venezuela, Peru, Ecuador, and Bolivia.

It was this symbol of independence that compelled Oliver Jardine and Veronica Velasco to think of their own independence. A year earlier they had moved to Spain to run a small rural guesthouse. Their move had been the result of Jardine quitting his intelligence analyst position with MI6 in Bogotá and Veronica leaving her position as a lawyer at the prestigious firm *Garcia y Velasquez*. A string of past events had shaken their lives, and they had come to the realisation that the usual rat race wasn't for them. Leaving two well-paid, stable jobs to buy and run a small guesthouse in rural Spain was just the shake-up they needed. Now as they rolled into a small colonial town in Colombia for a friend's wedding, they felt as if they'd never left.

Arriving in town and disembarking from the bus, they found their hotel, unpacked and decided to stroll through the town centre to grab a quick bite to eat. Later they were due at a small get-together on the wedding eve for drinks. Entering the *plaza mayor*, the enormous cobblestone square at the centre of town, the stars hovered close as if they were a ceiling. In the distance, fireworks erupted, peppering the night sky with an extra fizzle of light. Families strolled the square eating ice cream as two men dressed in thick woollen *ruanas* played guitars on the church steps. A group of teenagers sat beside the musicians swigging from a hidden bottle of *aguardiente*— an anise-flavoured liquor made from sugarcane. In front of their group, a father and son attempted to fly a kite as a mother and daughter stood by, laughing at their unsuccessful attempts. Jardine and Veronica wobbled over the large cobblestones as they breathed in the peaceful surroundings. Moments later they found a Venezuelan *arepa rellen*a restaurant in a small interior courtyard.

The *arepa* is a thick cornmeal tortilla-like disc, a staple in Colombia and Venezuela. A fierce battle rages between Colombia and Venezuela over who invented it and whose is better. A popular Venezuelan version involves slicing the disc open and stuffing it with your chosen ingredients, known as an *arepa rellena*. After perusing the menu and ordering, two stuffed *arepas* arrived promptly.

Jardine took a bite and chewed. He waited for Veronica to take a bite of hers and then said, "Venezuela wins."

Veronica chewed, swallowed, and then asked. "What do you mean?" She eyed him suspiciously and took another bite of her cheese and ham stuffed *arepa*.

"The *arepa* wars," replied Jardine.

Veronica continued chewing and didn't speak, frowning at Jardine.

Before she could respond, the owner of the restaurant approached. "Is everything to your liking?" The man's expression was sincere; his eyes open wide like two large saucers, his smile a wedge of ivory gleaming at them.

Veronica's expression changed from icy to warm as she smiled at the owner. "Of course. These *arepas* are delicious."

The owner exhaled, relieved, and then smiled. "I'm glad you are enjoying them. From where you are visiting us this fine evening?"

"I'm from Bogota," said Veronica, the daggers still

converted into a brimming, charming smile. "And he," the warm smile converted back to ice as she looked towards Jardine, "is *English*." She punched Jardine's shoulder playfully. "But we live in Spain now. We're here for the wedding. Just up the hill at the Hotel..." Veronica stopped as Jardine kicked her softly under the table. "A hotel just up the hill..." she finished, her voice trailing off.

Old habits don't disappear overnight and Jardine's preference for discretion still prevailed, despite having left the employ of MI6 more than a year ago. It was never a good idea to let a stranger know where you were staying or going.

"*Que bueno*. Can I get you another drink?" asked the owner, filling the awkward silence.

Jardine ordered a Club Colombia Roja beer and Veronica a glass of Cabernet Sauvignon. The owner turned and walked to the bar. A few moments later, he returned.

"Are you from Caracas?" Jardine asked the man as he received the bottle of beer.

"*Sí, señor*," he replied, placing the glass of red wine in front of Veronica.

"This might sound like a silly question, but how are things there?"

The owner exhaled loudly and shook his head. "It can only be described as chaos, pure chaos. I'm lucky to have gotten out and set up this restaurant." The owner looked around the room. "It has become something of a refuge for fleeing Venezuelans."

Jardine nodded. It was true. He had heard that approximately five million people had left Venezuela since ex-President Sánchez came to power. At first, those with means escaped to areas such as *Cedritos* in Bogotá (unofficially renamed '*Cedrizuela*') and Doral in Miami (unofficially 'Doralzuela') or Spain, where a large exile community had formed. However, more recently, a flood of less fortunate

Venezuelans had traipsed across the Andes on foot, all desperate migrants who preferred to chance it abroad rather than remain in a country with a minimum monthly wage of four dollars and shortages of the daily necessities.

"Hopefully there will be a change in the future," said Jardine.

"I hope so," replied the restaurant owner.

After finishing their meal and standing to leave, Jardine noticed a message board at the entrance to the restaurant, a mishmash collage of business cards, brochures and posters offering all kinds of services. He walked towards it and motioned to the restaurant owner, who arrived promptly. "Is it okay if I pin up my business card? We have a small guesthouse in Spain."

"Of course, go ahead, with pleasure." The man swept his eyes over the board. "This message board has become something of an informal network for Venezuelans passing through. Jobs, accommodation, almost everyone who passes through uses it."

Jardine pulled a business card from his wallet and stuck it onto the board. It read: *Hotel Casa Bosque — Granada, Spain*.

"How is Spain? There are many Venezuelans living there now?" asked the restaurant owner.

"I've heard there are. Mostly in Madrid, I suppose."

The man clicked his tongue, shaking his head. "My great-grandfather came from the Canary Islands. He left Europe for a better life in the New World. How things have changed."

Jardine nodded solemnly. "Thank you for the meal; we'll be sure to recommend it."

The owner took Jardine's hand and shook it. "Thank you, *pana*. I appreciate it."

CHAPTER 3

Villa de Leyva, Colombia

THE WHITEWASHED WALLS AND TERRACOTTA ROOFS flashed by in the tinted windows of the grey Chevrolet sedan as it rattled over bumpy cobblestones. Pulling up outside a large wooden door, the driver sounded the horn twice and then waited. The pink bougainvillaea cascading down the walls nearby swayed gently in the breeze while the vehicle stood idling. After a few moments the doors swung open, and the vehicle lurched forward into a courtyard surrounded on three sides by a verandah. Colourful hanging potted plants lined the verandah, and an elegant fountain trickled in the centre. The groundskeeper for the house approached the vehicle with an extended hand as the doors of the vehicle flung open. *"Bienvenidos a Hotel Sol,"* began the humble man as he beamed a welcoming smile.

"Gracias, very kind of you," replied a large thick-necked

man in Spanish emerging from the driver's seat. A second man with wide shoulders, dressed in a navy shirt, exited from the front passenger door without speaking.

"A pleasure," said a third, equally large, figure as he got out of the back seat.

The groundskeeper nodded to all of them and continued smiling. *Costeños?* He thought. Their accent had a more Caribbean feel to it than he was used to in the mountainous department of Boyacá. "This way, please." He gestured with his hand and helped them with their suitcases, showing the three men to their rooms.

Hours later, as the sun set, the men walked down the hill to the town centre. They located a small restaurant situated on a corner of the town square, and each ordered steak with *papas criollo*s, sharing a bottle of red wine. An old man draped in a *ruana* sang and played guitar in the corner, belting out Colombian folk songs. Finishing their dinner, the men spent an hour strolling the streets, browsing local artisanal shops, and taking photos of each other in front of the large church at the head of the main square.

It was important they maintained their cover: three Venezuelan tourists visiting a small historical town.

At ten o'clock, as the restaurants were closing, the men each bought a can of *Aguila* beer from a small shop and then sat on stone bollards fifty metres away from a small Venezuelan restaurant. As they sipped from the bright yellow cans, they monitored the entrance: watching and waiting. After thirty minutes, they observed the restaurant owner exit the building and take a few steps before stopping to zip up his leather jacket. He withdrew a packet of cigarettes from a side pocket, tapped out a cigarette, and cupped his hands around the tip as he lit it. He took a drag before meandering north-east on *Carrera 9* heading away from the main town square.

The three men waited until he had crossed a small stone bridge fifty metres away before they quietly stood, deposited their beer cans in a nearby bin and began to follow him.

The restaurant owner continued to stroll, puffing on his cigarette, occasionally whistling as he arrived at *Parque Ricaurte*. There he unexpectedly stopped to talk with an elderly couple sitting on a park bench. A young couple strolled around the park holding hands, a small group of university students sat in the middle of the square softly singing and playing a guitar and two policemen—each looked barely eighteen years old—stood at a corner scrolling through their smartphones. No doubt they were watching the latest football replay or a funny cat video. It was a quiet night in the town, and at this hour, the streets were thinning of people.

Approaching the park, the three men split. One of them walked past the restaurant owner as he spoke to the couple and sat on another park bench behind a small statue. He pulled out a horse riding brochure from his back pocket, which he'd picked up in one of the artisanal shops. The other two men held back and entered a small general store. One of them scanned the alcohol section as if looking for a particular item, while the other stood in the doorway nonchalantly watching the street.

After the restaurant owner finished his conversation with the couple, he turned left onto *Calle 15* and strode forward several blocks until he reached the edge of town. Here the streets were quiet and dark as the town morphed into the countryside. He stopped at a building which had a big wooden door. A thick bolt lock was fastened with a large padlock. A single streetlamp glowed from the nearest corner, straining to emit light down the street. Opposite the building was a small creek, and two large trees cast shadows over the man as he withdrew his keys from his jacket pocket.

The two men who had entered the general store had meanwhile followed the restaurant owner down *Calle* 15 and stood one hundred metres from him. The third man, having stuffed the brochure back in his pocket, had followed up behind. He stood at the nearest crossroads, scanning the street for potential witnesses.

At the door, the restaurant owner jangled a set of keys as he began to slot one of them into the large padlock. He turned the key with a satisfying click, unlatched the padlock and slid back the bolt. As he pushed on the heavy door, he heard a short, sharp whistle ring out. A human whistle.

A signal.

Looking to his right, he saw two dark shadows pounding towards him. He flung the door open and entered quickly, attempting to shut the door behind him, but it burst open as one of the shadows, a man, lunged forward, pushing the door and tackling him to the ground. The restaurant owner hit the paved floor with a slap as the second shadow entered, looming over him. The shadow pointed a pistol downwards. The restaurant owner's heart jumped as he heard a click.

Outside, the third man continued surveying the scene. After the initial scuffle, the night remained quiet. A dog barked in the distance, and the noise of a television with a football match wafted softly down the street. But otherwise, silence. No one had heard the commotion.

Inside, the man who had tackled the restaurant owner grabbed his jacket collar and barked a question. "Where's the general?"

The restaurant owner squirmed on the hard ground and looked at the man grasping his collar and then up at the man with the pistol. His eyes opened wide with fear and he managed to mumble a response. "I... I... I don't know what you're talking about. *Cual general*?" Which general?

The man with the pistol swung his arm low, pistol-whipping the restaurant owner across the face. "We *know* you know where he's hiding," said the man, his knuckles glistening with the restaurant owner's blood. "And, assuming you're not an *imbécil*, you know what we will do to you and your family if you don't comply."

"I really don't know what—"

The SEBIN agent holding the pistol pulled back the lever on the gun with a loud click and lowered it to the restaurant owner's temple. He spoke in a thick, guttural Spanish. "Sing like a birdy or I'll give you a seed of lead."

"I... I don't know anything about a general; I just—"

The second SEBIN agent slapped the man across the face with his right hand, his left still holding the restaurant owner's collar. "He was in your restaurant! We have witnesses. They saw you talking with him; you gave him something from your noticeboard."

The restaurant owner's brow twisted in confusion. "Oh, that? It was just a card, a business card. It had an address for a hotel in Spain. An Englishman pinned it there a few days ago... It wasn't important; it just—"

"Why did you offer it to the general?" barked the agent.

"The card? I didn't know he was a general. To me, he was just a fellow Venezuelan. He mentioned he wanted to get to Spain. I thought I would help a fellow *compatriota*. I'm sure you know what the situation's like in Venezuela. You sound like you're from *Barinas* department, right?"

"It's none of your business where I'm from." The SEBIN agent raised his hand to unleash another blow but stopped in mid-air. "You expect us to believe your little story? Are you part of the opposition?"

"What opposition?"

"You know what we mean! The opposition against President Madera. What did the card say?"

"It had an address, a hotel address."

"An address where?"

"*España*, I told you..."

"Where in Spain?"

"*Andalucía*, in the mountains outside Granada."

"What's the address then?"

"I... I... I can't remember it... This was several days ago now... I—"

"*Que coño...*" the agent holding the pistol pressed the cold metal barrel against the restaurant owner's temple.

"I... I can't remember the address, but I can remember the name of the hotel."

The SEBIN agent lowered the gun. "Well, what is it?"

"Hotel Casa Bosque."

"*Que sapo!*" What a toad! The SEBIN agent who had initially tackled the man released his grip on the man's jacket collar. In Latin America, snitches were known as toads. He raised the pistol again to the man's head and shot. A spray of crimson blood splattered against the whitewashed walls of the house.

Lowering his pistol, the SEBIN agent turned to the other agent. "You heard him. Hotel Casa Bosque in Granada."

The second agent retrieved a mobile phone from his pocket, opened an encrypted messaging app, and began to type a message.

CHAPTER 4

MIRAFLORES, THE PRESIDENTIAL PALACE — CARACAS, VENEZUELA

THE PRESIDENT OF THE BOLIVARIAN REPUBLIC OF Venezuela, Tomás Madera Toros, sat on a gilded Louis XVI chair, wearing an olive green *liqui-liqui* suit—a traditional Venezuelan tunic-like shirt and pants resembling a Mao Suit. Behind him loomed a large painting of *Simón Bolívar, El Libertador*, atop a white horse up on its hind legs in a Napoleonesque pose. The painting seemed to hover over the president, monitoring his every move. Leaning forward and spreading his arms wide, *el presidente* gestured to the members of his cabinet, who were crammed on two antique sofas surrounding a wooden coffee table in front of him. After clearing his throat, he began to speak. "*Muchas gracias*, comrades, for being here today."

A murmur of pleasant replies floated around the room—*de nada; con mucho gusto; a la orden*—as the cabinet members smiled and feigned enthusiasm to be in front of the president.

On the sofa to the left sat the Prosecutor General,

Guillermo Saeed, known as *El Poeta* (the poet). He reached forward for a white porcelain cup sitting on the table, flexing his large, tattooed biceps that bulged under his *Hard Rock Café: Isla Margarita* T-shirt. Beside *El Poeta* was Sindios Calvo, who held the rank of captain in the Venezuelan Armed Forces. He was the current President of the Constituent Assembly and Vice President of the United Socialist Party of Venezuela. He sat casually slumped on the sofa, running his hand over his closely cropped grey hair while puffing on a large Cuban cigar that was wedged tightly between his index finger and thumb on his other hand. Known as *El Pulpo*—the Octopus—he was the behind-the-scenes power broker in the country. Rumours swirled that he was the real brains of the republic, the president simply a stooge.

On the sofa opposite *El Poeta* and *El Pulpo* was Margarita Romero, Vice President of Venezuela, and head of SEBIN, Venezuela's intelligence service. She was noted for her superb skills in manipulation and cunning plans, despite her poised and naïve demeanour. She was yet to acquire a fun nickname. She smiled politely, picked up a manila folder sitting on the coffee table, and handed it to the person next to her, Lenin Gómez, nicknamed *The Godfather*.

The Godfather was a large overbearing man with dark hair and bushy eyebrows. As the Minister for Defence, he was a four-star general that had trained at the United States' 'School of the Americas'—the infamous training school for Latin American military leaders. He sat rigidly on the sofa, his military hat resting on his left knee.

An empty wicker armchair with plush white cushions sat empty at the other end of the coffee table. Margarita Romero, the vice president, noting its presence, asked the president, "Are we expecting someone, *Presidente*?"

President Madera nodded knowingly, his thick black moustache rising in a smile. "In good time, my dear Margarita, you will see what I have planned." The smile disappeared as his face turned solemn, and his moustache twitched, a trait that signalled to others that he was upset. "As you know, we live in troubling times for the Bolivarian revolution." He rose to his feet and ambled over to a nearby window, the echo of his foot-steps on the marble floor reverberating throughout the room. He arrived at a large bay window and peered out at Caracas, then he glanced up at the sky. His eyes darted around as if he were looking for something in the clouds.

The group remained seated and silent, not knowing whether to fill the silence with chitchat or to wait for the presi-dent to continue speaking. One of his bodyguards scurried across the room and approached him as he gazed out into the sky. "Don't worry, *señor Presidente*; there won't be any more helicopters."

"It's not that, Rodriguez. That was over a year ago now." The president continued to scan the sky. "I'm looking for *Him*."

"*Dios*?" asked the bodyguard.

"No, *tonto*! The late President Sánchez. He comes to me sometimes in the form of a *pajarito*—a little birdie—to deliver an important message or suggest a way forward."

The bodyguard nodded and followed the president's gaze into the sky. A pigeon swooped down near the window and defecated onto one of the grey government sedans below. They both watched as it splattered on the shiny grey paint like an exploding marshmallow. The president turned to his body-guard now. "That's it! That's the message, Rodriguez!"

"*Sí*?" questioned the bodyguard, looking confused.

"If the world shits on *you*, *you* shit on the world." The president's gaze focussed on the gates of the presidential compound. A group had gathered outside and had begun chanting in protest, but the large grilled gates and lines of the *Guardia Nacional* troops were keeping the protesters at bay.

"Tell me," he said, raising his voice and addressing all the cabinet members in the room. "What is it these people want?" He turned to face the group; his arm extended towards the window.

"They're trying to start a revolution, *Presidente*," offered The Godfather, the defence minister.

"*Una revolución*?" questioned the president.

"*Sí, mi presidente*," came the reply from the Godfather, who peered at the floor, not sure if he should have spoken out or not. He nervously adjusted the military hat on his knee.

"We are the revolutionaries, *coño*!" screamed the president, his face rapidly becoming red, his moustache twitching. A vein bulged in his neck. He pointed towards the window. "*They're* counterrevolutionaries."

The vice president spoke now, channelling the image of the smart girl in class who sits at the front and continually questions the teacher. "But what if a third group rises to counter the counterrevolutionaries? Due to the double negative, they would be classified as revolutionaries?"

The whole group of ministers looked sideways at each other, perplexed.

The president eyed the vice president with a seething, penetrating gaze. She looked at the floor, wishing there was a hole she could crawl into. There wasn't one.

Then he smiled and casually returned to the gold-leafed chair next to the ministers, who were still crammed awkwardly on the two sofas. "It doesn't matter anyway. *W*e are the ones in charge." He sat back in his chair, chuckling.

In that moment, the large double doors to the presidential office opened and a waiter arrived carrying a tray of sliced mango, papaya, banana, and figs with caramel. A second waiter followed with a tray of coffee and tea.

The vice president stood and spoke to the group, playing the role of host. "Would anyone like a coffee or some fruit?"

Before taking in the responses, she glanced at the fruit tray, did a double take, and stepped towards the waiter, covering the tray from the president's view. Her face reddened, and she hissed in the waiter's ear. "What have I told you, *carajo*! Don't bring mango to the president, it frightens him." She spun around to the group. "Who would like some guava? Anyone?"

"That would be delicious," said *El Pulpo*, placing his cigar in an ashtray on the table in front of him.

"*Claro, delicioso!*" confirmed *El Poeta*, the prosecutor general.

The vice president grabbed the server's arm firmly and spoke loudly for everyone to hear. "Manuela, could you bring us some guava?" The vice president then whispered in the server's ear. "Get rid of the mango and replace it with guava!" The vice president put her hand on the server's shoulder and firmly spun her around, ensuring the president wouldn't see the mango. The vice president then turned back to face the group and spoke more audibly. "Thank you, Manuela. Very kind of you."

It had been several years since the president had been struck with a flying mango. It was an attempt by a citizen to get his attention to fund her son's healthcare costs. He had managed to spin it positively, making a show of his willingness to help the everyday Venezuelan, but it had the unfortunate effect of making him petrified of mangoes, even sliced mango on a tray.

He sat back on his throne, cleared his throat again, and commanded attention. "Gentlemen and lady." He smiled at the vice president. "We've wasted enough time already, so I'll cut to the chase. The reason I have reunited us here today is because I would like to execute a plan to deal with a recent problem that has befallen us. I see this great country of ours like a giant bus, and I am the bus driver, ensuring that everyone gets on and off at the right stops and arrives at their correct destination." A flurry of serious nods and murmurs agreed and encouraged the president to continue. "As you all know, a political dissident, a general, has recently escaped *Ramo Verde* prison before claiming asylum in the residence of the Spanish Ambassador."

"Was it *El Pollo*?" asked the vice president, in reference to the nickname of a recent defecting member of the government.

"No, it was not The Chicken," replied the president. "He defected last year. It was General Angel Fernando Pereira Gallegos. I'm afraid he doesn't have a fun nickname."

"Neither do I..." huffed the vice president.

The president continued. "Anyway, we believe this general has now fled the Spanish Ambassador's residence and is in Colombia. We have a small team there following up on some leads as to his whereabouts and future movements, but we can assume that he will be in contact with other dissidents, and it's likely he will attempt to attend sessions at the United Nations Human Rights Council in Geneva. That's where all the snivelling dissidents head. Fortunately for us, many of the Europeans are very diplomatic and don't say much about the current situation in this country. Many were fans of the late President Sánchez and sympathise with our anti-imperialist cause. In any negotiations they just say they want peace and dialogue at all costs. However, we suspect the general may also attempt to travel to New York to speak at the UN headquarters in late September. If he does, the whole world will listen, especially those *Yankee Imperialistas*. It might even spur the gringos into action, and we don't want that, especially with the current orange-haired ogre in charge. We cannot allow it."

"The Devils! They just want our oil," said *El Pulpo*, shaking his fist.

The president nodded. "As you well know, we are all heavily sanctioned by our *amigos norteamericanos*. Likewise, since the *Acuesta Nogara* affair, our agencies are on the radar of the FBI and the CIA. Therefore, it's vital we deal with the general while he's in Europe. We cannot use the National Guard or SEBIN for this purpose. They are too close to us."

"What about using the *colectivos*? Someone loyal to the cause?" chimed in the vice president. The *colectivos* were armed paramilitaries loyal to the Madera regime.

"Those oafs couldn't organise a fiesta in a rum distillery. No, we need professionals. Besides, anyone connected directly to us will raise too much suspicion. All of us in the Bolivarian Republic of Venezuela must remain with our hands clear from this operation. Remember, this is all strictly for the revolution. I know it sounds drastic and not within our moral and ethical guidelines, but it's what the Yankee imperialists would do, and so we need to beat them at their own game."

"Well, that would rule out any of our military departments," said the minister of defence, motioning around the room.

"Yes, quite right," replied the president.

"How about *el vasco*? The former Basque member of ETA that now works in security for the Ministry of Agriculture. Alberto Castillas, isn't it? He's supposed to be an expert bomb maker; he taught the FARC and ELN in Colombia and previously advised the IRA. I'm sure he would get the job done," offered *El Pulpo*.

The president stroked his moustache, thinking. "A tempting option, but a bomb? Very messy." He shook his head. "No, not ideal. But I'll keep him in mind, perhaps as a backup plan."

A lull in the conversation followed and allowed the Prosecutor General, *El Poeta*, to speak up. "Actually if you don't mind, *Presidente*, I've written a haiku about our current situation that I thought might cheer everyone up."

The president sat up alert in his chair, his eyes open and welcoming. "Well, let's hear it, *Poeta*."

El Poeta stood and withdrew a crumpled piece of paper from his jean pocket. He cleared his throat and then began.

> *Strife in Caracas*
> *How will we fix this problem?*
> *What would Sánchez do?*

The group was silent and sat there blinking, not quite sure how to respond.

"*Entonces*? What do you think?" *El Poeta* asked, looking vulnerable, his eyes wide open with emotion.

Everyone swung their heads towards the president who sat semi-squinting, his hands forming a triangle in front of his face as if weighing up the quality of the poem in his head. Then, he stood and began to clap enthusiastically. "*Excelente, Poeta*!" he yelled, swiftly moving his hands in an upwards motion encouraging the others to shout similar encouragement. "That's exactly what we need to consider! What would Sánchez do! It's brilliant! My sentiments exactly!"

As the clapping and encouragement died down, a bearded man dressed in military fatigues rose from a darkened corner of the large presidential suite. "I know what he would do," he said. They all swivelled their heads abruptly towards him, not realising he'd been in the room. He was dressed in military uniform and strolled with a slow clop of large military boots. He raised a hand, taking a cigar from his mouth before speaking. "I was Special Security Advisor for Sánchez from 2002 onwards, so I know *exactly* what he would do." It was immediately apparent that the man's Spanish accent was different to those in the room. A Caribbean Spanish accent without doubt, but not Venezuelan. "Give me a few days, and I'll have someone who will do what you are asking, *señor Presidente*."

He sat in the wicker chair, leant back, and took a large puff on his cigar.

The president shifted nervously in his seat. "Yes, sorry, *compañeros*," he said. "Allow me to introduce you to *Comandante Lazo,* a special advisor acting as Military Attaché from Cuba."

The group nodded their nervous approval, not quite sure how to respond. A Cuban sitting in on a high-level government meeting?

Comandante Lazo leant forward, blowing a large plume of smoke across the room. Then, he spoke. "It's time *la revolución cubana* taught our Venezuelan brothers how we deal with defectors. It is time we employed *medidas activas.*" Active measures.

CHAPTER 5

Madrid, Spain

As the pilot announced the descent into Madrid's Barajas International Airport, the assassin reached down under the seat and prodded the violin case. It wasn't going anywhere, but it was prudent to be sure.

The plane promptly landed and then taxied to the gate. After a short wait and shuffle to exit, the assassin disembarked and strode through the walkway from the plane to immigration, pulling out a navy Cuban diplomatic passport from a jacket pocket. The photo looked stern, the skin lifeless and the stare vacant. It had been taken at the last minute as this assignment required a new alias. A new character. Like a chameleon changing its colours, only it took more than that to be successful in this profession. Each assignment necessitated a new personality, a new walk, a new smile and a unique tailor-made solution.

Passing through customs and immigration effortlessly, the assassin hailed a taxi and travelled to the Cuban embassy on the aptly named *Paseo de la Habana* in Madrid. "Wait here," said the assassin, darting inside and fifteen minutes later walking out holding a metal diplomatic briefcase. A five-minute drive later, the assassin checked in to the Hotel Zenit Conde Orgaz, rode the elevator up to the room and placed the metal suitcase on the end of the bed with the violin case next to it. Opening the case, the assassin extracted the violin—a cheap Stradivarius knockoff—to reveal a false bottom. Then, the assassin unlatched the metal diplomatic case and transferred the contents into the purpose-built inlay in the false bottom of the violin case. Before replacing the false bottom and the violin, there was a quick rundown of its contents: a 9mm PB pistol with a suppressor and two small, modified plastic cases. One of the cases contained a poison-laced retractable syringe, the other a retractable sharp metal point. Each of the three objects served their purpose. The method of elimination the assassin would choose was still unknown; it would depend on the circumstances. Like a professional golfer choosing the right club for each shot, it depended on the conditions.

There was no shortage of kill options in the world of international assassination, the assassin thought. Traditionally, the most reliable method was an aeroplane 'accident' especially if one never finds the plane. Countless important humans have been taken care of in this way, although you'd be hard-pressed to find a person who believed it, outside of conspiracy theorists, that is. The aerial 'accident' would usually be followed by a clever disinformation campaign of crackpot online conspiracy theories, serving to suggest anyone who believed in such a thing should be considered crazy, *loco*, nuts, stunningly bonkers.

Of course, there were genuine air disasters which further muddied the waters. Nevertheless, nowadays, death by aviation was generally considered to be a wasteful option in the assassination game. It was terribly bad for the environment with excess CO_2 emissions and the like. And there was no chance the assassin would pay the carbon offset, that would leave a paper trail.

The unnecessary and tragic loss of innocent lives was also passé. Despite what the movies will tell you, a professional assassin only wants to eliminate the target. *Ni más, ni menos.* Nothing more, nothing less. Unnecessary death is sloppy and unprofessional. We're *artistes*, not animals, thought the assassin, replacing the violin and fastening the latches, then retrieving a small bottle of vodka from the mini bar and taking a sip.

The second most reliable option was a drug overdose. That involved slipping poison into a drink, a meal, a teacup or a vodka martini, but for this to work, it would have to be within reasonable doubt the victim would partake in drugs, thus it required a specific type of target: a celebrity, a rock star, or a kinky politician with a reputation for partying. In this particular assignment, as the target was a strait-laced, patriotic general, the tool didn't fit the task. It would be like putting with a seven iron.

The assassin stepped back and moved over to the window to watch the clear blue sky, a slight shimmer on the horizon of the Madrid skyline. *That leaves me with three options, hence why I've chosen these tools.* The pistol was the last resort. Clunky, old-fashioned but fail-safe. A bullet is a bullet and, aimed correctly, it does its job. If worst came to worst the pistol would be deployed. Second to last was the plastic implement holding the spring-loaded metal spike. A swift stabbing motion into a vital vein, followed by a quick pull, was all that was needed. The result, of course, would be a quick loss of blood before the victim knew they were hit. Effective, yes. But messy? *Dios mio.* The blood could erupt like a geyser. That's at least what had happened in Istanbul on a recent assignment during an attempted coup in Turkey. Luckily the hit took place on Turkish Republic Day, and with a sea of red Turkish flags, no one seemed to notice a man stumbling around covered in blood.

The assassin took another sip of vodka. The preferred implement for this assignment, the choice *numero uno*, was the final implement. A retractable syringe housed in a plastic case that contained a deadly poison that could be administered at close range. It was not novichok—the nerve agent that put the small English town of Salisbury on the map, the town now known as the quaint town with the beautiful cathedral and where someone tried to murder the Russian defector and his daughter. God no. That was too unstable. Aconitine, or *devil's helmet*, was much more suitable for a job like this; not entirely untraceable, but the death is usually a result of organ failure and asphyxiation. Much more appropriate; novichok was for thugs. This was professionalism, not barbarity, thought the assassin, draining the remains of the small vodka bottle.

Turning away from the window, the assassin exited the hotel room, descending to the foyer of the hotel and heading towards the front doors. It was time for a real drink in a bar. A small girl ran along the marble floor, attempting to catch up with her mother who strode ahead, lugging a heavy suitcase as she spoke on a mobile phone. The little girl tripped and hit the floor with a loud slap. The assassin approached and looked down at the small girl writhing in pain on the ground. The mother continued without noticing, chatting away on her mobile phone. The girl looked up, helpless, her small brown eyes starting to well with tears. The assassin reached down and grasped the girl by her small backpack, then, with a strong, firm grip, lifted her back onto her feet. Leaning down closer and looking directly into the little girl's eyes, the assassin smiled. "Are you okay?" The voice was Cuban-accented Spanish.

The girl nodded.

"You look like you're a strong little girl, *cierto*?"

The girl nodded again, now with the beginnings of a small smile starting to form.

"Run along and help your *mamita*, she looks like she needs your help. Do you think you could do that?"

The child nodded and giggled as the assassin raised a hand to which the small girl high-fived and scurried over to her mother. The assassin looked up above the reception desk now. A large flatscreen TV played a news clip from RTVE, the Spanish state news channel. On the screen the reporter stood at the United Nations in Geneva, a fluttering row of flags flapping behind her.

"The dissident Venezuelan general arrived two days ago in Geneva and has met with the UN Commissioner for Human Rights whose report on Venezuela is soon to be published. The Commissioner mentioned that her office stands ready to assist in ensuring the human rights of all Venezuelans and that the Human Right Council will continue to advise and work with the state institutions of the Bolivarian Republic of Venezuela and opposition groups to improve the situation on the ground. The general thanked the Commissioner for her visit and her support but stressed the importance of increasing the monitoring of the situation and increased collaboration to move towards a more permanent solution to the crisis in the South American country. This comment and the presence of the dissident general—who the current government of Venezuela consider a traitor to the fatherland—drew arguments from the current Venezuelan government who currently holds a seat on the council, causing confusion and discomfort at the tense meeting. Due to this tension, it is rumoured that the general left Geneva yesterday en route to Madrid where he will meet with important Venezuelan dissident groups in Spain." The screen reverted to the RTVE studio as the weather report began. "Today in Madrid, the temperature will rise to..."

There was a small vibration from the assassin's pocket, a text message. The assassin took out the phone and peered at the screen.

> *MADRID IS COVERED. YOU'RE BEING REDIRECTED BASED ON NEW INTELLIGENCE. HOTEL CASA BOSQUE NEAR GRANADA. TRACK, MONITOR, AND WHEN WE CONFIRM, ELIMINATE. WE'RE SENDING YOU ANOTHER AGENT TO ACCOMPANY YOU.*
>
> JOAQUIN

The assassin stared at the screen, taking a moment to think before replying. Track, monitor and then eliminate. Like a jaguar that stalks and plays with its prey before the final kill. A useful strategy thought the assassin. To go in guns—or poisons—blazing and kill straightaway was ruthless, without class. Not the mark of a professional. It was more the domain of gangsters, mob hit squads and uncouth hitmen. The assassin would seek the general out, follow him and then take him out slowly. The assassin grabbed the phone with both hands and replied.

> *CONFIRMED. EN ROUTE, I'LL MONITOR FROM THERE. TELL AGENT TO RENDEZVOUS IN GRANADA.*

Hitting send and still looking at the screen, the assassin sighed and thought, *I do my best work alone*, then turned abruptly and strode to the reception desk of the hotel.

"How can we be of service?" the desk clerk asked.

"I'm going to need to hire a car ASAP. Can that be arranged?"

"Leaving us so soon? Change of plans?"

"Yes, you could say that."

The clerk eyed the assassin suspiciously. "Puerto Rican?"

"Cuban."

"*Muy bien*," said the clerk as he tapped away at a keyboard. "Your car will be with us shortly. We hope you have enjoyed your very short stay with us. If you'll kindly wait on those sofas over there, it won't be much longer."

The assassin smiled and replied. "No problem. I don't mind. I have time to kill."

CHAPTER 6

Hotel Casa Bosque — Granada, Spain

OLIVER JARDINE TAPPED AT HIS KEYBOARD, THE monitor illuminating his face. An invoice for grocery supplies —done; an inquiry for airport pickup—confirmed; a late booking—yes, we do have space. Hitting send on the last email, he sat back, exhaled, and reached for his cup of coffee. He took a sip and switched on the news on a large flatscreen TV that hung on the wall next to his desk. The room around him was part hotel common room, part reception, and part his personal office. His desk sat in the corner hidden by a divider. A cluster of leather sofas sat in the centre of the room, facing a long coffee table near the TV. On the other side, a large wooden dining table lay in front of a door which opened onto a large, paved terrace overlooking the hills of the Sierra Nevada. A hammock was strung up and swayed slightly in the breeze.

It was an idyllic location, five thousand miles away from the Andean metropolis of Bogotá. It was a week since Oliver Jardine and Veronica Velasco had returned from their trip to

Colombia. It had been refreshing to catch up with friends and family and take a small break. The past year they had spent setting up a small guesthouse in Spain had begun to take its toll. Despite the initial excitement in escaping their nine-to-five jobs, it had dawned on them just how draining and busy their lives had been since becoming their own bosses and assuming all the pressures that it entailed. Jardine enjoyed this new life, yes, but there was still a part of him that missed his former job as an analyst for MI6. The return to Colombia had triggered it. He missed having his finger on the pulse, being privy to important world events, and the intrigue and insights he could discover each day as an intelligence analyst, something which dealing with guest bookings, complaints and watching *CNN en Español* on repeat did *not* bring him.

Jardine turned his attention to the flatscreen TV now, as red and blue lights flashed on the screen. Next, a black tarp covering a body lying on the ground appeared, a dark red smear of blood visible on the ground next to it: the aftermath of a terrorist attack in France. He rose from his desk and moved closer, sitting on one of the leather sofas. The newsreader announced in Spanish how the scene had unfolded and the grim circumstances of the headless woman lying hidden under the black covering. As the story finished, the screen turned to a female journalist standing outside the UN gardens in Geneva. She had just started to speak when there was a sharp knock at the door.

Jardine crossed the room and opened the door to reveal a tall imposing figure standing in front of him. The man had a long face and dark stony eyes that darted inquisitively around the room. Behind him stood another man who leant against a *Guardia Civil* patrol car.

"*Buenos días, Teniente Muñoz*," said Jardine. "Please come in."

The lieutenant nodded and stepped into the office, taking

off his khaki cap. After taking a few steps, he swivelled and faced Jardine once again, asking, "I was just wondering if you or your girlfriend knew anything about a certain incident that occurred in *La Línea* last night?"

Jardine put his hands on his hips. "Why would we have any knowledge of what was happening in *La Linea*? It's a few hours' drive from here. And besides, we're hotel owners not criminals."

La Línea de la Concepción—known as *La Línea*—was a small coastal town bordering Gibraltar in southern Spain. Employment ran at around forty percent and its position on the Bay of Algeciras meant it was the perfect European landing point for drug-packed, high-powered speedboats depositing Moroccan hashish, South American cocaine, and Khyber Pass opium.

Lieutenant Muñoz nodded and smirked while continuing to stroll around the room as if searching for a clue or some incriminating evidence, and then he offered a response. "It's just that a man in the village mentioned that your *mujer* is Colombian and that you may have links to narco-trafficking in the area."

Jardine rolled his eyes and tried to remain calm but underneath, he was seething. "Was it Don Anibal?"

The officer froze, and his eyes widened as if Jardine had guessed correctly, then he shrugged, trying to play it cool. "I'm not permitted to say, *señor* Jardine."

"I bet it was. You know he also owns a small hotel in town and since we've set up here, he's been spreading rumours about us and trying to discredit our business. Resentment and jealousy are strong motivators in these parts."

"I see." Lieutenant Muñoz withdrew a small notebook from his breast pocket and scribbled with a small worn pencil. Then, he replaced the notebook, smiled, and stepped towards Jardine with his hand extended. "Well, thank you. You are quite right; I don't see why you would have anything to do with events in *La Linea*."

"Not all Colombians are narcos, you know?" said Jardine.

The officer nodded and forced a smile. "Yes, quite right you are. Thank you for your time, señor Jardine." He walked towards the door.

The *Guardia Civil* had changed significantly since the days of Franco, but still, for some officers, a heavy hand and hard-line policing were still the order of the day, especially for an up-and-coming lieutenant looking to make a bust in the ever-increasing drug trade in Southern Spain. The trade in Moroccan hashish and other narcotics across the straits of Gibraltar involving the 'Ndrangheta from Calabria, the Spanish Clan Los Castaña, the Russians, the Albanians, and smaller Colombian criminal organisations didn't help to alleviate their suspicions. The movement of South American cocaine through Guinea Bissau northwards to Spain also furthered the suspicions, and where cocaine was mentioned, Colombia usually followed close behind. Stigma was hard to break, especially when the product was as popular as glow sticks at a rave.

Stepping out of the office into the sunlight, Lieutenant Muñoz turned and spoke for the final time. "I am sorry for the intrusion, but in our war against drugs, we must leave no stone unturned and unfortunately, the Colombian involvement has only increased."

"Understood. Although it's important you understand that not all Colombians are involved in drugs."

"Very well," came the reply. "*Buen dia, señor* Jardine." And with that the two officers climbed back into their patrol car and drove down the windy guesthouse driveway.

Jardine shook his head, purposely inhaling and exhaling deeply trying to calm himself after the encounter. He returned to his desk and sat in front of his computer, opening the room booking software knowing full well that he'd already checked it moments ago. Anything to take his mind off what had just occurred and distract himself. After a few clicks, a grey box with an error message appeared on the screen. His face began to burn as he felt his pulse quicken and the vein in his neck pulsate. "Bloody booking software!" He slammed his fist down hard on the desk, trying to release his fury.

A few moments later, Veronica arrived at the office door smiling. "*Mi amor*, are you okay? Who was just here?"

"That idiot officer from the local *Guardia Civil*. I don't know what he has against Colombians, but he sure as hell likes to push that we're involved in something."

"Pilar at the taverna in town says he has a lot of anger issues and is known for his relentlessness in finding crime, even when there isn't any. Something about him wanting a promotion? Don't worry about him; no need to get angry about it. Maybe you need to lie in the hammock to calm down?"

"Oh, it wasn't just him. It's this booking software; it doesn't connect with the payment platform, which in turn, isn't compatible with our calendar. The whole system is corrupt and has been mismanaged from the start. I knew we shouldn't have taken on the old reservation system. The whole system needs to be torn down and rebuilt in a more efficient and effective way. A completely new system to wipe out the bugs and glitches and then rebuilt with a more robust system. Honey, I think our system mainframes need a revolution!" He smiled and slumped back in his chair.

Veronica walked towards the desk sitting on the edge of one of the leather sofas. "A new revamp of everything sounds like a good idea; then we can set it up the way we want and the way it should be. It will be a lot better like that."

"I'd advise against that," said a voice in Spanish wafting in from the open door.

Jardine and Veronica turned their heads. A man wearing a

well-worn dark brown Panama hat and a sand-coloured button-up shirt stood in the doorway, a small roller suitcase at his side and a leather satchel over his shoulder. A dark stubble was beginning to form a beard, and when he took off his hat, he revealed closely cropped dark hair peppered with grey which appeared as if it had been recently cut.

"Excuse me?" asked Jardine gruffly.

"Sorry to intrude. What I meant was I'd advise against a complete revolution; in my opinion, that never turns out too well." Jardine and Veronica stood staring at the man as he continued. "I was hoping you might have a room available? I did reserve but it looks like you're having a little trouble with your software—I'm sorry can you turn that up?" The man indicated to the flatscreen TV on the wall as a red banner flashed across the screen with the words, "Breaking news". He stared past them, his mouth open.

Jardine reached for the remote control on his desk and increased the volume. The newsreader spoke quickly and in an authoritative voice. "This afternoon, at a military parade in Caracas, two drones were flown towards President Madera in an attempt to assassinate him..."

CHAPTER 7

HOTEL CASA BOSQUE — GRANADA, SPAIN

THE NEWSREADER SPOKE AS A LOOP OF FOOTAGE recorded from the drone attack played in the background. "President Madera of Venezuela was speaking live at a military event outside Fuerte Tiuna along Heroes Avenue when two drones packed with four pounds of plastic explosives were launched towards the president. It is reported that one of the drones was diverted by the military, crashing into an apartment building several blocks away. On the podium, bodyguards attempted to surround the president with large black bulletproof pads. However, on the parade grounds below, in a somewhat embarrassing scene for the president, soldiers scattered, clambering and scurrying as far away from the scene as they could manage."

"Who is behind the drone attack is still not known, although several opposing theories have been alleged from all sides of the Venezuelan political spectrum. The government alleges the drones emanated from Colombia, a plot by opposition members who had conspired with individuals in Miami,

Bogota, and Madrid to attempt to assassinate the Venezuelan leader. Opposition leaders believe the attack to be part of a 'false flag' operation conducted by the government itself to justify more draconian powers to shut down protests and opposition groups which have caused chaos in the South American nation for the last year. With little access given to the international press and previous crackdowns on freedom of speech in the South American country, getting to the truth has been difficult to ascertain. Much like the previous case of a helicopter attack on the capital's Supreme Court and Ministry of the Interior more than one year ago, this latest event shows the political and social situation has arrived at a point where violent action has become the norm while millions flee from social and political turmoil in the Bolivarian Republic of Venezuela."

"The attempt on the president's life also comes as Venezuela is in the grips of an economic crisis not seen since the great depression where inflation has soared 12,000 percent just this year. This follows years of economic mismanagement by the former government of the now-deceased ex-president *Comandante* Sánchez, whose Bolivarian Revolution was touted as the new hope for the oil-rich nation. As we speak, there are large-scale shortages in food, toilet paper and medicine, and an out-of-control crime rate which has propelled it ahead of Iraq and Syria—both war zones—with the highest homicide rate in the world."

"The road ahead looks bumpy as President Madera and his supporters in the Supreme Court have sidestepped the opposition-controlled National Assembly by calling a Constitutional Assembly made up largely of government supporters. The result has been almost total control of the executive, judicial, and legislative branches of government, leading to a continued flow of protest and unrest. It is thought that..."

The journalist's report continued on-screen with correspondents in Miami and Bogotá voicing their analysis and subsequent opinions from the Venezuelan diaspora.

Jardine's mind raced back to his time in Colombia. It was very easy to purchase a drone in the dusty market town of Maicao in Colombia, a tax-free haven for electrical goods close to the border with Venezuela. He had done it himself. It would then not be a stretch to smuggle it across the border, pack it with explosives and attempt to take the president's life.

As the news report finished, he shook his head and laughed nervously. Trying to fill the air with something light but on point, he said: "Welcome to the twenty-first century, where drone assassinations are *de rigueur* in world politics."

Veronica raised her eyebrows and then moved towards the computer on the desk.

The man looked seriously at Jardine but then, as if remembering something important, smiled and nodded. "It does not look good, what is happening over there in Venezuela."

Veronica, raising her face from the computer screen, asked: "*Señor Pereira*? Late booking from last night?"

"*Así es, señorita*," the man replied.

"We'll just need your passport and then we can direct you to your room."

The man handed his passport to Jardine. Portuguese, he noted and then passed it to Veronica who scanned it and asked the man to fill out a short form.

"Visiting us directly from Portugal?" Jardine asked.

"I've come down from Barcelona," said the man. "I'm on a business trip, thought I'd take the long way home." Jardine and Veronica listened intently as he spoke in Spanish.

"But your accent is not Portuguese; you sound like you're from somewhere in the Caribbean?" asked Jardine.

Señor Pereira's eyes widened as if he were guilty of eating the last biscuit in the biscuit tin. "Venezuela," he said. "I can see there's no fooling you. You have a keen ear."

"I'm something of an amateur linguist; guessing accents is a hobby of mine," said Jardine. "Anything to keep my mind alert."

The man fidgeted uncomfortably with his Panama hat and sighed heavily. "I *was* going to wait before identifying myself, but it seems you are both competent detectives. I came across this business card." He held up a crumpled business card for their guesthouse.

"Where on earth did you find that?" Jardine stood now, reaching forward, indicating to the man to pass him the business card, although when he thought about it, it could have been from any number of places. He left or pinned up the cards in every restaurant, bar, tourist office, beach kiosk and café he visited.

"I came across it on a stopover in *Villa de Leyva*. We were driving from Cúcuta." The man reflected on his dash across the border, the migrant family he witnessed, then the SEBIN agents, the shots fired and the final jump into the waiting SUV.

"From Cúcuta?" asked Jardine.

"We crossed the border and then worked our way down to Bogota. I picked up the card at an *arepa* restaurant. I thought it might be useful and well, it turns out, it has been most helpful."

They stopped what they were doing and looked at the man intently. Jardine said, "Sorry, I don't understand?"

"You have seen the news about an exiled Venezuelan general visiting the UN in Geneva and who's now, supposedly, in Madrid?"

They both shook their heads.

"Oh, well, there's a general that recently escaped from Venezuela."

Jardine and Veronica nodded their understanding.

"This man is supposedly in Madrid now, but really, he is not."

"Then who's in Madrid?" asked Jardine.

"A decoy," replied the man.

"Then you are...?"

The man smiled. "I am General Angel Fernando Pereira Gallegos of the Venezuelan Armed Forces. Well, ex-general now. I'm here because I need your help."

CHAPTER 8

Caracas, Venezuela

El Helicoide is a pyramid-like structure in Caracas acting as the headquarters for Venezuela's *Servicio Bolivariano de Inteligencia Nacional* (SEBIN). It also houses a prison for high-profile political detainees and is well known in Venezuela for all the wrong reasons. While its original design and purpose were that of a luxury mall, its current use as a maximum-security prison was anything but luxurious. It was feared in Venezuela as a place of systemic torture and human rights violations, and while it didn't hold the noble mysticism of other world-famous pyramids in Giza or the Yucatán, its history was just as macabre.

Bunkered down in a secure room at the heart of the building, President Madera slammed his fist on the large wooden table in front of him. "What do we know about this drone attack? I want names, theories and more importantly a plan of action to capture the perpetrators." Around the president, on a large wooden table sat the minister of defence—*the Godfather*, the prosecutor general—*el Poeta*, the vice president—

Margarita Romero (no funny nickname), the foreign minister —*El Cuñado*, and two highly ranked SEBIN agents.

"We believe elements of the military are involved, *señor Presidente*," replied the minister of defence, *The Godfather*.

"*Sí, es correcto*. It's just like the helicopter incident a year ago; they are trying to launch a coup against the government of Venezuela!" said one of the SEBIN agents, trying to project his enthusiasm into the meeting.

The Prosecutor General, *El Poeta*, stood and ran his hand through his luscious, manicured grey-black hair, the slight creak of his black leather jacket the only sound over the air-conditioning unit humming in the corner. He had thought about conveying his message through another poem but hadn't had the time to think of a good one. "You make a good point about the attempted coup. As the prosecutor general, I propose initiating a new constitutional law to make it illegal to effect coups on the Venezuelan state."

"Didn't ex-president Sánchez try to affect a coup in 1992?" asked the vice president.

The prosecutor general sat quickly and stared down at the table in front of him, embarrassed at having made such a blunder. "I meant it purely hypothetically that one shouldn't affect coups on—"

"Actually," the foreign minister interrupted, pushing his glasses up the bridge of his nose, "the man involved with the helicopter a year ago was an ex-member of the investigative police, nothing to do with my father-in-law ... I mean *Comandante* Sánchez. May he rest in peace. Now, if we are speaking of your loud-mouthed son, Prosecutor General, that is another matter..." Nepotism was as bountiful as the oil reserves under Venezuelan soil, as plum positions in the government were doled out to family members. The foreign minister, José Arriza, was a key cabinet member. He was unelected and simply there because of his marriage to one of ex-president Sánchez's daughters.

El Poeta sat up quickly and arched his back as the meeting became animated; a shouting match had erupted between himself and the minister for foreign affairs.

Finally, the president intervened. "*Basta!*" *Enough!* he said as his thick black moustache twitched. "I may look like Stalin, but don't make me have to invoke his fury to retain order in this room. Now, if the military are involved—in this drone attack, I mean—perhaps there's not enough incentive for them. It's high time I established more government ministries and appointed more generals as their heads. How many generals do we currently have, Godfather?"

The Minister of Defence looked at the ceiling as if thinking hard. "It must be around one thousand five hundred by now?" His voice trailed upwards, uncertain.

Despite the Venezuelan army being one-tenth the size of the United States military, it had double the number of generals and admirals, a tenfold increase since before ex-president Sánchez came to power.

"Let's add fifty more to the rank of general to ensure they are loyal to our Bolivarian cause and allocate them an important and vital duty like food or medicine supplies."

"Yes, Sir," replied The Godfather as he scribbled in a small notebook.

"*Un momento, Presidente.* May I be excused to use the bathroom?" asked one of the SEBIN agents nervously.

The president nodded and indicated to a door to his left.

The SEBIN agent stood carefully and strode over to the door and entered the bathroom.

The president looked across at the vice president. "Now, where were we with..."

"Ahem," the SEBIN agent had reappeared from the bathroom door, coughing to get attention. "Sir, there's no toilet paper; is it possible to—"

"You know there's a toilet paper shortage, do you not?" shouted the president.

"*Sí, Señor.*"

"Then what do you expect? Do you want a clean ass or to protect *la revolución*?"

"Protect the revolution, *señor*."

"*Entonces*?" Well?

The SEBIN agent nodded and retreated once again into the bathroom.

The president shook his head in disbelief. "Okay, back to this drone fiasco. What theories are we running with?"

The vice president stood to speak. "We have discussed this at length and we believe that the dissident general Pereira is behind it."

"General Pereira? How much closer are we to finding him?"

"Leading on from our previous meeting, we have traced him to Spain where he will be taken care of."

"Ah yes, the operation with *Comandante* Lazo, our Cuban friend," said the president.

"Precisely," replied the vice president. "We originally believed he was in Madrid after his meeting with the UN in Geneva. But we now have it on good authority that he has headed south."

"This is from the intelligence gathering mission in Colombia?"

"*Correcto*. It's thought he is in the south of Spain and it appears he has a decoy impersonating him in Madrid. As you mentioned, in working with our Cuban friends, we have an operation underway to rectify the situation."

The president enthusiastically slammed his hands on the table as he stood. "*Muy bien*. That settles the matter." He strode to the door, accompanied by the SEBIN agent that had since come running from the toilet. "As you can imagine, I have important issues to attend to." He turned back to face the meeting room. "Now that you mention it. It makes perfect sense," he said, nodding thoughtfully. "Of course, General Pereira was behind the drone attack! Pulling those puppet strings from Spain, no doubt. It's so obvious!"

The vice president smiled. "We are one hundred percent positive that General Angel Fernando Pereira Gallegos was behind this drone attack. Absolutely positive."

CHAPTER 9

The Albayzín Neighbourhood — Granada, Spain

"Of course, I had nothing to do with the drone attack!" said General Angel Pereira as he sat across from Oliver Jardine. "I wasn't even in the country. Besides, do you know how many different groups, factions and everyday citizens who want that *chamo* dead? I simply wanted a quiet retirement on my *finca* in Aragua but Madera wouldn't leave me alone."

"And now he wants *you* dead?" asked Jardine.

"That's what we suspect, hence why we set up a decoy while I lie low here in Granada. Perhaps we should drink to that?" The general raised a large wine glass as Jardine reached forward for his, and they clinked glasses.

The two men sat at a wooden table in *El Mirador de Morayma*, a restaurant in the Albayzín neighbourhood of Granada. A fountain trickled nearby filling the courtyard with the soothing sound of running water as light flamenco guitars trickled out from Bose speakers above. An outdoor firepit burned close by, encircled by large sword-like skewers holding rows of charred sardines, known locally as *espetos*. The salty smell of crisp roasted fish wafted across them, blending into the warm night air.

The general took another sip of wine and continued. "I suppose what President Madera really wants is my silence, but at this stage death amounts to the same thing. I decided I would speak for my country. I'm aware it's not a good look to the rest of the world, an ex-general speaking for democracy and truth, especially a Latin American general! We have had a bad rap, what with Videla, Pinochet, Batista, Trujillo and the like. But there was also Torrijos, Peron and Arvelado." He sat back and swirled the wine in his glass. "Although I guess even *they* had their detractors too and rightly so."

Before them, across the valley, as if hovering on a cloud of green foliage, stood El Alhambra. The setting sun cast streams of pink and apricot in the sky, basking the edifice in the late light of the day. The general took off his battered Panama hat and sat it beside them on the table. His dark hair was peppered with grey, making him seem more human, less a military figure and more grandfatherly. Jardine sipped his wine and looked out over the setting sun behind El Alhambra. He admired the general's courage as he spoke of enduring prison in Venezuela, his stint exiled in the Spanish Ambassador's residence and the tough journey through western Venezuela to Cúcuta in Colombia. Now he was here, as *un hombre buscado*. A wanted man. In a way, it made Jardine feel alive again. Excited, as if the general's arrival had plunged him back into a world he craved.

A waitress appeared at the table now. She wore tight jeans with a black halter top and had short, messy hair. Her arms were covered in sleeve tattoos; one of a dragon twisted around her forearm. She smiled, asking them if they were ready to order.

"There's really only one dish we need to try here," Jardine

motioned behind him to a row of large glistening silver sardines skewered around the open fire.

"*Un plato de espetos*?" she offered.

"*Sí*," replied Jardine. "And *patatas bravas*, *pulpo al gallego*, and more bread please."

The waitress nodded, memorising their order, and retreated to the kitchen.

"In Venezuela, we consider sardines a cheap fish, only to be eaten when one cannot afford red snapper. Of course, under the Madera regime, we've become quite accustomed to eating whatever we can to survive."

"Well, what's considered 'poor' peasant food is all the rage now. Offal has become affable, you could argue," said Jardine, smiling at his own wordplay. "I guess that trend hasn't made its way to Venezuela yet?"

The general laughed. "No, we have been living with our own government-imposed 'President Madera Diet.'"

"It's that bad, is it?" asked Jardine.

"You mean you don't know?"

Jardine shrugged. "I guess I know more than the average person, but it's always better to hear it direct from the messenger."

"Do you think they'll mind?" the general asked, pointing his lips in the direction of the waiters, then lifting his eyes in the direction of a cigar he pulled from his shirt pocket.

Jardine turned his head. He could see one of the waiters beside the kitchen door, sucking on a cigarette. Returning to face the general, he said, "I'd say you're good to go."

The general struck a match and got the cigar going, blew out a puff of smoke, and turned his grey eyes to Jardine. "The first thing you should understand is that ever since Venezuela has been a leading oil producer, it has always gone from feast to famine depending on the oil price. That is nothing new. This over-reliance on fossil fuels has meant that we never really developed other industries to be somewhat self-sufficient. When times are good, it's easier to import everything we need rather than produce it ourselves. So that is perhaps the crux of the issue."

"When did the recent troubles start, do you think?" asked Jardine.

The general recounted to Jardine the recent history of Venezuela. The economic troubles of the 1980s resulting in the Caracazo riots in 1989. The failed coup of ex-president Sánchez in 1992, a charismatic paratrooper who idolised the liberator of the northern half of South America: *Simon Bolívar*. After serving a short prison sentence, Sánchez was released, launching his political career with fiery, hypnotic and surprisingly refreshing speeches from a leader who spoke in the colloquial, storytelling talk of *los llanos*—the plains, a rural heartland mythologised in Venezuelan literature and its independence heroes. The sum of this led to Sánchez being democratically elected in 1999. At the time, his rhetoric sounded logical, the general told Jardine. On paper that is. He was hailed as a new messiah, someone who was adamant the country's oil wealth should be shared by *el pueblo*—the people—and not just the corrupt, oligarchic elites in Caracas.

The older man shook his head. "It was very hard not to like him at first. His smile, his way with words, his booming voice; it seemed as though he genuinely cared. That fooled a lot of people."

Elected as president and with booming oil revenues from high prices, Sánchez launched ambitious social welfare programmes where money was funnelled into schools, health, housing and infrastructure. Local councils were given more authority and funding to make decisions; the country—even the world—was abuzz with hopes for a bright future for Venezuela and for a new form of socialism. All seemed well. But like most things, it was all too good to be true.

The general took a puff of his cigar and smiled at Jardine. "But this all sounds like a fairy tale, a too-good-to-be-true *cuento de hadas*. Sánchez was like a lottery winner who goes out and buys all the luxurious products that one dreams of when being rich but doesn't save or invest for the future. Yes, he set up various future funds for the country, but they were under his direct control which soon meant money was syphoned off into offshore bank accounts. And yes, he did alleviate poverty and increase the situation of millions of people—for a while. He also spent on frivolous projects that never went anywhere. And then when the oil prices dropped and there was no more money? What do you do when you run out of money, but you are in control of the Central Bank? You print more. He printed money like an old-fashioned pyramid scheme prints flyers. And when people complained, his finance minister said that he didn't believe in inflation..."

As many fell under President Sánchez's charismatic spell, his cult of personality grew and grew. He set up his own television programme where he dominated the airwaves and spoke for hours in self-aggrandising stage shows that portrayed him as a man of the people. Soon he was making rash unilateral decisions, expropriating private buildings and land live on television, surrounded by nervous government officials who didn't want to get on his wrong side. It encouraged and rewarded loyalty to him, but not to the country. It was at this stage that many wealthier Venezuelans saw the writing on the wall and began to move out of the country, along with their money. The president's response? Capital controls. Capital controls on US dollars with stringent rules and regulations which led to currency manipulations and a flourishing black market in US dollars. By this time, the limits on private business, draconian rules and regulations on industry, and the price control of common everyday goods led to shortages, which enabled a cabal of government-connected operators to profiteer on food distribution.

In 2002, opposition groups with several branches of the armed forces launched a coup to overthrow him, but it back-fired and members loyal to Sánchez reinstated him. This only made him more paranoid, and after that, he became involved with Cuban Intelligence. He also began to politicise the mili-tary, putting them in control of food distribution, giving them a key role in maintaining the status quo of his government, and thus, keeping them onside.

Had the oil money kept flowing in, boosting the govern-ment coffers, it might have been okay, but then he began to fire key oil employees—those that disagreed with his nonsen-sical policies—from the government-owned, yet indepen-dently managed, oil company PDVSA. He fired thousands of executives and workers live on television as if he were Donald Trump on *The Apprentice*, replacing them with government cronies or supporters who mismanaged the infrastructure and the business, making it bloated and inefficient. With the oil taps turned down to a trickle, Sánchez still held onto power with his supporter base and through various constitutional rewrites, foreign influence and advice from Cuba and others, his grip on power and the country only strengthened. Later, as he passed away from cancer, he passed the baton to President Madera as the country was already in a downward spiral. Throughout all of this, six million Venezuelans left the country—more than one-fifth of the population. With further rewrites of the constitution, stacking the Supreme Court with government supporters and interweaving the military into key positions in the government, industry and supply chains, Venezuela had plummeted into authoritarian rule with little hope for the future.

The general sipped his wine again and spoke in an exasper-ated tone. "And that's not counting what has occurred under

President Madera today! He has managed to control the country through handouts of essential goods, manipulation of elections, arresting and locking up of opposition members, and control of the Supreme Court. It has only hastened the fall into a dictatorship."

"And that was the final straw for you? I mean, you've been there through all of this, and it's not until recently that you decided to act?"

The general sipped his wine and considered the question, then shook his head. "For me, it was the Cubanisation of the military that really started me on this path. Then, I guess, the crackdown on the opposition-controlled National Assembly was the last drop that overfilled the glass."

"The straw that broke the camel's back?"

"Yes, that's right. The final straw. *La ultima gota*. I remember Sánchez used to have a situation room, you know like you see in those American movies where the president sits, and people monitor screens and the events of the day. After the 2002 attempted coup against him, Sánchez became paranoid. I arrived one day to the bunker—that's what we used to call it—and there were men in military uniforms with Cuban accents sitting there. Many elected ministers didn't have access to this room, but these foreigners did! Then the Cubans moved into the high echelons of the military. First, they attended high-level meetings, then they became advisors, and then they were *giving* orders. Can you imagine? Taking orders from them, and if you don't follow, they accuse you of being traitors to your country? The Cubans know all about keeping a population under control. Counterintelligence against subversives, military integration into the power structure, and the use of propaganda, particularly when projecting an image abroad. I must admit, they are very good. Learned it all from the Soviets first, then the East Germans and Czechs."

"Not something you see broadcast on the front page of your daily newspaper."

"The over-zealous right-wing shout it from the rooftops, but they also overplay it and exaggerate it until no one believes it, except for their ideologues."

"And then Venezuela becomes the play toy for those in the West to illustrate that socialism does or doesn't work."

"Exactly, they never mention the finer points. It's either 'Socialism is a complete failure' for the right-wingers on the one hand, or 'The USA is to blame for the ills of Venezuela' for the leftists."

"Nuanced debate has been lost," said Jardine. "And how did the Cubans become involved with Madera?"

"Ex-*presidente* Sánchez spent his last days being treated in Havana. It's likely that succession planning was done with Fidel and Raul at his side with Madera the obvious choice as he had studied and trained in Cuba. A natural progression. Although, of course, I am merely hypothesising."

Jardine nodded and looked down at his wine glass, twisting the stem. The general had just offloaded a plate full of information. Some he knew, some was new. Jardine had always focussed on Colombia and he'd let Venezuela slip. Or perhaps his mind was becoming sloppy just one year out of the intelligence game. Eventually, he asked, "Why Spain? Why did you come here? I thought Miami was the exile capital of the world? Or at least the exile capital of Latin America."

The general shifted nervously in his chair. "There are a lot of hotheads in Miami. They're too gung-ho and militaristic. The wrong sort of people. The Bay of Pigs types who want revenge more than a free Venezuela."

"I get that impression too," replied Jardine, lifting his wine glass.

"But as you know I was in Geneva, and I thought it would be useful to do some digging in—"

A woman appeared at their table, her straight silky hair swaying slightly in the breeze. "Excuse me, might I have a light?" she asked as she smiled at the two men, her lips red and full.

"What about the lighter in your hand?" asked Jardine suspiciously, noticing she held a small plastic lighter.

The woman raised the lighter in her hand and flicked it several times. "It is..." she flicked it in quick succession, "quite dead".

"*No te preocupes. Aquí tienes,*" The general reached into his shirt pocket and produced a small box of matches, extracted one and with a flick, lit it.

The woman leant forward to catch the flame and wobbled, losing her balance, then stabilised herself by resting her hand on the edge of the table, knocking the general's Panama hat to the ground.

"*Ay, perdóname!*" said the woman as she knelt to pick it up, dusting it off and placing it back on the table.

"Oh, please don't worry; that thing has been through a war," replied the general.

The woman smiled and said, "Thanks for the light." She strolled away, weaving her way through the tables before sitting at a table by herself.

He looked across at Jardine, his eyebrows raised. "Seems I still have my attraction with the ladies, no?"

Jardine rolled his eyes. "So, what do you plan to do? What is it you're doing here?"

The general picked up his glass of wine and swirled it in his hand. "My plan?"

Jardine nodded.

"I plan to talk at the United Nations General Assembly in New York to..." He paused as if thinking of what to say next. "To call on the international community to help Venezuela and her people."

"Oh, so nothing too important then," said Jardine sarcastically.

"Actually, that is why I'm here, Oliver. I need your help. I want you to accompany me to Lisbon to make sure I get on a plane to *Nueva York*."

"Why me? I'm not sure I'm much use to you."

"You worked for MI6, no? At least that's what my sources have told me."

"How did you..."

The general smiled. "Some friends of mine with the Colombian government."

"They really can't keep a secret, can they?" said Jardine, shaking his head. "Well, it's not like I was an intelligence officer. Or an operative, for that matter. I'm better with a pen than a sword. So as an analyst—a former analyst, I'm afraid I won't be much help. Unless you need a report? A background check? An investigation? Besides, I have Veronica and our new business here. There's a reason I got out of *that* business." He spoke as if he'd already made up his mind, but somewhere within him, a small spark ignited, and he felt a surge of adrenaline seeping into his veins. It was the opium of adventure which he'd previously thrived in. Going out into the world without a worry except for what was in front of him. No lamenting the past, no planning the future, pure living in the here and now. He looked at the older man seriously. "I really can't. I'm sorry."

The general slumped back in his chair and moved uncomfortably. "Well, we'll see what happens. We still have several days before I'm due in Lisbon to catch my flight. I'm sure you're not going to kick me out just yet."

Jardine smirked. "You're welcome to stay if you want. As long as you leave a review on *TripAdvisor*."

He nodded, smiled back, and reached again for his glass of

wine. "Of course. I wouldn't want you to slip down in the rankings."

It was in that moment that he first noticed the two men sitting at a table across the courtyard, watching them. The two men, both tall—at least six foot, he estimated—with muscular builds and wearing large dark sunglasses—at night...

"I think we have company," he said, covering his mouth casually as he spoke. "Behind you, look when you can. Don't be obvious."

Jardine raised his hand and turned, pretending to call the waitress over. In doing so, he was able to see the two men he was talking about sitting at a table. Their gaze seemed to shift as Jardine turned. In that moment, the food arrived.

"Let's eat quickly," said Jardine, helping to arrange the plates on the table, "and then get out of here."

The two men ate quickly, trying to act naturally without arousing suspicion that they were rushing and planning a speedy exit.

Half an hour passed, and after chewing the last mouthfuls of *pulpo al gallego*, Jardine raised his hand again, trying to get the waiter's attention. He again took a causal glance towards the two men. One of them was staring straight at him, but when the man realised that Jardine was looking in his direction, he turned his head rapidly down to the menu, pretending to peruse it for a dessert.

The general let out a soft whistle. The waiter looked over and seemed to appear in an instant at their table. He handed over a one-hundred euro note. "The tip is yours, *pana*," he said, *pana* being Venezuelan for 'friend'.

Jardine stood. "I'll get the car. You stay here, make them think we're still here."

"Good idea."

"I'll meet you at the *plazoleta* we passed on the way over here in five minutes." Jardine walked casually towards the bathroom and when he was out of the line of sight of the two men, he dashed through the restaurant's kitchen and out into the street.

The general, meanwhile, rose from his seat and strolled towards the door, examining the sardines searing around the open fire while throwing the occasional glance back at the two men sitting in the back corner.

The men seemed not to care and only occasionally looked towards him. The lone woman who had asked for a light smiled at him from a distance.

He smiled back as he paced back and forth, not in a nervous shuffle but as if killing time, waiting. Looking towards the men again, he saw one of them mouth something to the other, and then they both turned to watch him. *Mierda.* Time to go. He turned and exited the restaurant without looking back.

CHAPTER 10

THE ALBAYZÍN NEIGHBOURHOOD — GRANADA, SPAIN

THE GENERAL LEFT THE RESTAURANT AND STRODE down the steep street towards an intersection. He reached the corner and stopped as a couple strolled past him followed by an elderly woman carrying a basket who shouted at two children to follow her. He glanced back up the inclined street to the entrance of the restaurant. A bar was opposite and a young crowd stood out in the street, laughing and talking with glasses of wine and bottles of beer in hand, enjoying the warm Andalusian night. He squinted hard and saw two figures emerge from the restaurant. Was it the two men? He couldn't see that far in the distance. After the two figures, a sole person waltzed out, followed by a group of four that exited and then joined the crowd in the bar. The crowd from the bar and the figures he had seen leave the restaurant all blurred into one. He still couldn't see clearly if the two men had left. Then, while still surveying the scene, he saw a pair of headlights illuminate slightly up the hill. His stomach sank; he suddenly had a bad feeling.

Trusting his instincts, he chose to run left at the intersection for a block before he arrived at the *plazoleta*. The cave houses of *Sacromonte*—the gypsy quarter—stood above him. A lone man with long flowing hair, carrying an acoustic guitar strolled up a twisting road. A small group of tourists followed, no doubt hoping to catch one of the area's famous flamenco shows. Standing in the small plaza, the general heard a slight screech of tyres and turned to see a small Peugeot pull up with Jardine at the wheel. He jumped into the passenger seat and they sped away through the narrow streets of Granada.

Jardine drove quickly and efficiently but not overtly aggressively. It was best not to stand out if they were being followed. As they weaved through the narrow, one-way streets of the *Albayzín*, Jardine noticed a pair of headlights appear behind them. After executing several nonsensical turns, and with the headlights following, he knew that they were indeed being followed. "Looks like those two goons from the restaurant have found us," he said, lowering his eyes from the rear vision mirror. "Dark sedan following us."

The general looked out the passenger window at the side mirror. "It's hard to see with the headlights so bright. But yes, it appears we are being followed."

Jardine continued, arriving at a T-junction, and stopped. He peered left into the oncoming traffic and noticed a large garbage lorry barrelling down the one-way street. He kept the Peugeot idling, motionless. He could have easily pulled out in front of the oncoming lorry with time to spare, but he waited.

"Why you wait, *coño*?" asked the general impatiently.

"Trust me. You'll see what I have planned."

The dark car behind them approached quickly yet cautiously, not quite stopping behind the Peugeot. Its headlights beamed through the back window, reflecting into Jardine's eyes. Its engine revved, purring like a tiger. He kept the Peugeot idling for a few more seconds; the lorry was now almost at the junction and picking up speed.

"*Vamos!*" the general yelled, looking impatiently into the side mirror at the bright light and hearing the revving engine of the car behind them. "What are you waiting for?"

Jardine continued to wait patiently and then, with a screech of the tyres, he launched the Peugeot forward swinging into the narrow street, turning just moments before the garbage lorry arrived.

The driver of the lorry tapped the brakes and slammed his hand on the horn. "*Que pasa, joder!*" he yelled as the small Peugeot fishtailed in front of him, speeding down the street. A few metres later, past the intersection, the lorry driver stopped as a man riding shotgun on the back jumped down to collect a pile of black plastic garbage bags which lay on the street. A few metres later it repeated the same motion.

Meanwhile, the dark sedan couldn't pull into the street before the lorry and was now trapped behind it. The narrow one-way street meant that it couldn't overtake but would need to hover behind, waiting as it stopped at every corner to collect garbage. The driver of the dark sedan blasted the horn, more to alleviate pent-up anger than expecting the lorry to miraculously disappear. Then the sedan driver muttered, "*Tranquilo. No importa*. I know where they're going." The sedan driver looked at a mobile phone perched in a holder on the dashboard. The screen showed a map with a pulsating blue dot.

Back in the Peugeot, the general turned to Jardine, nodding in approval. "Very crafty; they should teach that one at Fort Monckton."

"They do to a degree. Well, for the field officers, that is. Not the analysts. But I've picked up a few tricks. Most people think evasive driving is all about the speed. They never stop to think about the logistics—the physical limitations of the vehicles and the layout of their environment."

The general shook his head. "I didn't recognise the men in the restaurant, but I'm sure they were sent by the Venezuelans."

"Local thugs or *SEBIN*?" asked Jardine.

"Too early to tell," said the general, shaking his head. "All I know is that the Madera regime will try every trick in the book."

They continued to twist their way through the streets of Granada, passing through the *Universidad de Granada* campus and onto the E-902 highway towards the coast and the far side of the Sierra Nevada Mountain range. Eventually, they turned off the highway and began to wind up into the mountains. Here the narrow streets and laneways of Granada disappeared and morphed into winding and twisting mountain roads that clung to the hillside. After fifteen minutes of driving, their heart rates had returned to normal and they began to breathe more calmly. The general lowered the window slightly. The cool crisp night air blew in through the windows and the smell of the countryside seeped in, with scents of pine, citrus and manure. The roads felt lonely and dark, with only small farmers' pickup trucks passing by, carrying goats. It would not be long before they arrived back to the guesthouse and they could process what had happened.

As they approached a rare straight stretch of road, a flash of yellow in the rear-view mirror caught Jardine's attention. Looking again, he saw a pair of high beams that seemed to float at first and then grew larger and larger as a vehicle approached rapidly, like two golden orbs rushing towards them. He looked back at the road ahead and pressed his foot down on the accelerator, propelling the Peugeot forward as the general gripped the armrest tightly, his knuckles turning white.

"They're back. This time we'll need to be more aggressive," said Jardine, adjusting his grip on the wheel.

In just a few moments, the pursuing car had arrived behind them, almost kissing the back bumper of the Peugeot. It lurched forward and nudged the Peugeot causing Jardine to momentarily swerve into the left lane. The black sedan accelerated forward again, once more nudging the back bumper of the Peugeot like an aggressive bull charging at a matador.

Jardine's thoughts raced. *What other evasive tactics are there?* Another swift bump from behind brought his mind back to the road. He looked into the rear-view mirror again and saw a dark figure behind the wheel. The Peugeot rattled again as the dark car rammed into the bumper a second time. Then he had a thought, as if a small piece of the evasive driving course had dislodged from his long-term memory and slotted into his frontal lobe. *If you know the terrain, you have the advantage.*

Up ahead, there was an intersection where the road forked into two. To the left the normal asphalt road continued, chicaning before a sharp turn with a wall on one side, a small ravine on the other. This was the usual road that led to the small village near the guesthouse. To the right of the fork, however, was a rougher dirt track which was inclined but straight, and went up around the town and through an olive grove. Eventually, it snaked around, and via back roads they could arrive at the guesthouse. He decided he would swerve right at the last minute onto the dirt track. If the car managed to follow, he could easily lose them on those back roads. He knew the terrain; they didn't. However, it was likely their pursuer would miss the turn and be propelled forward with no choice but to take the chicane of the asphalt road. Separating them and allowing them to lose whoever was following them.

Jardine drove on as the fork approached, then he accelerated as the black sedan increased its speed to keep up. The intersection was moments away now, coming closer and closer. Approaching the fork, he tapped the brakes, slowing the Peugeot down slightly before spinning the steering wheel to the right and accelerating up onto the dirt track.

The black sedan failed to calculate the manoeuvre and hurtled forward towards the tight corner on the asphalt road. The driver slammed the brakes, desperately trying to slow the car down as it went into the tight chicane, but snaked along the road, eventually sliding sideways with a loud screech as smoke bled from the tyres. Helpless to stop itself, the car careered into the left lane just as a small goat-carrying pickup burst around the corner. The sedan attempted to brake and swerve out of the way, but the farmer's vehicle slammed into the side of the black sedan and skidded down the embankment, rolling and crashing down to the bottom of the ravine. The impact of the crash sent the black sedan spinning and swerving before thudding heavily against the rock wall on the other side of the road.

Having swerved right and accelerating up the dirt track, Jardine and the general heard the screech of tyres—metal on metal, rubber on asphalt— and then the muffled tinny sound of the crash below. They continued onward, reaching the olive grove, the shadows of the trees flashing beside them like soldiers in a line.

"Do you think they're dead?" asked the general after a few moments.

"I don't know," replied Jardine, eyes forward on the road. "Let's get back to the guesthouse. It wouldn't be a good idea to go back and check."

Ten minutes later, they pulled up at the guesthouse and entered the office where they slumped onto the leather sofa, their hearts still thumping. After a few deep breaths, Jardine rose to his feet, went over to a small liquor cabinet and poured two tumbler glasses of Laphroaig scotch whisky. He returned to the sofa, handed one to the general and sat down.

Jardine's hand was shaking as he took a sip. "General, I'm sorry. I know you asked me to help you. But I can't. I'm no longer in the intelligence game and besides, I was always just an analyst, never an action hero. James Bond doesn't exist, I'm afraid."

The general took a long sip of the whisky and looked down into the glass. "I understand. It's just that I thought with your experience in Colombia you could..."

"My experience was as an analyst. Well, there was one event I got caught up in, but that was for stronger motivations..." He looked sideways at a photo of himself with Veronica on his desk. "I'm not sure it's in my nature to be a man of action."

"Then what are these photos?" The general stood up and stepped towards a wall of photos Jardine and Veronica had arranged of their travel. "Mountaineering? Scuba diving? Here you are, perched on a scooter on some sort of mountain road." He gesticulated with his index finger; his other fingers wrapped tightly around the whisky glass.

"That's all a piece of cake compared to being chased by ... whoever those people were!"

"Your *maniobra* with the car was quite unique?" offered the general. "Let me handle the action. You can provide the brains and the ideas, the contacts. That's if we need them. By all accounts we're now safe."

"Look, I care about what's happening in Venezuela, I really do. And I want to help. But in this situation, I just can't. I mean..." A thought suddenly occurred to Jardine. "Look, we can contact the *Guardia Civil*. They'll take you in, provide security, they'll—"

"I can't do that," the general interrupted. "My cover will be blown. I'll be a sitting duck. They'll realise the person hauled up in the hotel in Madrid is a pretender. A decoy."

"It seems someone already knows you're here, or at least

they did, but they don't know where we are now. Tomorrow morning they'll find the crashed vehicle that was following us and its occupants. If they aren't already dead... By then you'll be able to make your own way to Lisbon with no threats. There! Easy fixed. You won't even need me."

The general frowned as if thinking over what Jardine had just said. He stepped forward and placed his hand on the younger man's shoulder, like a father comforting a son. "You're right. Look let's sleep on it. All will be clear in the morning. And we can go from there?"

Jardine nodded. "Agreed, let's sleep on it. We're safe for now."

THE NEXT MORNING, JARDINE WOKE EARLY AT SIX o'clock and walked out into his office to find the general already sitting on the sofa with a cup of coffee. His mind was cloudy as if what had occurred the previous night was a dream. He felt it hard to process that it had *actually* occurred, yet adrenaline still coursed through his veins and he felt full of energy.

Veronica entered and sat on an armchair in the corner, a large mug of green tea cupped between her hands.

Jardine was the first to speak. "General, Veronica and I were talking over what happened last night. You know she has considerable legal experience? We think it's best if we contact the *Guardia Civil* and explain the situation."

The general frowned.

Jardine continued. "It's best to come out with the truth and we think—"

"Ollie?" Veronica interrupted.

Jardine didn't hear and went on. "—it's the best solution to go forward. Vero, what's the local number for the *Guardia*?"

"Ollie, *mira*!" said Veronica, grabbing his arm and then pointing at the flatscreen on the wall.

The men turned to watch the flatscreen TV hung on the wall. The news reporter stood at an intersection, the scene of a traffic accident. Jardine picked up the remote control and turned up the volume.

The newsreader's voice boomed through the room. "We are here at the scene of a crash overnight where a farmer has tragically died as his pickup was pushed off the road by what police believe was a case of late night drag racing along the windy mountain roads in the Sierra Nevada outside of Granada. Authorities have recovered a body, believed to be the driver of the pickup, and can confirm that the man died at the scene. A second body, believed to be the driver of a black Audi sedan was also recovered and rushed to hospital in Granada. It is thought that the patient is in a stable condition in hospital, with only superficial injuries sustained. Police, along with the *Guardia Civil*, are now looking for a second vehicle they believe was involved, which they insist is still in the local area. Local *Guardia Civil* Officer Lieutenant Muñoz will be making a sweep of the area later this morning to conduct a door knock to ascertain further information. Those with any knowledge are encouraged to come forward."

Jardine felt a cold rush of blood jolt through his body. *A farmer had died?* He knew the car had crashed, but not that a farmer was involved. He turned to Veronica. "We've got to get out of here. If Muñoz sees the Peugeot, he'll instantly know we were involved. He already has it in for us with his drug trafficking theory."

The general sat watching the screen, his face thoughtful, mulling over the information. Then he spoke aloud. "You are right. We must leave immediately and go to Lisbon. From there we will have time to get ourselves out of this mess."

"It's too far in one day. We'll need to stop somewhere on

the way, lie low for at least today. If we leave, they'll know we were involved. I know this Muñoz character. He'll have a notice out for our arrest based on his silly suspicions alone. We'll need new IDs in case we get stopped. We'll..." Jardine's voice trailed off as he paced back and forth, muttering to himself.

Veronica stood up and placed her mug on the table. "What about our man in Ronda?"

He stopped pacing and stared at her, his eyes lighting up. "That's it, Vero." He turned to the general. "We have a contact in Ronda that can help us. I'll make a call and we could leave in fifteen minutes?"

"Is easy for me," replied the general. "I travel light these days."

"Count me in; let me pack us some things," said Veronica.

Jardine ran to the garage with his mobile phone pressed to his ear. It rang several times before a voice answered. "Haven't heard from you since Colombia. You always say you'll visit but you never do."

"It's been a while between drinks," replied Jardine. "Listen, got a situation here. Feel like a visit now? Need a place to lie low for tonight and I need a cobbler. Happen to know of any?" *Cobbler* was the espionage term for a forger.

"Yes, I could probably help on that front."

"Good. I'll text you the details within the hour. We're headed your way."

"Okay, I'll let Dolores know," came the reply.

"Ciao, see you soon." Jardine ended the call and stood outside the garage when he heard the crunch of gravel.

The general approached from his room. "I have a thought."

"Yes?"

"I'd imagine they'll have your Peugeot on file somewhere. How are we going to travel in it?"

Jardine smiled. "I've thought of that." He opened the rusty garage door which groaned as he lifted it. A large object stood in front of them, covered by a tarp. He stepped forward and with a few calculated flicks and pulls withdrew the tarp revealing a battered Land Rover Defender.

The general stared. "That's your idea of a getaway car?"

"It's the best we've got," he replied. "It came with the property."

The general began to laugh and strolled away slowly, shaking his head.

Jardine entered the garage and approached a locked cabinet in the corner of the garage. He unlocked it with a key attached to his car keys and took out some euros and a pre-paid burner phone which he threw into a small satchel. Then he took out an old hunting rifle. A housewarming gift from his neighbour, a keen hunter. Not an uncommon object in the mountains of Spain.

He slid it in the Defender under the front passenger seat.

CHAPTER 11

RONDA, SPAIN

IT WAS JUST AFTER SEVEN-THIRTY IN THE MORNING by the time the Land Rover Defender sped out of the driveway of Hotel Casa Bosque.

Before leaving, Veronica had arranged with their neighbour to manage the guesthouse while they were gone. Paz already rented out her own villa in the foothills of the Sierra Nevada on *Airbnb* so it was no trouble for her to organise the slow flow of bookings they had coming in and organise their small staff. Paz also didn't trust Lieutenant Muñoz, so she wouldn't mention anything to anyone. Jardine purchased two airplane tickets online—Granada to Rome with EasyJet. He hoped it would be noticed if the authorities checked, leading them in the wrong direction. He had also sent a passport photo of each of them to their contact in Ronda. Just before leaving, they had each switched off their mobile phones, removing the batteries and placing them in a small metal toolbox Jardine had in the back of the Defender.

Now as Jardine drove, with Veronica in the front

passenger seat and the general sitting in the back, they watched as the windy mountain road brightened before them and the sun slowly rose. He couldn't help but feel the addictive seeping of adrenaline trickling through his veins, like a child anticipating a Christmas present. It wasn't that he didn't enjoy his new life as a guesthouse owner; it was just that he thrived in new environments, new people, new places, and new smells. Never knowing what would come next. It was something he had always felt, as if the normal routine of work, rest and play wasn't enough to satisfy his curious nature. The allure of action, adventure and the unknown was ever-present in his psyche, nagging at him. This characteristic had served him well in his previous occupation as an intelligence analyst with MI6, no matter where he found himself. He had never been stationed in the spy capitals of the world: Geneva, Vienna, Moscow, Hong Kong, Washington DC. For Jardine, it had always been the slightly off-centre places: Bogotá, Seoul, Guatemala City. The places no one wanted to go to as they wouldn't have enough impact for their careers. That much was true. His intelligence reports in these places had never garnered more than a three-star rating which meant they were rarely perused by the JIC—the Joint Intelligence Committee —and therefore rarely landed on the prime minister's desk. Except for one or two slightly embellished reports—the phrase 'slightly embellished' itself being grossly understated—in Colombia that had been rated five stars and had been seen, read, and acted upon by the JIC, the Foreign Office and the PM.

As the sun warmed his back, Jardine looked right to Veronica sitting beside him. She had given up her position at the prestigious Bogotá law firm, *Garcia y Velázquez*, to move to Spain with him. She had always envisaged herself climbing the corporate ladder, advancing quickly and showing her brilliance along the way, proving to all those who said she wouldn't amount to anything that she was capable, smart, and intelligent. She had been nervous to give it all up and move to Spain, but in the end she had realised that the corporate life wasn't at all as it seemed to outsiders and she had quickly realised that putting your life—and your heart and soul—into an organisation that didn't really care for you, was not something she strived for anymore. She was invaluable, of course. "The place wouldn't run without her," her boss Dona Alejandra Velázquez had said. But like all organisations, even when a crucial member leaves, it continues. She, like Jardine, had set her sights on something more independent and personal, something they could build together, something tangible they could throw all their efforts into and say, "That was all us." Something they wouldn't mind working towards and made them leap out of the bed in the morning without thinking that it was a chore to live, breathe and work.

He looked in the rear-view mirror and saw the general peering out the window as if mulling over his situation. If he was honest with himself, it wasn't only the adventure that pushed him to what he was now doing. There was something in the man that reminded him of his grandfather. Jardine's parents had died when he was young and his grandfather had raised him for a time until he was sent to boarding school. An old military man, his grandfather was strict and disciplined but slightly eccentric. He lived in an old country house full of books and had never remarried after his own wife had died before Jardine was born. His grandfather had read him fairy tales when he was young and then classical literature as he got older. He was always firm in developing good habits in his grandson, yet open in letting him explore without imposing a great deal of boundaries. The general had the same qualities.

The sun had fully risen now and was a fiery orb penetrating the windows. The Defender continued along the A7 Highway, hugging the southern coast of Spain before passing through Málaga and sliding off onto back roads venturing further into the mountainous interior of Andalucía. They passed through the small town of Ronda, famous for its Plaza de Toros, high cliffs, and former residents Ernest Hemingway and Orson Welles. They crossed the *puente nuevo*, the bridge that hovers over the *Tajo* gorge and Guadalevín River, splitting the town in two, before reaching the outskirts and pulling off onto a twisty mountain road towards the hamlet of Grazalema. Higher and higher into the rural mountain landscape they drove before finally arriving outside a small finca with a converted barn just after ten in the morning. A small olive grove spread down the hill to a deep valley of orange trees. A row of hills and mountains cascaded off in the distance behind.

Pulling up with a soft squeak of the brakes, the dust settled around them to reveal a group of whitewashed buildings. An array of cacti and succulent plants surrounded the building giving it the feel of a lonely ranch in a spaghetti western. A door on their left opened and a man appeared. Jardine smiled and switched off the engine as the group emerged from the Defender, stepping forward towards the approaching man. The man wore a navy-blue linen shirt with cargo shorts and a pair of crocs. A salt and pepper beard hung on the man's square face, giving him a dignified air.

Jardine strode forward, his hand outstretched. "Sorry to bother you in these circumstances, but I knew you'd be the right man for the job."

"You couldn't just let a man retire in peace, could you, Ollie?"

Jardine smiled and then turned to face the general. "General Pereira, allow me to introduce you to Ronald Ambrose, former MI6 head of station in Colombia."

. . .

RONALD AMBROSE HAD MADE THE MOST OF HIS retirement; he'd bought a small parcel of land on the outskirts of Ronda with a dilapidated finca and abandoned olive grove with his Spanish wife, Dolores. Previously, he had ridden the career ladder of MI6 as far up as he wanted before bowing out gracefully and deciding to enjoy life while he was still able to. The quiet life suited him. He was not one for sitting on the board of BP, Shell, Morgan Stanley, or the other large companies that recruited former SIS men. He preferred to put his hands to work on something tangible, something he could touch. Something he could develop and work hard at, a trait he had had drilled into him from a young age by his father who had moved from Jamaica to the UK in the 1960s. The generous pension he received also helped his decision; it went a lot further in Spain than in the UK.

Now, as the Defender pulled up outside his home, Ronald Ambrose shook hands with the general, hugged Jardine and Veronica, and then invited them inside. They passed through several rooms before emerging onto an outdoor terrace overlooking an olive grove. Wooden chairs sat around a Moroccan mosaic table while grapevines overhead provided shade. A metal pot of tea sat on a cork place mat at the centre of the table.

"Pot of tea going here if you fancy?" Ambrose motioned to the table. "Or head inside; Dolores will help you out if you'd prefer *un cafecito*."

Veronica and the general decided on coffee and slipped past Ambrose and Jardine, heading into the kitchen.

Jardine stood beside the table and poured tea into a chipped cup, splashed some milk, stirred and then sat on one of the wooden chairs which creaked as he sat. He scanned the scene in front of him: olive groves lining the hills like neat hedge rows, the smell of citrus in the air, all below the clear Andalusian morning as the Grazalema mountains spread out in the distance. He turned to Ambrose. "How does this compare to sitting beside a desk in an embassy in some far-flung corner of the world?"

Ambrose took a sip of tea and turned to Jardine. "You mean do I miss it?"

"I know you don't miss it."

Ambrose smiled. "When you join the Service, you think you're going to change the world. It's not until later that you realise that you're just another cog in the wheel and that you're not exactly sure you like where the vehicle is taking you. One often wonders if one is doing the right thing. What is it le Carré said? 'Patriotism is quite different from nationalism; for nationalism you need enemies.'"

"I'll take that as no."

"How's Veronica doing?"

"She's good. On top of all the paperwork, sorted all the contacts and legal aspects."

Ambrose smiled. "Speaking of paperwork, there's a delivery this afternoon. My contact in Marbella is one of the best. His clients are mostly—let's say—a tad outside the boundaries of the law. As you well know, Marbella has become something of a hub for nefarious criminal groups. Everyone's there: the Russians, the Albanians, the various Italian mafias, the Irish and British firms, of course. It's rather like Hollywood for criminals. If there were an Oscars or BAFTAs for crims, it would be in Marbella. The place to be seen and wheel and deal."

Jardine nodded his thanks. "It seems the Costa del Sol is becoming the Ibiza for the underworld. Thanks for organising everything. I'll fix you up when things have calmed down a little."

Ambrose swatted his hand in a 'don't worry' gesture as the general, Veronica, and Dolores came out onto the terrace with a tray of coffee.

The day passed with the group discussing their plans, taking a long siesta in the afternoon, and wandering Ambrose and Dolores' property. Later that evening they sat on the terrace as the sun drifted down towards the horizon, eating strips of *jamon serrano* and *cabrales* cheese while sipping on rough local red wine.

"They practically give away a dozen bottles in the local tienda," said Ambrose as he sloshed wine into their glasses, laughing as he did so.

After, they ate *morcilla*—a blood sausage—and shared a large plate of *remojón granaíno*—a light salad comprising spring onions, black olives, boiled egg, orange and codfish.

During a slight lull in the conversation, Dolores spoke: "So who do you think is following you?"

The general took a pull of his wine and then swirled it on the table as he spoke. "The order will have come from Madera himself, but I imagine the Cubans are running the logistics. They've been in this game much longer than we have."

"And what game is that?" asked Dolores with a smile.

"The intelligence game," replied the general, cutting into his blood sausage and lifting a forkful to his mouth.

Ambrose spoke now. "It wouldn't be the first time the Cubans have dabbled with an operation in Europe. They were more than capable in the assassinations of Bolivian Ambassadors Joaquin Zenteno in Paris and Roberto Quintanilla in Hamburg due to their involvement in the capture and death of Che Guevara in Bolivia. That was in the seventies and eighties, of course, but it showed just how effective they could be and how far their network stretches."

"The Cubans have a long arm," agreed Jardine. "Just ask the CIA."

Headlights appeared coming up the long driveway to the *finca*. The general reached his arm down instinctively to a non-existent pistol in a holster, an old reflex.

"This the cobbler, Ambrose?" asked Jardine.

"That's him, not to worry." Ambrose placed his wine glass on the table and jogged over to meet the approaching vehicle. An old, battered Renault came into view and stopped in the driveway; the group watched as Ambrose approached. A man dressed like an Andalusian sheep farmer got out and shook hands with him as the group returned their attention to the table and their conversation. Dolores asked Veronica how she had found it living in Spain. Jardine and the general listened and laughed along with the conversation as Veronica told them of the experiences they'd had. Just as she was recounting a particular story about their first guests, a loud bang caused the group to jump out of their seats and they quickly turned their attention to Ambrose.

"It's okay," shouted Ambrose from the driveway. "Just the car; thing's almost had it." The old Renault performed a U-turn as he pushed it, and then it puttered off down the driveway.

The group breathed a joint sigh of relief as he returned holding a large brown envelope. He placed it on the table and slid it across to Jardine, who opened it and poured the contents onto the table. The hologram enlaced photos of the driving licences gleamed back at them. He picked one up and examined it.

"I could only get EU driving licences; that's his speciality," said Ambrose. "You'll have no backstop, so hopefully no one is going to check your bona fides. But it should tide you over for a while. He's the best cobbler I know."

"*Gracias*, Ronald," said the general. "You know the *Sánchez* and *Madera* regimes were also very adept at making false documentation, especially for our more nefarious visitors. Fake passports were given to ETA and Catalan separatists, Hezbollah members, refugees fleeing from Iraq and Syria who paid a bribe to the Ambassadors. We used to call them Monopoly passports."

Ambrose chuckled. "Well, let's hope these IDs don't send you directly to jail without two hundred dollars. They should suffice for hotel check-ins and will keep your names from being blasted across the reservation system which the *Guardia Civil* may have access to. We wouldn't want Interpol breathing down your neck as well as Cuban and Venezuelan Intelligence."

At this the group laughed before continuing to eat, drink, and converse around the table as a cool breeze blew through the hills. Later, after the dishes had been cleared and washing done, only Jardine and Ambrose were left on the terrace, now both drinking from large tumblers filled with *Dictator*-brand rum from Colombia.

"Before I forget," said Ambrose. "I have a contact in Seville who might be useful to you. Ex-CIA, retired to Spain, like me. But he's an ex-operative, a man of action, not like me."

"How do I get in touch with him?" asked Jardine.

"You don't."

Jardine looked confused.

"He'll find *you*," said Ambrose, smiling.

Jardine opened his mouth as if to say something, then closed it, frowning.

Ambrose went on to explain the slightly ludicrous cryptic conversation he would need to engage in to establish the identity of his ex-CIA contact. After ensuring Jardine understood, he finished with: "And Jardine, do me a favour?"

"What's that?"

"Don't get yourself killed. Try to remember what we taught you in the Firm: the basis of your self-protection is good information."

"Define 'good'," replied Jardine, sardonically.

"Don't get all analytical with your never-ending questioning of the status quo. Don't go full millennial..."

"Ok, Boomer," replied Jardine with a smile.

"Just remember all the basics. If you're anything like me, you'll be rusty."

"One year out of the spy game seems like a lifetime," said Jardine. "So, what tips have you got for me?"

"I'm old school, you know that. We were trained on the old Special Operations Executive Manual. World War Two stuff. It suggested you should be inconspicuous. Become an 'average' citizen in your appearance and conduct. In these parts, that means you'll need to appear as a regular Englishman living in Spain. In wartime, on the continent, you would've wanted to be seen as anything other than a typical Englishman. Here in *Andalucía*, you should appear to be just that."

"Duly noted," replied Jardine, taking a sip of rum.

Ambrose continued: "Be observant and deduce situations before you get into them. If you see the same face or hear the same voice twice, it's likely you're being followed. And if you *are* being followed, remember the easiest trick in the book to avoid surveillance: boarding public transport at the last minute. This, of course, depends on how many are following you. Failing that, use elevators in big stores—I'd recommend *Corte Inglés* in Spain— it's a good way to evade someone following you. Or if you enter a restricted area which has its own security, say a public attraction in which you need a ticket, that can buy you some time."

Jardine nodded. "Don't worry about us. We'll be going grey, keeping a low profile. Besides, I think whoever was following us is currently laid out in a hospital bed."

CHAPTER 12

Hospital Virgin de las Nieves — Granada, Spain

A SLOW RHYTHMIC BEEP SOUNDED, REPEATING EVERY few seconds, the kind of artificial sound heard in hospitals around the world. The assassin woke with eyes wide open like two emeralds glistening in wet rock. A glance downwards showed an intravenous drip was taped to the forearm, the winding tube twisting its way up to a transparent bag hanging above. Still lying down, it took a few moments for it all to come back: receiving the target and location, driving to the small guesthouse outside Granada, monitoring and then following the two men—the general and the hotel owner—from the guesthouse to the restaurant in Granada. Then, as they left pursuing them, and giving chase, following them up into the windy mountain roads, missing the turn and then propelling forward into the oncoming headlights of the farmer's pickup. All this followed by: complete blackout. Then a vague memory of being spoken to in the car and walked to an ambulance. An EMS paramedic had declared they would go to the hospital for observation overnight.

As the assassin lay there, a slight fog clouded the mind, straining to recollect more about the previous night's events. There was something missing. Something important. *My partner? Where is he?*

The assassin sat up and looked around the room, then it hit her.

She was working alone.

Her handler had later messaged saying there was no one to send; she would be flying solo. The world of freelance killers could get lonely, but in some ways, it was better that way. Last night's interaction played through her mind now in more detail. After asking for a light, she lost her balance on purpose and knocked the general's Panama hat to the ground, then she picked it up and attached a small tracking device under the hat's black band. Earlier in the evening, she had also placed a device on the undercarriage of the Peugeot as it sat parked outside the guesthouse—Hotel Casa Bosque. She had also entered the dilapidated garage and placed a device under an old Land Rover Defender. It had seemed overkill, but she'd been caught out with a change of vehicle before and didn't want to repeat the same mistakes. She had considered going in for the kill at the guesthouse, but her orders were clear: follow and monitor and only when prompted—eliminate.

She sat up, her head throbbing. It seemed like the worst that had occurred was a concussion. She thought back again to last night and remembered the paramedic saying her vital signs were okay; she just needed rest. With each second, her heart began to beat faster and faster. But she couldn't rest. Not now. There was a job to be done, an action to be completed. A target to be found, followed, and terminated. In the world of revolutions and political upheaval—her world—it was *assassinate or be assassinated*. The general was a traitor to *la patria* and the sentence for that was death. *Patria o muerte* were the words that echoed through the groggy fog of her mind as if it were a Yogi's mantra rattling in her brain: *fatherland or death*. She smiled to herself but then quickly frowned as she interrupted the mantra with a question: *but whose patria?* For the first time she questioned her beliefs as if the concussion had caused a break in the loop, knocking a kernel of contradiction into her mind. It was then that she also realised the hypocrisy within the empty slogan. As a Cuban and as an elite member of the G2, Cuba's *Dirección de Inteligencia*, why was she targeting a Venezuelan? Why was she targeting a man whose only crime is a complaint against his own government?

She shook her head from side to side to try to dispel her thoughts as if they were made of sand and a quick shake would disperse them. Then, as if a reflex from something drilled into her mind at school, the words of *Ernesto 'Che' Guevara* entered and answered the open questioning that had suddenly fallen on her. "We must struggle every day so that this love for humanity becomes a reality." The assassin smiled. That's why I am doing this—for the Cuban people, for the Venezuelan people, for *los pueblos* of Latin America and for revolution. To rid the world of Yankee imperialism and emancipate the free world. It rang through her head like a childhood earworm invading her thought process, like an annoying advertisement jingle that one remembers decades later. She was satisfied with her response, reasoning it was nothing more than a small sprout of cognitive dissonance seeping in. *The modern world, with all its complexity, has us all guessing what is true and what is false*, she thought.

After a while sitting upright, she felt light-headed as if she could lie down and sleep for the rest of the day, but then another of *El Che*'s quotes rang out in her mind. "Better to die standing than to live on your knees." Looking to the right, a wooden door led out to a corridor, the occasional flash of people in white coats visible in a small circular window. Looking lower at the bedside table, she saw a glass of water and a packet of *aspirina*. She swung her legs around and planted them on the cool tile floor, reaching for the glass and the aspirin. She extracted three tablets and gulped them down with a large swish of water. Moving her right hand across to her left arm, she pulled firmly on the needle of the intravenous drip, extracted it and placed it under the covers while also putting several pillows underneath the blankets to provide the illusion of a body in the bed. Now she stood for a minute, slowly regaining her balance, readjusting her body to the upright world, and gradually gained strength by breathing deeply and lightly stretching her limbs. A pair of dark jeans and white T-shirt lay over an armchair in the corner and sitting on the chair itself was a small leather shoulder bag that contained her belongings. She slid into the jeans and T-shirt and placed a pair of white Converse which she found under the bed on her feet, then flung the small bag over her shoulder. Hearing voices outside the door, she swung around rapidly and then ducked behind the bed. Popping her head up and glancing at the round window of the door she saw two figures dressed in white speaking outside, their muffled voices barely audible. After a few moments the figures disappeared and she approached the door. Pulling it towards her, she peered outwards and swivelled her head from left to right, ensuring no one was coming, then stepped out and walked with purpose down the corridor, quickly found an exit and waltzed out of the hospital. Outside in the sunlight she looked up at the name above the entrance, seeing it briefly before being temporarily blinded by the sun: *Hospital Virgin de las Nieves*. She rummaged in her satchel for her Ray-Ban Wayfarer sunglasses. Slipping them on, she sifted further through her belongings in the leather shoulder bag, and she was relieved to find a mascara case and lipstick. The violin case was still in her hotel. She would need to collect it before moving on.

From the hospital, she strode down *Avenida de la Consti-*

tución eventually crossing the busy avenue into *Avenida de Andaluces* before arriving at the *estación de ferrocarriles*—the train station. She organised a hire car—the other had been totalled in the crash—and while waiting for it to be brought around, she fished out a mobile phone from her satchel. She held the side button until the screen lit up. Flicking her fingers across the screen and with the phone now unlocked, she opened a decrypted mapping app. She peered at the screen, hoping the blue tracking dots would illuminate. One of the tracking devices she had planted shone on the screen. It appeared to be the one she had attached to the Peugeot, its location revealing it remained at the Guesthouse outside Granada. The device she'd attached to the Land Rover Defender was no longer visible. Ditto, the device on the general's Panama hat. With a few deft taps and swipes she came across the last known location information for the Panama hat and the Defender trackers—*Calle Santa Maria la Blanca*, Seville.

Some more swiping and pinching the screen to zoom in on the map revealed a plethora of hotels in the area: Pensión Javier, Hotel Rey Alfonso X Sevilla, Hotel Las Casas de La Judería, Hotel un Patio en Santa Cruz. *They could be holed up in any one of them*, she thought. Or in an apartment. An *Airbnb*. They must be underground? Or maybe they found the tracking devices?

She decided it was best to wait until they moved, then she could easily trace them. But at least for now, she had a destination. She closed the app and opened her contacts, scrolling to the name *JOAQUIN*, the alias for her Cuban intelligence handler from the MV department of G2. MV—or M5—was the department responsible for assisting and supporting 'illegals', those Cuban agents that worked without diplomatic cover and who entered countries on false passports.

The phone rang several times before she heard an answer. "*Sí?*

"*Soy yo.*" *It's me,* she replied.

"What's your status? We lost communication with you. Someone was dispatched from the Embassy in Madrid to check up on you."

"Tell them not to worry. I've just left hospital."

"Hospital? What happened? We can send a doctor; you know we have the best doctors in the world. We could—"

"No!" she interrupted before responding more calmly. "It's not needed. I'm fine; I will finish the job. I am ready to re-engage."

"Has a tracker been placed?"

"*Sí.*"

"On *every* vehicle? We don't want a repeat of Jakarta."

"*Sí.* There was an old 4X4 in the garage; it's being tracked."

"*Muy bien.* Then you should have no problem fulfilling your objective."

"*Ninguna.* I'll get a car and I'll be back in operation by this afternoon."

"Very well. You are now authorised to terminate. Remember it must look like an accident unless, of course, you have no other options."

"*Entendido.*" Understood.

She hung up as the hire car approached. She reached into her satchel one last time, grasping the modified mascara case which contained a retractable syringe loaded with aconitine.

Here is your accident, General, she thought as she smiled and softly laughed.

CHAPTER 13

SEVILLE, SPAIN

THE ROAD FROM RONDA TO SEVILLE WAS WINDY AND hilly at first as they descended from the southern Andalusian mountains. Olive groves and citrus orchards stretched out over the undulating countryside like a carpet of green cotton balls tinged with glints of orange and yellow. Mountains covered in pine trees sat behind barren yellow hills with craggy ravines that punctured the landscape like ancient scars. These were not the flat plains and windmills of *Castille* or *La Mancha*, but the parched, rugged mountains of southern Andalucía: baking hot in summer; snowy with a bitterly cold wind in winter. Occasionally in the distance a small white village would appear, clinging to the side of a hill or blending into the rocky peaks like a white fungus.

Jardine, Veronica and the general had left Ronald Ambrose's *finca* after an early lunch, deciding to drive during the heat of the afternoon. It was not recommended practice to drive at that time, but it meant that activity would be low during the *siesta* hours. There would be less traffic and less chance of coming across a *Guardia Civil* patrol on the open roads. Twisting along a valley road, the white village of *Zahara de la Sierra* came into view like a medieval fort of white stone blended into a rocky outcrop on the top of a mountain.

The general spoke. "You know, for a Latin American it's always strange passing through Andalucía. The landscape, those villages. They feel like home, like something familiar to us. You've been to *Villa de Leyva* in Colombia, no? That," he pointed to the mountaintop, "reminds me of *Los Nevados* outside of *Mérida* in Venezuela. A small white village just like that one." He laughed. "It is only when I listen to the people speak, that I realise I'm not at home. We are so similar but so far."

"It sounds like you miss Venezuela already, General?"

He sighed. "Is it that obvious? I don't know when I will return. Sometimes I even contemplate doing nothing, throwing in the towel. For a time, I did this in Venezuela, you know? After years of crisis. No food, no medicine, no security, the sense of society lost. After years of that, *día tras día*, it wore me down. The whole system was crumbling; Madera's regime gained control of the electoral and judicial system; even the opposition gaining a majority in the National Assembly couldn't overcome it. And I know what you're thinking, I'm just a privileged ex-general lamenting the loss of my power, but it's not that. *Para nada*. Everyone agrees: Amnesty International, Human Rights Watch, and the UN Human Rights Council. Even Sánchez's former supporters have abandoned his ideas. But all that didn't seem to matter. That's when I truly lost hope. I didn't even want to read the newspaper anymore, something I always did, every day, *sin falta*. I even thought about whiling away my days watching *telenovelas* to escape the horror that only got worse day by day. And if you know me, I detest *telenovelas*."

They both sat in silence for a moment before Jardine

asked, "Then why make this trip? Why the change of thought? You could've comfortably rested in exile out of harm's way."

"I did think of that," said the general as he shuffled in his seat. "But I thought if everyone was like me, then that would be exactly what Madera would want. Everyone lacks so much hope that their attempts seem futile. After mulling over this for days, you know, there's only so many *telenovelas* one can watch. I realised that any small step towards regaining democracy in Venezuela would be enough. *Poco a poco*. Day after day, we could get our country back on track. *Y así fue. And that was it.*" He shook his head, chuckled, and then continued, "It was also personal, in a sense. I thought of my father who had worked for years to establish his bakery. He was an immigrant from Portugal. I know you probably thought I was using a fake Portuguese passport when I checked in, but no, it was real."

"I did wonder," said Jardine with a quizzical look on his face.

"My father immigrated to Venezuela during the beginnings of the oil boom in the 1950s. He set up his bakery and it became a success. The Portuguese are well known for their bakeries in Caracas. Then later, much later, as Lieutenant-Colonel Sánchez came to power and established price controls, bakeries were designated 'special contributors' and they had to pay double taxes for the basics of milk, eggs and cheese. In most cases they couldn't even get flour! Then the people from the SUNDDE came—the so-called National Superintendence for the Defence of Socioeconomic Rights. They were government-appointed 'volunteers' who came in and told you how to run your business and what prices everything had to be. Only they had no idea and made ludicrous suggestions based on ideology rather than what practically works. That is when you realise how hopeless the situation is when you have such incompetents in control."

"It doesn't sound very effective."

"Exactly. But anyway, you could say that was the tipping point when small family run businesses couldn't survive, the economy collapsed." The general's mood had lost its earlier melancholy and he smiled with watery eyes. "Everyone deserves a chance to better themselves, to deny that is inhumane."

As they approached Seville, the land flattened out and the heat became visible, shimmering on the horizon like white gold. The general had dozed off in the front passenger seat and Veronica was stretched across the seat in the back, snoring slightly. It was only a little over two hours before the Defender began to rattle over the cobblestoned streets of the barrio of Santa Cruz in Seville, or as the city was famously known, The Pearl of Andalucía. As a former gateway to *Las Americas*, Seville once witnessed all the riches of the American continent pass along the Guadalquivir River to its port as it was granted a royal monopoly to trade with Spanish colonies. Huge quantities of gold, silver and other products pillaged from the continent were offloaded and spent by the King and his family in Spain. It was a theme that continued to this very day. Latin America had freed itself from colonial rule, but the pillaging of natural resources continued. The Spanish King had been replaced by home-grown *caudillos* and powerful oligarchs converting into a small elite who owned large swathes of land and production, a fact that had caused a wave of revolutions and insurgencies throughout the twentieth century. But like the pigs in *Animal Farm*, the revolutionary movements that were successful—through force or elections —were usually no better than the power they deposed. In the case of Venezuela, the oligarchs had been replaced by the *boli-garchs*, the tongue-in-cheek name for the new rulers of the

Bolivarian revolution. The Spaniards had pillaged the Latin American continent while charging taxes, much like Sánchez used the Venezuelan Central Bank, brimming with oil revenue, to consolidate his power. It became a piggy bank for false promises and ultimately people suffered.

Jardine parked the Defender in the underground car park of the hotel and switched off the engine. He turned to the general as he awoke from his nap. "Let's hope that one day Venezuela will be democratic and prosperous as it once was."

"*Ojalá*," said the general. "I hope so."

CHAPTER 14

Barrio Santa Cruz — Seville, Spain

The small lobby of the *Hotel Las Casas de La Judería* was air conditioned, providing crisp cool air, a relief from the heat outside. The hotel itself was a string of old houses linked together by a labyrinth of tunnels, inner laneways, passages, and patios dating back to when *barrio Santa Cruz* was known as the *la judería*—the Jewish quarter. The property was littered with plant-filled courtyards, trickling fountains, and lush gardens and although it was a well-known hotel in the area, it was secluded and private and the underground rooms with the network of passages and laneways offered a hidden sanctuary and a variety of escape routes if needed.

As the group approached the reception, a man in his early twenties looked down at a computer screen. He received their EU driving licences without question and another employee showed them to two adjoining rooms. After a few hours settling in and resting from the drive, Jardine phoned the general on the hotel phone and mentioned that he and

Veronica would head out for an early dinner. Early by Spaniard standards meant eight o'clock, that is. Most Spaniards wouldn't think of dinner until ten at the earliest.

The general, in reply, said he would stay in and order room service. It wasn't worth the risk for him to be seen outside again. The incident in Granada had caused him to reassess the hazards. If they found him once, they could find him again, he reasoned, but it was likely Jardine was not yet on their radars so Veronica would not be compromised. Besides, the general could use the time to make some calls and ensure everything was in order for his arrival in Lisbon.

Showered and changed, Jardine and Veronica checked in with the general at seven-thirty. After a brief exchange to finalise their plans for the next morning, the general looked at his watch and then flung his battered Panama hat towards Jardine. "You might need this." The hat floated briefly through the air and he caught it on the brim. The general continued, "The sun is still out and strong and I imagine your complexion doesn't work well with this Andalusian sunshine."

Jardine slapped the hat on his head and smiled. "I promise I'll bring it back in one piece." He went to grab the door handle to leave but turned, taking off the hat and holding it up as if on display. "You know it's called a Panama hat but really it's from Ecuador."

"I know. *Sombrero de paja toquilla*. Where do you think I bought it?"

Jardine nodded his approval. "Good to know it's authentic." And with that, he and Veronica left, weaving their way through the hotel's warren of tunnels, before exiting the hotel and turning right onto the narrow *Calle Maria la Blanca*. They crossed through a small plaza of open-air cafés, glancing at the chalkboard menus as they passed and then continuing into *Calle Ximenez de Enciso*. They were now firmly in the labyrinthine alleyways of the *barrio Santa Cruz*. The neighbourhood was the former Jewish quarter, a haven for the Sephardic Jews who flourished in Spain until being expelled in the fifteenth century with the grave choice: convert, leave or die. Their general destination was Seville cathedral and *La Giralda*, the famous bell tower atop a former minaret. They knew the streets nearby were filled with small tapas bars and would provide some options for them to have a low-key dinner.

The smell of fried fish wafted through the air, reminding Jardine of the men in the restaurant in Granada. It caused him to arch his back, his eyes darting. As he walked, holding Veronica's hand, he scanned the crowd, looking for familiar faces, someone following him. He'd rarely needed to employ this type of tradecraft in Colombia; usually those following him were so obvious it didn't require advanced training to shake would-be pursuers. They were usually stocky in an ill-fitting suit or dressed in a leather jacket with aviator sunglasses, moustache optional, as if they'd stepped out of a B-grade spy movie set in a fictional Latin American country.

His eyes continued to dart from left to right. He wasn't sure if he was just being paranoid or just overly cautious. He wasn't so worried about the *Guardia Civil*. Being away from Lieutenant Muñoz, they should be safe. It was more the unknown threat of Madera's regime that hung over him. The two men they had seen at the restaurant and who had chased them through the hills outside Granada. He didn't know what had happened to them. Had they been killed? Injured? Even if they had been put out of the game, there would be more, so it was best that he remained alert.

In thinking this, Ambrose's voice suddenly rang in his head, reciting the archaic tips from the SOE training manual. "Assume that you are being followed." Then, if a follower is spotted, "Spend time in large stores and use elevators." *That wouldn't be possible here in the old part of town*, he thought. "Get into crowds," was next. *That's more likely; September in Seville is swarming with tourists.* "Walk up a side street and take a sudden turn." This was the pièce de résistance in this environment. The rabbit warren that was Santa Cruz would be to their advantage if they were followed.

Turning the corner and passing a window displaying tourist menus, Jardine stopped and pulled lightly on Veronica's arm, directing her to look into the window. Pretending to peruse the menu, he waited as three teenagers passed by dribbling a football along the ground. They passed without stopping and continued down the street. A small group—two middle-aged couples, who appeared to be German tourists, wandered slowly looking at the menus outside the restaurants on the opposite side. The shorts and socks with sandals were a dead giveaway as to their country of origin.

"Everything okay, Ollie?" Veronica asked as she peered into the window.

"Just running a quick surveillance check to see if anyone stops or does something suspicious in the reflection."

Veronica raised her eyebrows with a look of 'what-the-hell-are-you-talking-about?' Then she smiled. "Yes, do watch out for those four with the socks and sandals. They looked particularly suspicious."

Jardine smiled, surprised. "You are paying attention."

"I guess I'm a quick learner." Veronica smiled and tugged at his arm as they walked further down *Calle Mateos Gago*—a touristy pedestrian street leading to the cathedral. The Giralda bell tower loomed ahead like a watchtower, at least that's how it felt, as they saw a small crowd gathered in the street on the corner of *Calle Rodrigo Caro*. People spilled out of a small tapas bar. It was now well past eight o'clock and still much too early for the locals to be thinking about dinner. But like most places with high influxes of tourists in Spain, they offered an 'early bird' discount for those diners eating before the standard Spaniard dinner hour.

Approaching the tapas bar, they saw a yellow building with a red awning which sat opposite a string of scooters parked outside a pharmacy. An *artesanías* shop selling tourist T-shirts, mostly red with depictions of bulls and flamenco dancers, sat on the other corner. Written on the red awning above the bar was: *Bodega Santa Cruz*.

"This looks popular," said Veronica.

"A good place to blend in," replied Jardine.

The windows on either side of the entrance to *Bodega Santa Cruz* were plastered with *Tripadvisor* 'Certificates of Achievement', *Yelp* recommendations, health regulation certificates, and a solitary 'Golden Tapas Award 2012'. Surprisingly, and despite the early hour, a scattering of elderly Spaniards sat at high round tables, men in open-neck shirts with gold chains and women with permed hair. A large group of Sevilla FC fans in red and white striped football kit filled the rest of the space, the colour of their tops matching the red Coca-Cola branded serviette holders sitting on each table. It seemed some Spaniards did venture out early or perhaps it was the UEFA Cup game that evening. The tapas menu was scribbled on a chalkboard above the bar and Jardine ordered a glass of *rioja* for Veronica and a cold *caña*—the name for the small glasses of beer in Spain—from the bartender.

The bartender acted swiftly, pouring the glass of wine while simultaneously pulling a beer tap releasing frothy beer into a glass before promptly pushing both towards them.

Jardine smiled in appreciation.

"They call me *bala*, you know?" said the bartender in Spanish with a smile. *Bala* being Spanish for bullet. A name straight from a gangster novel. "But not because I'm involved in anything to do with guns, no *señor*. It's my speed with serving drinks."

"I can see you are worthy of that name," said Jardine. "To eat we'll have the *solomillo al whisky, sardinas fritas, berejenas con miel* and *patatas bravas*."

The bartender nodded, and Jardine went to the table in the corner that Veronica had found. The food arrived almost as quickly as the drinks had been served, soon filling their small table.

Veronica picked up her glass and spoke. "You know I thought we'd left all this trouble behind after your last little adventure in Colombia." She sipped the wine and placed the glass back on the table before holding up a slice of crusty baguette with a fried sardine balancing on top. "And I hope this doesn't affect the hotel's rating. You know how fickle the comments on those travel review sites can be. If a person doesn't like the temperature of the toast, it's cause for complaint."

"Hot toast is important, you know?" said Jardine with a smile, sipping the small glass of beer. "If anything, it could help us. Once all of this is over, we can advertise it as the 'Hotel of famous wrongly accused fugitives'."

"Assuming the *Guardia Civil* learns the truth and nothing more happens. What has the general said to you? What's his game plan?"

"If we can get to Lisbon, he's home free. He said he would be meeting his people at the airport, and from there, he'll be in good hands."

"Well let's hope that's the last of it," said Veronica, biting into the baguette.

At that moment, a group of English football fans entered the bar. At first glance Jardine thought they were a typical 'lads on tour' posse, but on further inspection, he noticed they all had matching tattoos. Perhaps a more sinister group of hooligans? As the group entered their eyes darted around the room. Jardine sensed a hint of violence in the air. On a flatscreen in the corner, a banner for tonight's EUFA Europa league match spread across the screen: Sevilla vs Liverpool. That would explain the invasion of red-shirted Liverpudlians, with equally red faces, flooding into the bar. Jardine felt strangely relieved as another of Ambrose's SOE spy manual refrains droned through his mind. *Try to blend in with your surroundings.*

This is panning out nicely, he thought.

THE ASSASSIN PEERED DOWN AT THE SCREEN OF HER smartphone as she heard a chime. A blue dot appeared on the map of her encrypted tracking application. She watched as it darted through the alleyways of *barrio Santa Cruz*. Jumping up from the bed in the small *pensión* where she was staying, she slung her small leather bag over her shoulder and strode out into the street, jogging with the mobile phone in hand. She was several blocks away on the other side of the cathedral and pushed forward arriving within ten minutes at a small tapas bar with red awnings, flooded with a sea of ruddy-faced men in red Liverpool football shirts who blended into a sea of red and white striped Sevilla FC tops.

Two waiters at a nearby restaurant eyed her as she stood outside taking in the sights and smells of the *noche sevillana* beginning as the tapas restaurants, *churrerías*, Italian restaurants and Irish pubs of *Calle Mateos Gago* began to serve the crowds. She entered the bar and pushed forward, cutting through the drunken antics of the crowd like a shark fin through water. The scent of sweat and fried food filled the air as she watched groups engaged in conversation, laughing and slapping each other on the back before the big game. High in the corner, a large flatscreen TV broadcast the introduction of the teams.

She still wore the sunglasses, black jeans, a white T-shirt, and white Converse she'd been wearing since leaving hospital.

She shuffled forward through the crowd arriving at the bar itself. Two men—part of the Liverpool football crowd—stumbled their way through the crowd, bumping shoulders with other patrons as they sidled up beside her. "Hello, love. Fancy a drink with us?"

She turned to look at them, her face blank behind the sunglasses. "No, thank you," she replied, in English, rolling her eyes before looking away with an uninterested look on her face.

The second man grabbed her wrist. "Come on, we'll look after ya. We don't bite."

She spoke again. "*Por favor*, let go of my hand and..." She pushed her face closer to theirs and hissed, "Leave. Me. The. Fuck. Alone."

One of the men tried to put his arm around her waist and pull her back towards him, but in an instant, she grabbed him by the belt, reached into her leather shoulder bag, and produced a sharp knife-like instrument protruding from her lipstick case. She held it firmly, pushing it against the man's jeans just below the waist. The tip poked into his jeans' zipper as she whispered in his ear, "Do you want your appendix extracted, right here, right now? Or how about your balls chopped off? Oh, and it won't be covered by the NHS's agreement with the Spanish National Health System because you voted to leave the motherfucking EU. So, what'll it be, *pendejo*?"

The second man stood back, his eyes open wide and his mouth ajar. The man she was threatening tried to arch his body away, but she held onto his belt and pushed the sharp pointed object a little closer towards his skin. "Are you leaving, or shall I have your balls?" she asked finally.

The man stammered. "I... I... I think we'll just head back with the boys, yeah?"

The assassin let go of his belt and smiled. "Good idea.

That's a good boy, jog on" —she said this in a perfect Cockney accent — "and how about you behave yourself this weekend in Seville? It's quite common for a girl to carry sharp objects these days. You never know who you might run into. Oh, and *viva Sevilla FC*!"

The two men clambered through the crowd back towards the group as the assassin shook her head slightly and then turned again to the bar, ordering a glass of sangria. She took a large gulp and then swivelled, resting her back and both elbows on the bar while surveying the room. Lowering her glass, she reached with her right hand into her leather shoulder bag and stowed the small knife-like object—the lipstick case with retractable razor-sharp point—a quick stab and pull with that implement in a high-pressure area would cause a large volume of blood to flow with minimal entry wound. *Didn't expect I'd need to use that so soon*, she thought, as she took another sip and let the breeze blowing down from a ceiling fan cool her body. With her hand still inside her shoulder bag, she grasped the mascara container. *Hopefully it won't come down to using this*, she thought. The mascara held a more serious apparatus.

She placed the glass of sangria on the bar and continued to scan the room. After she'd taken in her surroundings, she couldn't see the general anywhere. She took out her mobile phone again and saw that the blue dot was flashing in her exact position. She looked up again. *He must be here*. She bit her lip and tapped her foot impatiently while again surveying the room when her head stopped. Her eyes widened; her pupils dilated. It wasn't the general, but a man in his mid-thirties sat at a small table in the corner; the woman accompanying him stood up and moved towards the bathroom. She picked up her glass again and took another sip, chancing a look again as she mulled over her next move.

I recognise him from the restaurant in Granada.

. . .

Jardine had just taken the last forkful of *patatas bravas* as Veronica was returning from the bathroom when he noticed the woman in sunglasses eyeing him from across the bar. Usually, he'd be flattered but it became immediately apparent to him that she wasn't 'checking him out' at least not in a romantic way. His stomach sank, his skin became hot as he recognised her as the woman who had asked the general for a light in the restaurant in Granada. Ambrose's voice floated through his mind again. "If you see the same face or hear the same voice twice, it's likely you're being followed."

Is she following us? This dawning realisation caused him to grip his fork tightly as he lowered his hand, discreetly slipping it into his back pocket. There was no spy manual mantra for weapons, but he guessed a fork would be a useful implement to have when your back is against the wall. Seeming to notice that Jardine was watching her, the woman flinched and looked towards the door as if watching the pedestrian traffic outside. Nearby, two men from the hooligan posse were pointing at the woman and swinging their arms in pantomime, animatedly talking to their friends. Their faces grew angry and a large group of them moved forward towards the woman, surrounding her. Their heads arched forward, shouting as bubbles of spit flew through the air. It was clear they were agitated about something and she was their target.

The woman paid them no attention, ignoring them while trying to step away and gesturing with her middle finger and a smile. She managed to slide slowly through the crowd, landing a few metres from Jardine and Veronica, but the group of men persisted and surrounded her again, blocking her path and forming a cordon around her. The woman still seemed unfazed and focussed her gaze on Jardine, like a pair of lasers burning a hole in them from behind her sunglasses.

Veronica returned to the table from the bathroom, and Jardine spoke through gritted teeth at her. "Time to go, Vero. Keep walking and exit like you don't know me. I'll follow. Act natural." Another tradecraft axiom floated in his mind. "Never give any sign (either by sudden, undue haste or looking round) to show a follower that you suspect you are being followed." *Too late for that now*, he thought.

"But I've barely touched my wine, couldn't we—"

"Now, *vámonos ya!*" he hissed through gritted teeth, trying not to move too quickly or suddenly.

Veronica sighed and continued walking past him, leaving via the main door.

Jardine stood up, took out two twenty-euro notes, and then wedged them under a serviette holder and moved towards the exit. He saw Veronica outside already turning to the left.

The group of four men still blocked the woman as she tried to move forward but they wouldn't let her pass, taunting her and occasionally pushing her. The bartender and several other patrons began to pay attention to the tussle between the woman and four men. The bartender wiped his hands on a tea towel as if preparing to intervene.

The next movement took everyone by surprise.

In an instant, the woman swung her left arm around connecting her fist with the cheek of one of the men to her right. The sound was a meaty thwack which made everyone in the bar flinch as it rang out. Almost immediately after the punch, she pivoted backwards, letting her right elbow fly backwards, landing square on the nose of a man standing behind her. The two men crumpled, both wincing in pain as blood trickled down their faces. Anticipating that the remaining men would lunge at her—which they did—she crouched as their wild roundhouse swings missed, setting them off balance. While they wobbled, she stood and swung her right fist forward in swift punches to their throats, causing them to rasp and wheeze and fall to their knees, clutching their windpipes. As the last two men fell, the bartender—who had seen it all unfold—began to clap enthusiastically and shout, *Bravo! Bravo! Bravo!* Other patrons either nodded in surprised appreciation or clapped along not knowing what was happening. A few elderly ladies pulled out white handkerchiefs and waved them in the air as if they'd just watched a bullfight.

As the ruckus unfolded inside the bar, Jardine and Veronica quickly left. Jardine broke into a light jog, extending his arm out to hold hands with Veronica. After a short while, they were soon lost in the maze of alleyways of the *barrio Santa Cruz*.

"Where are we going? Why are we running?" asked Veronica.

"That woman ... I think she's the one that followed us in Granada."

"I thought you said it was two men?"

"That's what we thought, but I remember her now. She must be the one after the general. Or maybe they all are? I don't know. But we need to lose her somehow." Jardine swivelled around; they were surrounded by narrow pedestrian streets and alleyways.

Ambrose's words came flooding back to him: "the easiest trick to avoid surveillance: boarding public transport at the last minute. This, of course, depends on how many are following you. Failing that, use elevators in big stores."

The tram is several blocks away and it's not exactly very fast. And there's not a department store in sight, thought Jardine.

"I have an idea. The *Alcázar*," said Veronica.

"Vero, now is not the time for sightseeing we—"

"Just trust me, okay?" Veronica interrupted as she pulled out the burner phone they had packed and began to tap rapidly on the screen. After a moment, a small ping sounded, and she smiled. "Come on, follow me."

. . .

THE ASSASSIN BURST OUT OF THE BAR LEAVING THE group of men nursing their broken noses, bruised cheeks and damaged voice boxes as they rolled and writhed on the ground. The cheers of 'Bravo! Bravo! Bravo!' had died down but many of the clientele were still cheering with laughter and commotion, replaying the scenes in animated conversation. Outside, the assassin peered to the left and saw a flash of a couple jogging down *Calle Rodrigo Caro* and turning right.

She sped off in pursuit.

CHAPTER 15

Hotel Las Casas de la Judería — Seville, Spain

General Angel Fernando Pereira Gallegos found himself sitting on the queen-sized bed in his basement room in the *Hotel Las Casas de La Judería*, feeling like a parrot in a cage. He had eaten a club sandwich, spoken with his small team in Madrid, and now sat with his legs stretched out in front of him, remote control in hand, flicking through various news channels. He reached for a cup of instant coffee sitting on a bedside table, sipped it and sighed. In the call he had previously made, he had confirmed the last part of his plan was still in play. There was one last source to meet in Lisbon before his intelligence-gathering mission was complete. He would then have all the evidence he required to present at the United Nations in New York. He felt slightly guilty that he was purposely withholding this pertinent information from Jardine and Veronica because if they really knew the magnitude of his plan and the information he already carried, they may not have been convinced to help him.

Mulling this over, his hand trembled slightly as he again

drank his coffee. On returning the cup to the bedside table, he sighed once more. A year locked up in *Ramo Verde* prison, followed by months in the Spanish Embassy in Caracas, then his daring escapade across the Colombia border and now here he was—still locked in a room, only this time with a nicer bed and *CNN En Español* to accompany him. He shook his head slightly at the thought of his predicament. *It wouldn't hurt if I ducked out of the room for an hour. Not really outside, just outside this room. The hotel is full of small discreet courtyards of lush vegetation and fountains. Surely, it wouldn't hurt to get some fresh air, be surrounded by plants? At least escape this hotel room for un momentico.*

Swinging his legs off the bed, he slipped into a pair of loafers, grabbed a copy of *El Pais* newspaper, picked up his reading glasses from a desk in the corner and slid out of the room in search of a secluded alcove with some fresh air. Strolling through the small passageways of the hotel, he headed for a small courtyard he remembered passing on the way in. Approaching, he turned a corner to see an elderly— what he assumed to be—French couple sitting on a metal bench with glasses of wine in hand. Both were reading well-worn copies of *Don Juan Tenorio*. The novel was set in Seville, and they were no doubt indulging in a romantic getaway to follow in its literary footsteps. Continuing to the next court-yard, he stumbled across three women in their late twenties speaking in animated voices which echoed throughout the courtyard. Americans, he assumed as two of them wore jeans with sneakers. A dead giveaway. He was beginning to regret leaving the room. *Perhaps I should return?*

Then he remembered a bigger courtyard which housed several sofas and chairs closer to the front entrance. It wasn't as secluded as he had hoped, but still, it would be better than the stuffy hotel room. He continued down a small flight of stairs, along a narrow tunnel which ran under the hotel and then semi-jogged up a small set of steps, arriving at a larger partially covered courtyard containing a gushing fountain in the centre. In this courtyard, a man in his late forties sat at a metal table, typing on a laptop. An iPad was propped up next to him. *A journalist or writer, perhaps?* On the wall opposite him was a flatscreen TV showing the news of the day. In the corner, under cover, sat a leather sofa and two large leather armchairs. A plump man in a pink polo top and chinos sat in one of the armchairs, an iPad on the coffee table in front of him. *The sofa,* thought the general. The plush sofa sat empty as he moved towards it. He nodded to the man in the pink polo top and sat down, shaking the newspaper in front of him and began to read. Large potted palms were spread around the courtyard like a small tropical forest. Bougainvillaea dripped down from balconies above like a green and pink waterfall cascading into the courtyard. A slight breeze blew in from above, cooling the air from the remaining heat of the day. He breathed in the fresh air and smiled to himself as he set in to read the paper. *Mucho mejor. Much better,* he thought.

After a few minutes of reading, he heard movement and noticed the man in the pink polo top had shuffled along to the armchair opposite the sofa. He was now sitting directly opposite him. The general lowered the paper as the man looked towards him, smiling. In locking eyes with the general, he reached out his hand. "Bob McAdams from Houston, Texas. Where y'all from?"

The general rustled the paper nervously, not sure how to respond. "Portugal," he said finally.

"Portugal? Ain't that something? I was just there with my wife, beautiful spot. We did Oporto, Coimbra, and then Lisbon. Then we decided to come down this way to see old Chris Columbus's tomb in the cathedral down there near the Alcazar and that bell tower. Thought it was about time we visited the roots and founder of our great nation, America."

A muffled snort followed by sardonic laughter emanated from the man at the laptop in the corner but neither the general nor the pink polo man noticed.

"Ah yes, Cristóvão Colombo we say in Portuguese. A complicated figure with regard to—"

The general stopped mid-sentence as news from Venezuela flashed on the screen.

The newsreader spoke from the top of an International Hotel in Caracas. "Today in Caracas, riots have broken out in the aftermath of an attempted assassination on the Venezuelan president via drone." Footage of the drone attack played on a loop as the newsreader continued. "It comes after years of crisis in the embattled South American nation, thought to possess the largest known oil reserves in the world. This event has occurred just over one year after the government was accused of a 'self-coup', as the president, Tomás Madera Toros, ordered the Supreme Court to usurp the opposition-controlled National Assembly, paving the way for a new constitution written by a parallel Constituent Assembly, a body which is largely made up of members of the current ruling socialist party and its allies. It is thought—"

"Well, I'll be damned," the pink polo man interrupted and pointed to the screen on the wall. "Wanna thank our lucky stars we didn't head down to Venezuela for our vacation. What a goddamn mess." He shook his head. "I used to travel there back in the seventies and eighties; I was in oil, you see. It's a darn shame what they've turned that country into."

The general muttered a reply. "Yes, a shame indeed." Then, wanting to steer the conversation away from his home-land, he asked, "How did you find Lisbon?"

The pink polo man continued, not having listened to the general's question. "You see, that's what people don't get. Communism or socialism, whatever you want to call it, it don't work! You got price controls, secret police, and then you gotta have a bureaucracy the size of ... well, size of Texas to keep it all in check. Which, of course, eats up all the government revenue and then meddling in the market knocks out the economy and the motivation to produce anything. Then everyone gets down in the dumps because everyone's tattling on everyone else to please the secret police. It's a corrupt system from the top down. It's a one-way ticket to totalitarianism."

The general nodded without uttering a word. He wished he could somehow vanish, teleport back to his room to be in peace and escape the diatribe from pink polo man.

"Now isn't that just an absolute load of bullshit!" The younger man—whom the general assumed was a journalist or writer spoke up now. He had shortly cropped hair and glasses and wore a dark-coloured shirt buttoned all the way to the top. "What's your solution? Capitalism?" The man huffed and crossed his arms. "A system whose never-ending quest for economic growth is destroying the planet, squeezing the middle class and shifting all the profit and value to the one percent. A system which sucks value and autonomy from people as they try to eke out a living by screwing over others."

"Geez, where'd you read that?" said pink polo man, then adding with a pompous twang, "The Commie Daily?"

"If you'd taken a small iota of time to step outside your neo-con bubble and stop listening to corporate propaganda machine of one of the most powerful countries on earth, you might be better informed." The man finished his sentence in a flurry of sneering condescension and a trickle of sardonic chuckling.

"Powerful countries?" asked the pink polo man. "You mean like China? Russia? India?"

The spectacled man huffed and puffed. "No! The US of A. The capitalist ruler of the free world. You know, *home of the greed, land of the depraved!*"

Pink polo top's face turned the same colour as his shirt and his eyes seemed to bulge as his back arched. "If you love those commie countries so much, why don't y'all live there?"

After a few moments, the general spoke, addressing both the men and trying to calm the situation. "I agree with some of what both of you have said, but let's not forget about the Venezuelan people. Five to six million Venezuelans have left the country."

"Oh yeah, how would you know?" The man in glasses stood and walked towards them. "You probably only watch the mainstream CNN, Fox, BBC, yada yada yada media. Like a neo-liberal sheep. I imagine you just soak it all up, don't you?"

The general didn't want to respond or continue speaking about his country but muttered: "I have some friends who—"

"Oh yeah, great. Your friends who know friends who said some bullshit. I've heard that argument before. Besides, we all know, the only reason that everyone has left Venezuela was due to the draconian US sanctions."

"What was the excuse before you blamed everything on sanctions?" asked pink polo top, his voice rising.

"He's right in some ways to question the sanctions; they don't always have the intended consequences," added the general now, trying to reason with pink polo top man. "It's a tricky balancing act to apply pressure but not hurt the people."

"Sanctions my ass," said pink polo.

"In his defence," the general pointed to pink polo, "I think you'll find that the problems in Venezuela began much earlier than the sanctions."

The spectacled man leant over his laptop and typed rapidly on his keyboard, and then, picking it up, approached the general and the pink polo guy who were sitting on the sofa. "Look, it says it right here." The title of a news article was on the screen:

'Recent anti-government protests are part of a CIA-backed coup to unseat the democratic government of Venezuela.'

"Which website is that?" The general squinted, before finally seeing the publication title. "*The Grey Area*?"

"Yeah, well, like I said, you probably only follow CNN or Fox or one of those mainstream networks. Have you ever thought to follow the money? See who's funding them?"

"Who funds the '*The Grey Area*'?" interjected the pink polo man.

The man at the laptop frowned and froze, before muttering, "They received funding from a variety of independent sources that are anonymous. They..." His voice trailed off.

"Sounds mighty transparent," replied pink polo top man.

The general's mind was spinning. This was just what he didn't want, a shouting match to draw attention to himself. He slid down in his seat hoping the conversation would die down, dissipate, and float off into the evening. But it was the twenty-first century and everyone had an opinion. With a flood of 'news sources' curated on social media to show only what people already agreed with, it meant that many lived in echo chambers, unable to agree on basic facts. And it seemed when Venezuela was the topic of conversation, everyone had an opinion. Not because they care about the country or its people, but because it helped them to amplify their own political worldview.

Pink polo man stood now, aggressively pointing a finger like he was poking a swarm of mosquitos. "How about you take your piece of shit news source and shove it up your ass!" he said, now visibly angry, his face having fully blended into his polo top.

The man in glasses perched one hand on his hip, the other still balancing the laptop, and replied, "Yeah? Well why don't you make me, porky?"

And with that pink polo man pushed forward, attempting to wrestle with the bespectacled man as they both engaged in a match of push and shove until, eventually, two hotel employees came in and tried to calm them both down. The shouting match continued in full flight as the two hotel employees attempted to separate the men.

During the commotion, a tall man with a grey moustache and wearing a cowboy hat slid into the room. He sat on the sofa opposite the general and ignored the two men's shouts as they faintly echoed into the background and smiled at the general. His deep blue eyes gave him a friendly demeanour. In addition to the large Stetson hat which had a Pueblo tribal design band, he wore dark jeans and a denim shirt. Edging forward, sitting on the edge of his seat, back upright, he nodded towards the general. "What a mess."

"Venezuela or those two?" replied the general.

The man considered his response for a few moments before replying. "Both, I guess." He nodded towards the doorway where the shouts still emanated. "Politics?"

The general smiled and nodded. "It's always politics."

"Or religion," replied the man in the cowboy hat as he sat back, extending both arms out along the top of the sofa. "What is it with people these days? Why can't everyone just get along?" His moustache twitched as he spoke.

"I blame social media," said the general as he and the cowboy hat man turned their heads to continue watching the news report.

"Kids these days," replied cowboy hat, shaking his head.

"Drink?" asked the general, motioning to a passing member of the hotel staff.

"Sure, why the hell not."

The general ordered and a few moments later two frosty bottles of *Cruzcampo* beer arrived.

The two men held up their bottles, both saying *"Salud!"* as they each took a large gulp while listening to the distant echo of shouts still trickling into the courtyard.

CHAPTER 16

SEVILLE, SPAIN

JARDINE AND VERONICA JOGGED THROUGH A STRING of alleyways and then along *Calle Joaquín Romero Murube* until they reached *Plaza del Triunfo*. The General Archives of the Indies stood in front of them with the Seville Cathedral rising on their right. A row of horse-drawn carriages stood along one wall of the Archives and a driver approached them.

"Tour of Seville, *señor*?"

They shook their heads. "No, *gracias*."

On their left stood the *Puerta del Leon*, a pastel red wall between two castle-like turrets with a crowned lion grasping a cross above the large arched doorway. The entrance to the *Royal Alcázar of Seville*. A large line of sunburned tourists snaked out from the doorway and around the corner. Groups of Chinese tourists held parasols while red-faced Scandinavian couples waited next to American families with fanny packs. The heat was still intense and many sucked on cool bottled water while waving recently purchased *Sevillana* fans.

Veronica pointed at the entrance and cocked her head towards the *Alcázar*.

"That's your idea? Enter the *Alcázar*?"

"*Sí*," replied Veronica.

"What about the line?" asked Jardine, not letting the pressing urgency of the situation diminish his British preference for orderly lines. "It will cause a commotion if we just waltz through without lining up."

"I told you I had an idea." Veronica held up the burner phone, smiling. "Two express entry tickets purchased."

Jardine blinked as he glanced at the screen. "Well, why don't they just do that?" He pointed to the line of tourists. As with many famous monuments in Europe, a simple purchase online can—with a higher price, of course—gain one express entry. No line-up required. It still didn't stop hordes of tourists politely lining up to buy their entrance tickets the old-fashioned way.

Veronica shrugged. "I often wonder that myself."

"I knew you'd be able to weave your magic," said Jardine as he leant in and gave her a kiss on the cheek as they both strode towards the entrance. After a few steps, he turned abruptly to Veronica. "Wait, where did you get that phone? We said we weren't going to use any phones."

Veronica shrugged again. "It's a burner phone, no? I found it in the bag we packed. I know you always have a cheap pre-paid phone ready to go."

Jardine nodded impressed. "You're a quick learner, aren't you? Well let's get inside before she catches up with us."

The *Royal Alcázar* palace complex was a mix of buildings in *Mudéjar* (Moorish) style architecture with Renaissance and Gothic thrown in for good measure. Surrounded by high walls and dotted with courtyards and lush gardens, it would provide a useful place to hide. And once inside, Veronica and Jardine reasoned that they could potentially sneak out a backdoor, allowing them to return to the hotel and alert the general. Or at the very least lie low until the woman following them lost the scent.

Veronica scanned their tickets via the burner phone, and they entered the *Alcázar*, picking up a map of the layout and two audio guides. They paced forward into a large square of trees surrounded by low-lying hedges and propelled themselves forward through the various patios and terraces: *Patio de la Montería*, *Patio de las Doncellas*, *Patio del Crucero*, and the decadent interior rooms of the palace. Slipping on the audio guide headphones, they rambled under elaborate archways with *Mudéjar* plasterwork and briefly admired the decorative ceilings of royal iconography and the unique blend of Iberian Islamic art and tiles dotted throughout the complex. Jardine lamented the fact that there wasn't an express version of the audio guide where one could have the history recounted in a speeded-up format, one suitable for those being chased by an assassin.

Ten minutes had passed by the time they reached the palace gardens, an immense stretch of paved walkways sprinkled with fountains and lined by low-lying hedges with pines and palm trees swaying in the breeze. They arrived at a small fountain where a large Asian tour group huddled around as a guide spoke energetically into a small lapel microphone. Passing the group quickly, Jardine recognised the language as Korean from his days spent in South Korea. An easy beginner posting, ideal for new recruits due to its relative safety in terms of political stability and a friendly government. Much like its neighbour, Japan, the Republic of Korea experienced one of the lowest crime rates in the world, yet with a potentially nuclear-armed, volatile dictator as its other neighbour—North Korea—it meant the stakes were still high enough for a young MI6 recruit who was cutting his teeth.

As they paced through the gardens, Veronica grabbed

Jardine by the wrist and pulled lightly, indicating to stop. Jardine stopped and turned, keeping one eye on the entryway to the garden and the other eye on Veronica.

"*Mi amor*, can we stop for a moment?" asked Veronica. She let go of his wrist and propped both hands on her hips, sucking in air. "I just think we should stop and think about what we're doing for a moment."

"Sure," said Jardine.

While Veronica caught her breath, Jardine paced back and forth. His mind raced and he felt his heart rate increasing, his heart bouncing in his chest. *She was right; time to take a small breather and plot the next move*. It wouldn't hurt to clear their heads for a moment. "I guess we need to find an exit? A back door or somewhere we can slip out and evade that woman."

"Do you think she saw where we went?" asked Veronica.

Jardine shrugged. "I don't think so. But what I don't know is how she found us in the first place."

"Maybe she's been following us since Granada, only we didn't see her until now?"

"Either way, let's get back to the general and we can work out our next move."

They both gazed around at their surroundings; the sun still blazed down but under the leafy trees of the garden and near the cool trickling water of the fountain it felt fresher. The soft scent of pine filled the air, a sweet, fragrant odour in contrast to the heat and waft of fried foods and beer they had been running through moments earlier while escaping the small tapas bar. Here, it felt as if their predicament had suddenly vanished, and they could spend the rest of the evening wandering the gardens.

In another hour, the sun would set, the soft twilight a perfect background for photographers. Around them, young tourists snapped selfies from protruding 'selfie sticks' and small tripods, no doubt hashtagging with a reference to the popular series *Game of Thrones* which had been filmed in the garden, increasing its popularity with a younger crowd which may have otherwise overlooked it.

A young couple walked past them and after a few muffled comments from the woman, the man laid down on the ground, twisting and turning his body while aiming his phone's camera towards his girlfriend who posed and grinned. Once the photo was taken the woman's smile disappeared and she barked orders as the boyfriend dutifully followed in tow. By all accounts it would have been an outstanding photo for his girlfriend's *Instagram* account, but the split-second change from smiley pose to grouchy seriousness struck them both as psychopathic.

As the couple left, Jardine noticed a figure emerge from under a large, sand-coloured archway a hundred metres away. On further inspection it seemed to be a woman, moving slowly, a pair of self-guided audio headphones perched on her ears as she swept her gaze across the gardens. Then she stopped momentarily, lowering her head to glance at a mobile phone in her hand. To anyone else she was an innocent tourist taking in the sights of the palace gardens, but to Jardine it became immediately obvious she was not admiring the view. No, she was scanning, analysing and tracking. Like a female terminator crunching data on which humans to kill and which to let live.

"Vero," said Jardine, lightly grabbing her wrist. "Is your mind clear enough now?"

"Crystal, why?" she replied as she knelt to smell a pink rose.

"The fox has entered the hen house."

"*Qué?*" she asked.

"The eagle is tracking the mice."

"Have you got too much sun? It was rather hot back there..."

"Vero, that woman's here. Time for thinking is over. We need to get out of here now."

Veronica turned swiftly from admiring the rose and sprang to her feet, scampering towards the high stuccoed wall wall behind them. Jardine followed, trying not to draw attention to their sudden movements. A small archway appeared on their left and they jogged through it into the outer reaches of the gardens. A terracotta-coloured boundary wall ran along on their right. Jardine looked down at the map in the brochure that came with the audio guide to confirm that it was a wall which ran along *Paseo de Catalina de Ribera* on the outside. If they could find an exit through that wall, they could leave the *Alcázar* and return to the hotel. The ground was sandy gravel here and it crunched slightly under their feet as they ran along the wall, occasionally glancing back to see if they were being followed. So far, nothing. The crowds had thinned out in this section and it felt empty and alone.

They propelled forward to the north-west corner where they saw a large dark-green door surrounded by another sand-coloured archway. It appeared this door would lead out of the garden and on to the streets outside. There were bags of cement next to the door and a large blue skip bin. They were well and truly in the outer reaches of the garden, where few tourists roamed. Two groundsmen in khaki uniforms stood nearby chatting, one sitting in a golf cart, the other leaning on a shovel next to him. A security guard walked down towards the two men, jangling a set of keys. The three men, preoccupied with each other and no doubt almost at the end of their shift, didn't notice as Jardine and Veronica stood in front of the green door, not fifty metres away.

Jardine observed the large metal door and saw a type of latch mechanism halfway up. He lifted the latch and tried pulling on it, but it was stiff and rusted and didn't move. He tried again; it creaked this time but still didn't budge.

The two groundsmen were now speaking with the security guard, but they had still not noticed them.

Jardine turned hard on the door latch again. The door still didn't move but he could feel its latch loosening.

Veronica tapped him on the shoulder. "*Cariño*, how are we going?"

"Almost there; I can feel it moving a little."

"Okay. Well, not to alarm you but she's approaching ... rapidly."

Jardine turned his head to see the assassin semi-jogging towards them now. The absence of people had obviously emboldened her and she was working up to a fully-fledged gallop, like a cheetah winding up to pursue a gazelle. He twisted the latch and a loud creak escaped as it moved slightly.

The assassin sped up, moving closer and closer with each spring of her legs.

Jardine turned the latch again using all the strength of both arms. His biceps burned from all his efforts.

She was almost upon them now; they could hear the crunch of gravel rumbling under her feet as she got closer and closer.

With a final turn, a loud satisfying click emanated from the door as the latch unhooked and Jardine pushed the heavy door open. It groaned with a metallic creak. But after it opened a metre, it stopped and held stiff as if stuck.

"Go, go, go!" Jardine hissed.

Veronica shuffled her feet on the sand and managed to squeeze her body through the opening. Jardine followed, breathing in as he pushed his body through. Once through, he turned quickly and tried to push the door closed, heaving his shoulder against the door as it slowly moved. The groan of the rusty metal cried out, mixing with the sound of a skidding crunch of gravel and then a loud thud that banged on the door from the other side.

She's here.

He repositioned his hand to get a better grip, pushing against the door with his shoulder. He readjusted his hand once again, placing it midway up the door when suddenly he felt a small prick on the back of his hand. His eyes darted down and he saw slender fingers with dark red nail polish quickly withdraw from the other side of the door. He heaved harder and with a final push, the large metal door finally clanked shut. He turned the outside latch with a satisfying click and was about to collapse in a heap after exerting all that energy when he realised there was nothing to hold the latch in place. "Vero, find something to put through this hole to hold the latch," he said, still leaning against the door.

He heard shouts, Spanish voices, and loud footsteps from inside the garden grounds as it seemed the two groundsmen and the security guard had heard the commotion.

Jardine looked down at his hand. A small trickle of blood dripped down to his fingertips.

"Your hand!" said Veronica.

"It's nothing, just a small pinprick. It must have been that woman; she scratched me!"

"I don't have anything to hold the latch," said Veronica.

Jardine's eyes darted around then he suddenly realised he still had the fork he'd pocketed from the restaurant. He fished it out and jammed it into the latch, stopping it from moving. Once it was firmly in place, he took a step back, took off the general's Panama hat, and wiped his sweaty brow. A smear of blood spread across his forehead.

Veronica stepped forward and examined his hand. "It doesn't look too serious." She reached into her small handbag and produced a packet of disinfectant wipes. "Here, let me clean it; we don't want it getting infected." She wiped the wound clean, but a small trickle of blood still dripped slowly from it. She leaned forward and wiped the blood from his forehead.

"Vero, I feel fine. Let's just get back to the hotel," said Jardine, replacing the hat on his head.

She nodded as they both set off and began to jog along the *Paseo de Catalina de Ribera* towards the hotel.

CHAPTER 17

Royal Alcázar of Seville — Seville, Spain

THE ASSASSIN SAW THE COUPLE PASSING THROUGH the *Puerta del Leon* gate and followed in pursuit. A quick sweet-talking of the middle-aged man at the express ticket counter and a one hundred euro note later, she gained access, along with an audio headset.

She looked down at her mobile phone, following the blue dot and quickly realised it was stationary in the palace gardens. She smiled and strode through the various rooms, patios and terraces of the *Alcázar* before reaching an open garden. She placed the audio guide headphones over her ears but did not turn it on. Looking up from the phone screen, she saw a trickle of tourists strung around the gardens like confetti. There was a small group huddled together near a fountain and then, next to that group, she saw them. The man was watching her from afar like a curious rabbit. A second later he turned and walked quickly along one of the garden paths. She glanced down at her phone to confirm. The blue dot was now moving. It was them.

She strode forward, not wanting to draw too much attention to herself, but then, as the couple were about to pass through a stone archway into another section of the garden, the man chanced a backwards glance.

They *had* seen her.

She pushed forward as the couple disappeared into the outer section of the gardens. She picked up the pace, weaving her way along the path. She pulled off the audio guide headphones, letting them hang and swing around her neck. She arrived at the archway, looked through it to see a row of pine trees swaying in front of her, and scanned this new section of the garden.

In the distance, she could see the couple next to a blue skip bin, wrestling with a large green door. Glancing to her left, she noticed two khaki-clad groundskeepers and a lone security guard waddling on the other side of the garden. Swivelling her head back to the couple, she figured she could easily get to them and, with the method she had in mind for dealing with them, the security guard wouldn't even realise what had occurred.

She sprang forward, her feet crunching under the gravelly sand of the walkway. She reached into her shoulder bag and ran her fingers over the mascara case and lipstick, caressing the two smooth cylinders, both implements at the ready to withdraw as she pounced: the mascara for administering poison and the lipstick case for stabbing.

The cylinders were not a new design by any means. Based on a CIA plot to kill Castro in the 1960s, the mascara case had been modified with a poison-laced hypodermic syringe. The Cubans had managed to foil the attempt on Castro's life, stealing the technology. The original was housed in a *Paper Mate* brand pen, but no one carried pens anymore. Back in Cuba, she'd floated the idea of bringing an umbrella loaded with pneumatically propelled ricin pellets, as the Bulgarians did, 'taking care' of dissident writer Georgi Markov. But that technique was old hat and much too obvious. Intelligence Services around the world had a rational fear of umbrellas. The lipstick case was a much simpler design. It wielded a small, retractable steel spike that—placed in the correct point and with a slight pull—could open a vein like a sharp knife through warm Brie.

She was close now, moving forward with her eyes fixed on the couple as they struggled with the door. She heard the scraping of metal as the man fiddled with the door latch.

She drew closer and closer. Three metres... two metres...

She was barely a metre away, almost ready to punch, when she saw them shove the heavy door open. The woman had squeezed through the door opening and now the man, his body sideways, wriggled through the gap.

In this moment, the assassin lunged at the door, trying to wedge her foot in the gap to stop it from closing. Her killer instincts surged just as they had in Istanbul, in Asunción, in Havana, in Miami and in Jakarta on previous operations. As she slammed against the door, the metal rattled and she felt the man pushing the door from the other side.

She reached into her shoulder bag, withdrew a small cylindrical object, taking off the lid with her teeth, and thrust it forward, pricking the hand of the man as he wrestled, trying to push the door shut from the outside.

Once she felt the contact with the metal point on flesh, she withdrew her hand, replacing the lid she had retrieved from between her teeth, as the metal door clanged shut. She replaced the implement in her shoulder bag without looking and then grasped the metal door latch, jiggling it, hoping it might open, but it didn't budge. Heaving against the door proved equally unsuccessful.

Frustrated, she slammed her fist against the door. She went to pound it again but stopped. *Don't draw attention to yourself*, she thought. She heard footsteps crunching behind her and turned to see the two groundkeepers and the security guard running towards her.

Inside, she felt like yelling an expletive but instead she smiled and asked politely if one of the men could open the door for her. She swung her shoulder bag around behind her as if it were transparent and they could see inside it.

One of the groundskeepers responded, "*No señorita*, we cannot open these doors. They are for emergencies only."

The second groundskeeper and security guard nodded solemnly.

Her face flushed as she felt her temperature beginning to rise. She reached behind her back, slipping her hand into the shoulder bag. She clutched the cylinders and stepped aggressively towards the three men.

They shuffled awkwardly backwards, their mouths agape. Then she stopped, withdrawing her hand from the shoulder bag and slowly raised her hand to her long, dark hair, casually pushing it behind her ears. "Very well. Thank you. *Buen dia*, gentleman."

She nodded politely at them and turned to leisurely stroll back through the gardens, replacing the audio guide headphones to her ears to give the appearance she was a genuine tourist.

The three men exhaled while muttering to each other and wishing her a pleasant evening as she walked off.

The dose has been delivered, she thought. *It should only take a few hours to take effect; by then he should have led me directly to the general. Without that man to help him, the general will be all by himself*, she thought. Her head began to throb just as it always did when she got angry. She raised both hands up to her face, massaging her temples. As she continued through the gardens towards the *Alcázar's* exit, she realised her ankle was also throbbing. She wasn't sure if it was a result of the lunge towards the door or an old injury of torn ligaments she had sustained as a teenager during a softball match in her first year of university. She had studied history and foreign languages at *La Universidad de la Habana* before she was recruited—in her second year—to the *Dirección de Inteligencia (DI)* of Cuba, more commonly referred to as G2.

The slight pain in her head and ankle caused her to wince and she instinctively reached to her chest and held the caiman tooth necklace her Russian father had given her. He was always travelling and had brought it back from a trip to the Orinoco River in Venezuela and she'd worn it every day since. She held it whenever she was stressed or anxious. Its smooth texture contrasted with the small, jagged points, helping her to reflect on the need for elegance and beauty with action and aggression, something she'd had drilled into her at G2.

At first, she hadn't wanted to join G2, but when she was presented with the opportunity, she reasoned it would be the only way she could travel and see the world. Regular Cuban citizens weren't allowed to travel, and for a student of foreign languages, that was similar to an engineer who would never get to build a bridge or a doctor who never saw a patient. What good was it to study languages if you couldn't practise using them?

It was then that she had accepted the offer, although her father had also given her a nod in that direction. Her father had been a KGB trainer who was sent to Camp Matanzas in Cuba to strengthen the scores of Cuban agents who had trained at the KGB's Moscow Centre. During a weekend off in Varadero, he had met a local Cuban doctor—her mother. They married and supported the then Dirección General de Inteligencia (DGI) and later the Dirección de Inteligencia (DI) in their efforts around the world. The caiman tooth necklace from the Orinoco River she now held had been picked up while he armed and trained guerrilla fighters in *los llanos*—the flat plains of Venezuela—on one of Cuba's many overseas missions to propagate their revolutionary ideals.

Letting go of the necklace, she took out her phone and watched as the blue dot moved swiftly along *Paseo de Catalina de Ribera*. *The tracing chip is still in place*, she thought. *There's no rush*. She relaxed her shoulders a little as she continued her way through the gardens towards the main exit. She closed the tracing app, opened her contacts and hit call on the code name: JOAQUIN.

She pulled the audio guide headset off and raised the phone to her left ear.

A voice answered after two rings. "*Sí?*"

"Target confirmed. Not the general, but his source. A dose was delivered."

"You're sure?"

"Positive. Who is he?" she asked.

"Our intelligence says ex-MI6. And you're sure you administered sufficient agent?"

"The usual dosage," she replied in a serious monotone.

"Enough to kill a pig?"

The assassin's voice brightened, and she smiled. "Enough to kill a bay of pigs."

"*Muy bien*. Now the general," came the reply, then the line cut dead.

The assassin put the phone back in her bag, replaced the audio guide headphones over her ears, and took a deep breath as she hit play. "The *Alcázar* gardens are part of the Imperial Palace compound which in 1646..."

CHAPTER 18

Hotel Las Casas de la Judería — Seville, Spain

A FEW MOMENTS AFTER THE ICY AIR OF THE HOTEL foyer hit them, Jardine and Veronica heard muffled shouts coming from somewhere inside the hotel. Entering the front courtyard, having already passed the reception area, they saw the general sitting quietly on a sofa opposite a man with a cowboy hat and greying moustache. Both men watched a flatscreen TV and each drank cold bottles of *Cruzcampo* beer.

A random American-accented yell echoed from one of the hotel's passageways as if a radio had been left on. "Piss off, you fucking neo-liberal shrill! You're CIA!" As if in response, a deeper, American-accented voice with a Texas tinge burst through from a different passageway. "Yeah, well screw you ya goddamn pinko!"

Entering the courtyard, Jardine and Veronica nodded politely and approached the general. Jardine indicated with a slight sideways nod of the head for him to follow them back to their rooms. He stood up and extended his hand towards the man in the cowboy hat. "A pleasure. Please enjoy your evening," he said, shaking hands.

"Likewise, shame 'bout the *telenovela* just now," replied the man in the cowboy hat, taking a swig from the frosty bottle of *Cruzcampo* beer. "Seems people these days have lost the art of civilised debate. Oh, and thanks for the beer."

Jardine and Veronica smiled at the man and they returned to their adjoining rooms. Arriving at the door but not yet entering, Jardine turned to the general. "We were just followed by a woman."

"A woman?"

"The woman from the restaurant in Granada. Remember? The one that asked you for a light?"

The general's eyes widened, his pupils dilating. "Are you sure? How do you know it was her?"

Veronica spoke now. "Even if it wasn't her, this woman that followed us, she's bad news. She found us into a tapas bar and then followed us to the *Alcázar*."

"Why were you in the *Alcázar*? Now is not the time for sightseeing," he said.

"We weren't sightseeing," said Jardine. "We managed to lose her momentarily and then enter to *Alcázar* to hide, but she somehow managed to track us before we escaped through a back exit and then hightailed it here." He looked down to see the trickle of dried blood across the back of his hand, like a faint henna tattoo, fading at the edges.

"What happened to your hand?" the general asked.

"Oh, it's nothing; it seems she scratched me or pricked me with something as we exited the *Alcázar*. It's nothing serious, just a small puncture wound; I don't even feel any—"

A voice boomed from behind them. "You might wanna get that checked out, *amigo*."

Jardine, Veronica, and the general turned to see the cowboy hat man behind them. He leant against the whitewashed wall of the courtyard, his cool blue-grey eyes twinkling as he gave a slight smile, causing his grey moustache to wriggle under his nose.

"Sorry, but who the fuck are you?" asked Jardine, in a polite manner with a touch of disbelief.

"Just a friend," he replied, taking a swig of the *Cruzcampo* beer.

"A doctor?" asked Veronica.

"No, but I know a little something about what you're up against."

"And what's that?" asked Jardine, still in disbelief.

The cowboy hat man looked at the ground and smiled as if remembering a funny story, then raised his head slightly. "Sorry, we should probably do this the correct way. Now I'm supposed to ask you, 'Are you a football man?' Then you respond: 'Yes, but which football do you mean?' To which I respond: 'I'm a Broncos man, myself. American football, you know, the NFL?' To which you reply, 'Why do they call it football if they almost never touch it with their foot?' To which I can reply however the hell I like because we've now established contact."

Jardine's jaw dropped. "You're Ambrose's contact?"

"Yessir. And that there looks like a Cuban kiss of death. *Beso de muerte*, they call it. The Cubans learned a thing or two from the Russians. They're using Putin's playbook as their modus operandi. Now, like I was saying, I can't be certain, but it's possible that small pinprick ya got there could be a tad more dangerous than a rattlesnake bite."

Jardine looked blankly at the grey-haired cowboy. "I'm sorry, I don't follow."

"Like I said, the Cubans are starting to learn from the Russians."

"They're drinking vodka now instead of rum?" offered Jardine.

The man with the cowboy hat chuckled. "Not quite. Although now that you mention it, ice-cold Siberian vodka would go down a treat under that blazing Havana sun." He peered sideways as if recalling a fond memory. After a few moments, he peered back at Jardine. "What I'm saying is, that woman was a Cuban assassin and I think she mighta just pricked you with novichok. You know, like Salisbury, St Petersburg? It might as well be Seville next."

Jardine's blood froze cold. He peered down at his hand as the blood began to drip slowly down his hand.

The cowboy hat man waved his hand in a 'follow me' gesture. "Don't worry I got a woman in a hospital, owes me a favour."

He gulped.

The general put his hands on his shoulder. "You should get it checked out."

He gulped again. "You stay here, general. Thanks for the hat." Jardine passed the Panama hat back to the general and then followed Cowboy Hat with Veronica in tow.

"We'll take my car; I know the way," said Cowboy Hat as the three of them descended to the underground car park.

CHAPTER 19

CLINICA SANTA ISABEL — SEVILLE, SPAIN

IT WAS DARK BY THE TIME JARDINE AND VERONICA arrived outside the *Clinica Santa Isabel* in Cowboy Hat's vehicle. The streetlights flickered outside as a nurse pushed a man in a wheelchair, stopping at the kerb as a taxi approached. Jardine eyed the woman suspiciously as if he were seeing the female assassin in the shadows. The man in the cowboy hat pulled up the handbrake and turned to them. "Don't go in the main entrance. Go down that alleyway to the side entrance. Press the button on the intercom and ask for Marta. Tell her Felix sent you. She'll get a handle on it."

Jardine and Veronica both nodded and descended from the vehicle. The sun was gone but the concrete still radiated heat. The streets were alive with people now coming out after the hot day as they scrambled down the alleyway. They arrived at a door and pressed the intercom. After ten seconds, a voice answered, "*Sí?*"

"We're here to see Marta," said Veronica. "Felix sent us."

A slight pause, and then the door buzzed open. They

entered a room with a closed door, a bench, a small water cooler, and a service window. The room smelled of disinfectant which filled their nostrils. They could hear the muffled sound of machines beeping and animated voices.

In the room, Jardine's legs began to feel like overcooked spaghetti. As he approached the window, his knees gave way slightly and he lunged forward, resting his arms on the counter to balance himself. His head began to throb as he felt acid rising like a churning sea, splashing in his belly.

Veronica looked sideways at him. "Are you okay, Ollie?"

Jardine tried to reply but couldn't manage to utter a word.

A woman appeared at the window in a protective suit.

"Please we need help," said Veronica.

"*Un momento, por favor,*" the woman replied.

Veronica looked again at Jardine and then said, "I think you should take a seat." She guided him to the bench and helped him to sit while trying to comfort him with her arm around his shoulders. As they sat, she placed a hand on his forehead. "*Estas quemando,*" she said. *You're burning up.* She stood and strode over to the nearby water cooler and splashed some water into a paper cup, passing it to Jardine. He gulped it down in a thirsty swallow, but it did little to lower his temperature. He was sweating heavily, and his skin became itchy; he began to feel nauseous and lightheaded. His tongue felt numb, and a metallic taste permeated his mouth, like he could taste blood.

His mind raced as he tried to recall the symptoms of novichok poisoning. He wished he had his phone with him and could quickly search the symptoms, although that usually resulted in Dr Google suggesting you were going to die. He didn't need that now.

"Vero, do you have the burner phone?"

"I left it with the general. We don't know how she tracked us, so I thought it best to leave—"

"My skin feels on fire," interrupted Jardine, his voice weak. "It feels like there's acid rising in my stomach and my head won't stop throbbing."

In that moment, a stocky, stern-looking woman with shortly cropped dark hair entered the room. Her face was visible behind the plastic shield of the protective suit. "Jardine, Oliver?" she asked. She pronounced the Spanish J sound, so it sounded like 'Hardine'.

Jardine nodded, stood and followed the woman. She spoke in a strong Andalusian accent, in rapid-fire Spanish, cutting off any trace of the letter S. "You are a friend of Felix?" she asked in Spanish.

Jardine managed to say a single word, "*Sí*."

"Then I will take extra special care of you." She smiled and winked, then guided them into a small examination room where she pressed a small red button on the wall. After a few moments another nurse arrived with a small array of medical equipment. The nurse began to prepare a needle before sitting on an adjustable office chair which let out a small squeak as she sat.

"Now roll up your sleeves, *por favor*," asked the nurse.

Jardine rolled up his sleeves as the nurse leant forward, holding the needle steady, she pierced the skin. She then pulled back on the plunger as it filled with dark blood.

As she did so, the nurse examined the wound on Jardine's hand. "Did you clean it?" she asked, glancing at Veronica.

"*Sí*," said Veronica. "I wiped it clean with a wet disinfectant towelette. I always carry them in my handbag."

The nurse eyed Jardine. "If you *were* poisoned," the nurse indicated with her head towards Veronica, "she may have saved your life." Then she frowned, "However, we will still do a test."

Jardine's mind swirled with possibilities. His mind flicked through a movie reel of potential poisons, toxins, and nerve agents. From the Tokyo sarin gas attack to the Kim Jong-Nam assassination, to the Skripal case in Salisbury. Arsenic, cyanide, ricin or maybe novichok? It had become the preferred toxin of choice.

If it was novichok, he would need immediate attention. He knew it had been developed by Soviet scientists in the 1970s, initially to avoid detection from NATO chemical detection equipment. Once administered it inhibits certain enzymes which prevent the breakdown of organic neurotransmitter chemicals which causes them to concentrate in neuromuscular junctions leading to contractions of muscles and resulting in cardiac and respiratory arrest.

As he waited, Jardine wondered if burning skin and feeling weak was the beginning of this.

The nurse stood and made for the door but just before exiting, she turned and asked. "Do you have a power of attorney?"

Jardine shook his head.

The nurse frowned. "If you are incapacitated, can she make decisions on your behalf?" She pointed towards Veronica.

Jardine gulped and then nodded. "Why, is there something you're not telling me?"

The nurse shrugged. "No, but it's better to be prepared for such events. We have a rapid-testing unit which will give us a base analysis in fifteen minutes, but we'll send it to a professional lab as well as a precaution. At least the rapid test lets us know if it's serious."

"*Gracias,*" said Veronica.

Marta, the CIA's hospital contact, entered the room. "I'm sure it's nothing," she said, trying to comfort Jardine, but she then shook her head. "Actually I shouldn't say that; the truth is we don't know!" She bit her lip but then stopped and gave an apologetic look towards Jardine. She fidgeted with her hands and then disappeared through the door again.

He had initially felt comforted by the matronly nurse helping him. It put his nerves at ease to know he was in the hands of a professional, one that was recommended by the CIA, no less, but this latest interaction with the nurse and Marta left him more anxious than ever.

A nervous wait ensued as they sat in the examination room. Once the fifteen minutes had expired, Marta entered the room again with a stern look on her face. She looked down at a clipboard and sighed, an action that caused both Veronica and Jardine to gulp. Veronica grabbed Jardine's hand and squeezed it.

CHAPTER 20

CLINICA SANTA ISABEL — SEVILLE, SPAIN

MARTA CONTINUED TO GAZE AT THE CLIPBOARD. SHE sighed and shook her head, then she looked up and smiled, saying, "We're fairly certain that you have not been poisoned and most definitely not with anything deadly."

"How do you know?" asked Jardine.

"Because if it had been any of the serious poisons, well, you'd be dead already... I knew that much when you came in. But we wanted to test just in case."

"But what about the burning sensation, the dizziness, the light-headedness?" asked Veronica.

Marta smiled again and stepped forward to feel Jardine's forehead. "We believe that you may have a touch of sunstroke. The sun is very strong here in Spain and you *were* out in the heat of the day."

"Sunstroke, that's it?" asked Jardine in a mix of surprise and relief.

"That's right." She stepped towards a small refrigerator and took out small bottle of hydrating fluid. "Drink this."

She passed Jardine a bottle of the light blue liquid. "Keep drinking juice and water tonight and you'll be fine by tomorrow."

Jardine looked towards Veronica who smiled from ear to ear, then stood, his legs now finding some strength. "Too much sun?"

Veronica and Marta both nodded.

AN HOUR LATER, JARDINE AND VERONICA WERE BACK at the hotel with the general and Ambrose's contact—the man in the cowboy hat. They all sat in the general's hotel room in the underground section of the hotel. Jardine sat on a small sofa with Veronica, the general in a plush armchair and Ambrose's contact on the end of one of the beds.

The contact introduced himself as Felix Aguilar, a former CIA technical operations officer originally hailing from New Mexico. He nursed a small cup of coffee in his right hand as he began to speak. "Well, I guess you'll be more careful now in the heat of the afternoon sun," he said with a chuckle.

Jardine smiled wryly. "It's lucky you arrived when you did. Thanks for the recommendation."

"Think nothing of it. Marta fixed up my wrist after I fell off a horse down near *El Rocío* a year back."

"Have you been in Spain long?" asked Veronica.

"A few years. I'm in semi-retirement."

"Didn't want to settle down in the States?" asked Jardine.

Felix shook his head. "Not now. My family owns a ranch outside *Las Cruces*, New Mexico. Had it since the days when it was known as New Spain, becoming part of Mexico then integrated into the United States after the Mexican American War. My old man used to run it, approaching ninety and he was still on the tools. Then one day, an SUV from south of the border turned up on the property, demanding he let them transport 'you-know-what' through his land. He refused—at least that's what it looked like in the CCTV footage—and so they shot him dead, then and there. That's why I'm here in semi-retirement instead of there at the ranch. After the funeral, I needed somewhere to lay low until the situation cools down a bit."

The group nodded in solemn silence before the general broke it with a question: "Where were you stationed with the CIA?"

"All over. Never anywhere important though. I was in the Technical Services Division. Forgeries, disguises, and what they call 'document support'. It's a lost art nowadays with everything digitised."

"You helped Ambrose get our EU driving licences?"

Felix nodded. "That I did. I set up the contact. I still dabble occasionally. *The Company* has a chequered history, I know, so I'm not too fond of dwelling on the past. Some operations I'm proud of, others not so much. It's only in old age that you reflect and make sense of everything." Felix took a sip from his coffee cup and continued. "Anyway, those days are behind me. Now my only worry is refining my flamenco guitar skills and working my way through the tapas bars at night. But I guess I still like to keep my finger on the pulse, so to speak."

"Any intel on Venezuelan affairs? Here in Spain, I mean?" asked the general.

"*Madera*'s cronies, the *bolibourgeoisie*, are buying up property in the Salamanca neighbourhood in Madrid." The *bolibourgeoisie* was a portmanteau of *Bolivarian* and bourgeois, a word used to describe those who became rich under the former Sánchez administration and his Bolivarian Revolution. "Lots of dissidents, like yourself, are exiled in Madrid too. More and more each day. And then there are the Cubans. G2 has its agents spread throughout, have done ever since Castro and the revolution. They punch well above their weight in the intelligence game." The Cuban *Dirección de*

Inteligencia (DI) had received training from the KGB, the Stasi and Czechoslovak intelligence, seeking to project their revolutionary ideals in conflicts around the world. They had developed expertise in complex intelligence operations, tradecraft, SIGNIT, HUMANIT, anything to wreak havoc on the Yankees. Felix continued, "The Cubans always kept us busy when I was in the CIA, what with Ana Montes infiltrating Defence Intelligence, Kendall Myers passing on intel while at the US State Department and *La Red Avispa*. You've heard of them, right?"

"The Wasp Network," replied Jardine.

"Exactly, they managed to worm their way into dissident Cuban exile groups in Miami. Hell, Castro even dripped spies into the US during the Mariel boatlift where thousands of Cubans fled the island to Florida. He was an expert strategist, Castro, I'll give him that." Felix chuckled and shook his head, then looked at Jardine and Veronica. "You mentioned a woman following you today?"

Jardine nodded. "She approached us in Granada at a restaurant two nights ago; only then we didn't know who she was."

Felix gave a pensive look and then reached down and picked up a leather suitcase from the ground he had brought in from his jeep. He placed it on his lap and clicked it open with both hands and shuffled some papers. "Ambrose mentioned you were in trouble, so I took the liberty of organising some material for y'all. When he mentioned the Cubans might be involved, well I got in touch with our people in Madrid—I still have the odd contact—and did some digging. It's not one hundred percent, but I think I know who this *chica* might be." He took out some documents, giving one each to Jardine, Veronica, and the general. "This ought to give you a snapshot of what you're dealing with."

All three started to read.

NAME: Alina Grinchenko Calderón

CODENAMES: Doña Bárbara, Lorenz

DESCRIPTION: Tall, approx. 1.8m, green eyes, dark chestnut hair.

BACKGROUND: Calderón studied history and foreign languages at *Universidad de la Habana* before being recruited into the Dirección de Inteligencia, more commonly known as G2. It's thought she has been involved in operations in Asunción, Istanbul, Havana, Hong Kong, Managua, the Southern United States and Jakarta. Not a lot is known of said operations, although her various aliases have appeared on our systems.

Her father was a former KGB trainer in Havana named Dimitri Grinchenko. He lived for several years living under an assumed identity in Argentina and Chile before transferring to Havana. There he encountered a Cuban doctor and spy by the name of Luisa Calderón, who had recently returned from Mexico City. It's thought that they had a brief relationship before Luisa Calderón was exfiltrated into the USA as part of the Mariel boatlift. After several months in Miami, they realised she was pregnant and consequently Alina Calderón was born in the United States, therefore,

holding dual American-Cuban citizenship.
Later, Dimitri Grinchenko would be assigned
to the Russian consulate in Miami, running
agents through the Southern US and maintaining links to the Russian mafia during
the 90s, many of whom were involved in
organising strip clubs in the Miami-Dade
area. Later, Calderón returned to Cuba
where she undertook her university studies.
It's thought that her mother now resides
outside Havana, a result of the uncovering
of *La Red Avispa*, the WASP network of Cuban
spies operating in the USA. Her father's
whereabouts are unknown, but we assume he's
in Cuba with Luisa Calderón.

EXPERTISE:
Like all Cuban spies, her forte is the non-
technical aspects of the profession. False
flag operations, deception, covert acquisi-
tion, the insertion of moles, intelligence
collection, and particularly in her case,
low-level assassinations.
She is also a very handy pitcher for a
local universidad de la habana softball and
baseball teams.

LANGUAGES: Apart from her native Spanish
and Russian, fluent in English, French,
Italian, with competence in Mandarin.

THE GROUP REMAINED SILENT AS THEY READ THE brief description of the female assassin following them. After several moments, the general raised an eyebrow asking, "Alias: *Doña Bárbara*?"

"That's the latest alias she was given by the Venezuelans."

"Does she know witchcraft?" the general asked with a smile. *Doña Bárbara* was a reference to a character from a novel by *Romulo Gallegos* a writer and former president of Venezuela.

"I wouldn't put it past her," said Felix, with a twinkle in his eye and a slight smile. "She sure can put men under her spell. Right before she slits their throats, that is."

"Isn't this forbidden?" asked Veronica, holding up the paper and examining it. "I mean holding physical copies of documents?"

"Well as you mighta guessed I'm old school. I never let this case out of my sight." Felix tapped the old leather suitcase. "And what with all the hacking, viruses, spyware, malware and whatnot these days, old school is back in fashion. Oh, and this material," he flicked one of the pieces of paper, "is water soluble. A light drizzle of liquid and she'll dissolve like cotton candy on your tongue. Good to know, just in case we're interrupted while you're reading it. Speaking of being interrupted, do you have any idea how she is tracking y'all?"

"We don't know..." said Jardine. "Since the crash, our phones have been switched off, dismantled and put in a metal box. We have a burner phone, but no one knows about that and it's not registered."

"Well, looks like you're gonna have to strip so we can test your clothes," said Felix.

"Our clothes?" asked the general.

"You said she approached you in Granada? She could've placed a small tracking chip on your shirts, your belt, or any other article of clothing that was on display."

Jardine and the general looked at each other in surprise and then they grimaced as if saying 'We're idiots' to each other.

An hour later, the group had gone through all their clothes, not a tracking chip in sight.

Felix shook his head in dismay. "Nothing in your clothes. She have access to your vehicle?"

Jardine looked confused and unsure. "Maybe? That would explain how she tracked us outside of Granada after leaving her behind the garbage lorry in Granada."

The group descended to the underground garage as Felix got on his knees, then rolled onto his back, shimming himself under Jardine's Defender. A few metallic clangs later, he slid out with a smile. "Bingo. Here you are. I'll give you the honours of destroying that." He passed a small magnetic tracking chip to the general who was about to throw it to the floor and step on it with his heel before Jardine interrupted. "*Espera*! Wait! I've got a better idea."

The general passed it to Jardine who swaggered over to a large red BMW on the other side of the underground garage. "Let's create some confusion for her." Kneeling next to the BMW, he reached his arm under the chassis, placing the device underneath. Then he stood, brushing the dust from his knees. "That should buy us some time."

Felix nodded, impressed, and said, "All warfare is based on deception."

"Sun Tzu?" asked Jardine.

Felix nodded again.

"I didn't know we were at war?" asked Veronica.

"When there's a tyrant involved, one's always at war," replied the general.

CHAPTER 21

La Casona — Caracas, Venezuela

THE DEFENCE MINISTER OF THE BOLIVARIAN Republic of Venezuela, *The Godfather*, knocked firmly and waited for the confirmation to enter. After hearing, "*Sí, adelante*," he entered and was surprised the president was not in the *Salón Mayor de Audiencia*. Instead, an assistant ushered him over the red carpet and through another door leading outside. Here, the president sat in a low deck chair on a black-and-white tiled verandah.

Hearing the defence minister approaching, the president stopped reading a document, placed it to his left and looked up at the defence minister. "*Godfather*, I've brought you here for an update on the search for our *querido general*."

The Godfather smiled and looked around the garden. "I thought this place had been made into a museum?"

"It is," said the president, holding his arms out and looking around the room. "It belongs to the people now." In a symbolic gesture, *La Casona*, the presidential residence had been made into a cultural site and museum.

"Then why are we meeting here?" asked the Godfather, sitting on a chair and removing his military hat and resting on his knee.

The president's moustache twitched. "It's preferable here than at Miraflores at the moment." The president took a quick look around the garden now. "We won't be interrupted here."

The Godfather opened his mouth to speak but stopped. He could smell the pungent stench of burning tobacco wafting along the verandah and turning to his right he noticed the bearded man in dark green Cuban military uniform chuffing away on a large cigar.

Noticing the Godfather glance at the military officer, the president offered an explanation. "You remember *Comandante Lazo*, no? He is my security advisor on such matters. I trust you don't object to his being with us today?" He cocked his eyebrow in question, as if daring the defence minister to object.

The Godfather stared at the comandante and then turned back to the president, saying, "*Buenos dias, Comandante*." He didn't want to give the *comandante* the respect or satisfaction of direct eye contact as he acknowledged him. As defence minister, the Godfather seethed at the fact there were Cubans calling the shots behind the scenes, but he dared not say anything. Not in this Republic.

Comandante Lazo blew out smoke, then walked towards the Godfather and the president, saying, "Godfather, we have tracked the general to Seville and our intelligence suggests he is en route to Lisbon. It appears our neutralising methods have eluded us so far."

The president squinted and raised his right hand to stroke his moustache. "Yes, it would appear the general is very cunning. Of course, he must be employing all those dirty tricks the Yankee Imperialists taught him at the CIA's School of the Americas."

"I don't believe General Pereira studied there," replied the Godfather.

"Ah, no? Well, nothing good for the freedom of Latin America ever came out of that school," chimed in the president.

Comandante Lazo let out a raspy, smoky laugh. "*Asi es, Presidente.* You are quite right."

The Godfather gulped before replying. "*I* went to the School of the Americas, *señor Presidente...*" His sentence trailed off as he nervously fidgeted with his military hat resting it on his knee.

A surprised look spread across the president's face which slowly converted into a menacing smile. "*Claro*! But you are different. You follow *my* orders now, Godfather." He shuffled some papers and picked up a single sheet of paper, looking down at it as he spoke. "Now, according to our tracking devices, it appears the general and his co-conspirators have split up. It seems as if one of the devices we planted is headed south from Seville, while the other remains on target to Lisbon. *Comandante Lazo* has eyes on Lisbon, but we may need some help to track the former which we believe is heading for Marbella or Estepona. We have some contacts in Marbella do we not, Godfather? The Albanians?"

"*Sí Presidente.* Although that is much more in the realm of Sindios Calvo, him being *El Pulpo* (The Octopus) and all. I believe they are helping him with 'distribution' through Europe."

"Distribution of...?" asked the president.

The Godfather again squirmed in his chair. "Distribution of the products supplied to us by our freedom fighter friends in Colombia."

"Ah yes, excellent. Our ELN brothers. Could you get the details from The Octopus and pass them on to *Comandante* Lazo here?"

Not on the grave of my mother, you pig, thought the Godfather, but he replied: "*Sí, sí*, of course, *Presidente*."

"Very good, Godfather."

Comandante Lazo blew out a cloud of smoke. "*Gracias*, Godfather. As you know, we Cubans are well resourced and have a great deal of operational experience in Europe. In fact, we just missed 'taking care' of Fulgencio Batista by two days, before his own heart gave way in Guadalmina," he said, grinning. "But in this case, we need a little helping hand."

The Godfather smiled meekly and nodded at *Comandante* Lazo. "An interesting detail, *Comandante*. We'll be glad to help. But it really will be *El Pulpo* who is assisting you."

The president stood now, signalling it was time for the defence minister to leave. "And remember, Godfather, we need plausible deniability at all stages. If anything goes wrong, blame the Americans. Ensure all our media contacts are shouting 'CIA assassination' from the rooftops should there be any mishaps. No one must suspect us or our collaborators at Cuban G2."

The defence minister nodded and smiled. *That's why he wants* me *to provide the details to Lazo. I'm the fall guy here. He wants my orders on the documents,* he thought, before replying: "Very true, *Presidente*."

The president walked towards the Godfather; his arm extended ready to shake the Defence Minister's hand. "And of course, if this next stage fails, we will launch Operation Cienfuegos."

"Operation *Cienfuegos*, sir?" asked the Godfather.

"If the need arises, the *comandante* here will fill you in on how this plan works."

The *comandante* lowered the cigar from his mouth and nodded. "With pleasure."

The Godfather received the president's hand and shook it. "If I may, *Presidente*."

"*Sí?*"

"This operation, I'm afraid we just don't have the funds, you said yourself, the US sanctions..."

"Don't be *tonto*, Godfather! We have plenty of money and besides this is to keep the Bolivarian revolution alive. Do you want to kill the Bolivarian revolution?"

"No, *señor*," replied the defence minister without thinking.

"*Entonces*, get your arse into gear and get this project on its feet."

The Godfather lowered his head slightly. "*Sí, señor*."

The president turned abruptly and returned behind his deck chair. "Now if you don't mind, I have a little situation in Cape Verde that I need to deal with. That'll be all, Defence Minister."

The defence minister bowed again before striding along the black-and-white tiles. He gulped loudly, knowing all too well that now he had been let in on the operation, if it were to head south, *he* would be the scapegoat.

CHAPTER 22

Undisclosed location between Seville and Lisbon

The general watched Jardine wrestle with the fuel hose before placing it into the side of the Defender. He approached the vehicle, leaning his back against it. Looking into the distance he said, "That smell reminds me of holidays."

Jardine looked quizzically at the general. "Petrol fumes?"

"My father used to fill up our Plymouth Valiant on the way to the beach and those fumes, that smell, always takes me back to those trips."

"Not the most delightful smell though, is it?"

The general continued to look longingly into the distance. "And when I think of all the trouble that resource has cost us." He shook his head, the pleasant memory gone.

Jardine looked up. "The resource curse. Dutch disease, the paradox of plenty. Nigeria, Angola, Equatorial Guinea, etc. It's a worldwide problem."

The general nodded and turned to face him. "Although I believe it's more of an institutional curse. Countries with strong institutions don't seem to have problems dealing with a plethora of valuable assets under their soil. Look at Norway, Canada and Australia. We had a good system at one stage, it wasn't perfect but at least it was well run, efficient and government owned. That was all before Sánchez ousted thousands of PDSVA employees, reading their names out as 'enemies of the state' live on television like a deranged reality TV host. He even blew a whistle each time while issuing a red card like a football referee. Pure theatrics with little regard for what the result would be."

"I think I've seen that reality show with a similar orange-haired character, what was it called? *The Apprentice*?"

The general chuckled. "*Sí, The Apprentice*. From that ogre of a president up there in *norteamerica*. It seems he learnt a lot from our former president Sánchez. For men on different sides of the political spectrum, they had much in common: appealed to the disenfranchised, understood the free media was the enemy of their propaganda, fervently nationalistic, and they understood the nature of a good political performance and playing it up to your audience."

"Both campaigned as liberators but ruled as tyrants," added Jardine as the fuel pump clicked, signalling the tank was full.

The general smiled. "That's a good summary. And as a tyrant, you need an enemy, a scapegoat for your country's woes. For us in Latin America, we have no shortage of scapegoats at our disposal. On the right, there's the fear of *la guerrilla*, communism, and Castro. Then, on the left, they're fond of using the oligarchy, Yankee Imperialists and sanctions. That's a favourite to defend the incompetence of Madera and his failings."

"The same in Colombia," said Jardine, replacing the fuel nozzle back into the pump. He then turned and glanced at the general as if something had suddenly occurred to him. "If the US has sanctions on Venezuela, how are they still selling oil?"

"Ha! Oil production has plummeted. But China, Iran and Turkey are still buying, not to mention the oil-for-doctors scheme with Cuba. And then there's *los bachaqueros*, the smugglers who make money from reselling price-controlled goods. They are also involved in petroleum trading. There is no shortage of commodity schemes being operated out of Venezuela: oil, gold and rare earths. Madera has an array of networks that facilitate these types of transactions. Sánchez and his cronies did too."

"But how are they moving funds in and out of the country?"

"Ah..." The general broke eye contact and became quiet, then he mumbled, "Offshore accounts, Panama, Cayman Islands; you know the drill."

Jardine nodded before looking at the ground, thinking. "But then—"

The general interrupted. "Would you like a coffee? I'll go inside and bring you one."

"Ah, yes, sure, I'll have a—" Before Jardine could finish, the general had swivelled and was striding towards the café entrance.

Jardine walked around the car and sat in the driver's seat. He couldn't quite put his finger on it but he had a strange feeling about the general. "I think he's hiding something," he said to Veronica who was sitting and waiting in the passenger's seat, doing a crossword in a magazine she had swiped from the hotel.

"What could he be hiding?" she asked, raising her head.

Jardine clicked his tongue and then replied, "I don't know, but we need to find out."

A few moments later, the general returned with coffee and several pieces of *tortilla española*. "I hope you're hungry. I think I got enough to last until Lisbon," he said enthusiastically. He opened the vehicle door and sat in the back seat, dishing out the coffee and tortilla to Jardine and Veronica.

After another hour of driving and after having turned right at the Algarve to head north on the E1 highway towards Lisbon, Jardine began to mull over the general's dismissive behaviour back at the petrol station. Several questions still swirled in his mind. The Cuban assassin, who they now knew was Alina Calderón, had hunted them with such ruthlessness that there had to be more to her relentless pursuit than just the general speaking at the UN. Jardine looked in the rear-view mirror to see the general sitting happily in the back, chewing on *tortilla española* and sipping coffee, as he watched the scenery flash by. Now seemed like a good time to poke the bear; nowhere for him to run or hide. Coughing to clear his throat, he asked, "General, why is it that they want to kill you? I mean, I know they're ruthless and they want to stop you speaking at the UN, but wouldn't it cause them more trouble if you were killed in Europe? I mean media attention and the like."

The general stopped chewing and met Jardine's eyes in the rear-view mirror. "They just don't like any dissent. And you're right; how they appear is very important to them and although it may not seem like it, they crave legitimacy. Russia, China, all authoritarians want that—legitimacy. So I guess my speaking at the UN will embarrass them and so they've calculated that it's worth the risk to bump me off, as it were."

Jardine frowned. "But there's a cacophony of loud dissenting noises against the regime in Venezuela, Miami, Madrid—all around the world, in fact. You're not the only one. Also, why didn't you just fly direct to New York from Geneva?"

"I told you I had to make some visits in Spain."

"But you said you took the train from Geneva to Spain? Why didn't you just fly? Surely that's quicker and safer?"

The general coughed as if stalling. "Oh, that? I was worried about a bomb on board the planes; you know that's how important people often disappear or die in a mysterious crash. They still haven't found Flight MH17. You know I also watched an interesting documentary on Dag Hammarskjöld's plane crash, it said that—"

"That's unlikely. In Europe, at least," interrupted Jardine, raising one eyebrow in a sign of mock belief.

The general mumbled, "Yes, well, I had to visit Andorra in person..."

"Andorra? What were you doing there?"

"Oh, nothing important." He swatted his hand as if to say, 'forget about it.'

Jardine locked eyes with the general in the mirror which caused the other man to sigh loudly before he spoke. "I suppose I should just be honest with you." He reached down and picked up a satchel that he had been carrying with him and passed it to Veronica in the front passenger seat. "I'll let your lawyer take a peek. *Vea la carpeta amarilla*, the yellow folder."

Veronica pulled out a stiff manila folder, opened it, and began to skim through the documents. For Jardine's benefit she read out what she was looking at. "Bank accounts in Switzerland, Andorra, Portugal and now Madrid. It appears to be large transactions from various Venezuelan companies. One called 'The Sun Corporation' and what looks like some large food importation contracts. Nothing here that raises suspicion."

"Try towards the back of the pile," the general suggested. "You'll find something a little more appealing."

Veronica shuffled the files until she reached the last document and again read aloud. "Company Directors of the Sun

Corporation: Juan Antonio Tafur Kabachi, Margarita Romero, Sindios Calvo, Guillermo Saeed, Cecilia Florencia. All arranged by a Jonathon Saeed, a dual Colombian-Venezuelan national, who seems to be a broker for the Venezuelan government."

Jardine slammed on the brake and pulled over the Defender, slipping and sliding on the gravel beside the road. "Vero, let me see that!" He looked intently at the document, his head hovering over the page, scanning, his lips faintly moving as he read. Then he looked up, his eyes wide like saucers. "General, these are members of the Venezuelan Cabinet." He looked down again, and read a little more. "Cecilia Florencia? Isn't that Madera's wife!"

"*Correcto.*"

"And Jonathon Saeed? He's the one who has been arrested in Cape Verde and is about to be extradited to the US?"

"That's right."

Jardine turned to face him in the back seat. "This is concrete proof of corruption at the highest level of the Venezuelan regime. *This* is why they're trying to kill you!"

The general exhaled with a puff. "*Pues, sí.* Sorry, I should have mentioned that. But I'm afraid that's not all." He pulled out more documents from his satchel and handed them to Jardine. "These show that the Venezuelan government is selling gold bars to the Iranians, and in some cases to the UAE and Turkey, in exchange for technical expertise on the PDVSA oil facilities. It's smuggled out through Guyana or Suriname. I'm no expert in such matters, but I believe that it's in direct breach of United Nations sanctions. And towards the back of that document, there are some environmental crimes, for good measure."

Jardine scanned these new documents. "This is huge. Are you presenting this at the UN in New York?"

The general nodded. "*Correcto.* It shows not only collusion between the Iranians and Venezuela, but it involves offshore banks in Geneva and Andorra and their subsidiaries in Panama and Uruguay, all helping syphon money out of Venezuela and into private offshore accounts of Venezuelan politicians. I also suspect some well-known US and UK banking institutions are involved, but that I cannot prove yet. It's a complex web that involves not just the Venezuelans, the Cubans, the Russians, and the Iranians; there are US companies implicated in some of the transactions. All roads lead to the 'The Sun Corporation'. That is why I came to Spain: to investigate Ricardo Guerra. He used to be the head of an important television channel in Venezuela, now he's the lynchpin in siphoning government money to Madrid, helping Madera and his cronies to fund purchases of assets for the *boligarchs* around the world. My contact in Madrid is investigating him there as we speak. It started when they moved money through the state oil company PDVSA with a complicated scheme of currency manipulations. Then when that stopped functioning—due to horrendous mismanagement of PDVSA —they turned to illegally mined gold and narcotics. There have also been missing funds from the Ministry of Planning and Finance and our national import-export agency, all taken by the regime or *los enchufados,* those that are connected or 'plugged in' to the Madera regime. As you can imagine, it's quite a complex web."

Jardine sat back in his seat abruptly and exhaled. "We need to get you on a flight to New York as soon as possible."

The general lifted a khaki green folder out of his satchel now. "But I guess this is the *pièce de résistance*, as they say." He handed the last document to Jardine. "This was very difficult to smuggle out. I carried it with me when I scrambled across the border from Venezuela to Colombia."

Jardine received the document, noting it read '*Ultra Secreto*' in Spanish—*Top Secret*. He opened it and started reading. After several minutes he stopped and flicked through some of the maps and images provided. "Is this...?"

"*Sí*," replied the general.

"A plan to invade Guyana and take back the Essequibo region?"

"I'm afraid so. It seems the recent actions of Putin in Ukraine have only emboldened Madera."

The Essequibo region was a large swathe of Guyana which Venezuela had claimed as its own since independence and the establishment of *Gran Colombia*. Rich in gold and other minerals and, potentially, vast amounts of offshore petroleum, it was often used as a nationalist rallying cry to distract the Venezuelan population in difficult times. It appeared Madera was taking it seriously this time and would act.

"Are you sure these are real?"

"I'm certain," replied the general. "It would start with a blockade of the coast and then advance from there. It's quite a remote area. Militarily it's crazy and I'm not sure it's actually possible but it looks like they're seriously considering it."

Jardine shook his head and then put his face down into his hands. "We need to take you direct to the airport and get you on a plane. Forget waiting and seeing your team."

"Yes, well, there's a slight problem."

"Which is?" asked Jardine.

"With regard to the financial aspects. I'm missing one piece of the puzzle."

"Isn't the potential invasion enough?"

The general cocked his head. "Not really; countries invade other countries all the time. No one stopped Putin when he took Crimea, no? Financial crimes, however, by the so-called 'Socialist Republic', will garner attention."

"So what do you need?" asked Jardine, raising his head from his hands.

"They move—well, they *moved*—their money through the

Ernvok Mosnak bank in Russia and the Banco Corporativo in Nicaragua. But those banks have now been blocked due to US sanctions. We know they're using a bank in Andorra." He held up one of the pieces of paper. "Here's the proof. But they are also using a Portuguese bank. I have a source from the Vitória bank in Lisbon. I am to meet with him and he will provide the final documents I need to finalise my case."

Jardine turned to face the general, his face blank and serious. "Surely email would be a better way to get your hands on those documents?"

The general laughed. "If only it were that simple. He has physical copies—the originals. He doesn't have faith in sending them online as he believes he'll be traced or that the information will fall into the wrong hands. He wants to hand them to me personally."

"This is heavy," said Jardine. "There are too many players here; that's why they want to get rid of you. That's why she followed us! They probably assume we—Vero and I—know all this as well."

"*Sí, exacto*. Well, now you *do* know it."

Jardine shook his head. "If I'd known you were about to blow up a corruption scandal involving the Troika of Tyranny and major international banks and announce a potential invasion of a neighbouring country in the same UN speech, I would've stayed at home, sipping coffee on my terrace and looking at olive trees." *Troika of Tyranny* was the new name given by a Trump advisor to the collaboration of Cuba, Nicaragua, and Venezuela.

"I'm sorry, I should not have gotten you into the pickles."

"Into a pickle," Jardine corrected. "It's an American phrase and I'm not too fond of pickles."

CHAPTER 23

*InterContinental Hostel Cascais-Estoril —
Lisbon, Portugal*

Sunlight beamed down, bouncing off the ocean and flooding the glass of the InterContinental Hotel Cascais-Estoril. The hotel was perched on a small cliff on the outskirts of Lisbon in the elegant enclaves of Cascais and Estoril; both places were no stranger to dissidents and ex-spies. Portugal's neutrality in World War II meant the area had been a haven for refugees and exiles waiting on exit permits or planning the next dash to Casablanca and then further afield. This —naturally—meant it had also been a hotbed of spies, mercenaries and diplomats of all persuasions, hoovering up intelligence to gain an edge in the war.

Having parked the Defender in the hotel's underground car park, the group checked in and made their way to their rooms. Felix had also arrived and was staying on the same floor in a separate room. It was he that had suggested the strategic location. The hotel gave them access to the city centre but also a clean run to the airport without getting bogged down in Lisbon's notorious hilly and windy streets. After descending from his room and borrowing a mobile phone from reception, Jardine walked out onto the sun-drenched terrace overlooking the Atlantic Ocean and dialled Ambrose. He wanted to check in and keep him abreast of the situation.

The phone rang twice before Ambrose picked up. "Hello?"

"Watching the olive trees grow?"

"Ah, Jardine, I see you made it to Lisbon in one piece?"

"Are you tracking us?"

"Not at all."

"Then how did you know we were here?" asked Jardine, his voice inflected with a hint of breathless paranoia.

"Now I *know* you're in Lisbon."

He remained silent for a few seconds, annoyed with himself for having reacted so emotionally and divulging his location.

Before he could speak again, Ambrose continued. "I knew that's where you were headed and assumed you would be there by now if all went according to plan, that is."

"Sorry. I'm a tad rattled at the moment if I'm honest."

"It sounds like it. Have a *caipirinha* to calm the nerves."

"Thought you were more of a port man, Ambrose?"

"I am. I was going to suggest a stiff glass of the stuff but figured that's more of an old man's drink. My sort of thing."

"You're right, though, I do need a stiff drink."

"The aptly named 'Spy Bar' in the Hotel Palacio is a good spot for a tipple—that, and the Casino Estoril next to it. In fact, that was where Bond author Ian Fleming witnessed the Yugoslav double agent, Dusko Popov, attempt to bankrupt a group of Nazis by beating them at the baccarat table with MI6's money before he—"

"I know the story, Ambrose," Jardine interrupted. "And

Fleming used it as inspiration for his first Bond novel *Casino Royale*."

"You've done your research," said Ambrose. "But I bet you didn't know it was also the inspiration for *Our Man in Havana*?"

"That I did not know," replied Jardine.

"Ha! Well, looks like we old blokes can teach you young guys something. Look up 'Garbo' online when you get a chance. You might learn something useful."

Jardine smiled and rested a hand on the terrace railing, looking at the sun on the sea as two seagulls flew by. "Thanks for setting us up with Felix," he said. "He's already helped us out on one occasion."

"Nothing serious, I hope?"

"Just a little bit of fun in the sun."

"You're in safe hands with him. The operational officers of *The Cousins* are good to have if you get into a tight spot." *The Cousins* was MI6's name for the CIA.

"He's shown that."

"You can rely on him. But there is one thing..."

"What's that?"

"Just don't let him near a casino..."

One of the most famous casinos in Europe is just down the road, thought Jardine. "You're saying I shouldn't let him near Casino Estoril. Why's that?"

"Why do you think? He likes to roll the dice."

Jardine rolled his eyes. "Good to know, I guess." *My advantage may have just become a liability*, thought Jardine. "Any word on the *Guardia Civil*?"

"Not yet, still trying with my contacts to see if I can clear the situation up. I'll let you know in good time."

"Thanks, old boy. Isn't that what you used to say in Colombia?"

"A bad habit," replied Ambrose.

Jardine turned and rested his back on the railing, looking back towards the hotel. "I'd better get a hold of the situation here. We've gone grey since we left Granada, so I'll contact you when I can."

"Take care, old—" Ambrose stopped short. "Sorry, like I said, bad habit. Take care, mate."

Jardine ended the call but didn't move, still leaning on the terrace railing. He looked back at the hotel and saw Felix sitting on a sofa adjacent to reception, reading a newspaper. Behind him, pacing and speaking on the phone in a hushed tone, was the general. Pushing off the railing, Jardine strolled across the terrace, returning the phone to reception, and then walked towards the general. As he saw Jardine approach, the general turned and looked away as if the action would stop Jardine from approaching. Standing next to him, Jardine tapped him on the shoulder. In return the general turned and lowered the phone, covering it with his right hand, smiling. A polite, fake smile.

"Everything okay?" Jardine asked.

"*Todo bien*," the general replied. *All good*. "Just confirming our meet with my contact."

Jardine nodded and moved towards Felix as the general swivelled on his heels and returned to his call.

A few minutes later, the general appeared in front of Felix and Jardine on the sofa. "We will meet my banking contact in the city. There is a small square, the *Largo do Carmo*, with a kiosk. That's where we will meet with the contact and receive the documents." He sat on a sofa next to Jardine and Felix. He looked away and waved his hand as if this next piece of information wasn't important. "Oh, and coincidently, it is also where they serve the best *pastéis de nata* in the world. They bring up a batch from the famous *Pastéis de Belém* café in the morning. My father, the baker, used to tell me stories about them when I was young."

Jardine raised an eyebrow. Everyone likes *pastel de nata* but meeting in an open space? "Will it be safe?"

"It will be safe, I promise. I, my country, need those documents. With the documents in hand, I will be all set for my flight this evening to New York. I've just spoken with my team and they will fly into Lisbon from Madrid; we will rendezvous at the airport."

"Are you sure he can't just send an email? Or get him to post it on *WikiLeaks* or something?" asked Jardine.

The general shook his head. "It's not that simple; we need the official bank seal and the special perforated stamp to ensure they're authentic, otherwise Madera will simply spread the rumour that they're *falso*, fake news, disinformation. Besides, it's safer to be in a crowded place rather than a quiet hotel room, like a sitting duck."

"I'll help draw up a plan on how we approach this. My speciality," said Felix.

Jardine held his hand up to his chin, thinking. "You're willing to risk your life for a *pastel de nata*?"

General Pereira smiled and winked. "*Sí señor*, but it's the documents I'm interested in. The pastel is just the sweetener."

Jardine shook his head. "I hope these documents are worth it." He smiled. "The *pastel de nata* too."

CHAPTER 24

*InterContinental Hostel Cascais-Estoril —
Lisbon, Portugal*

"It ought to be a simple operation," said Felix
Aguilar, as he spread out a large map of Lisbon on one of the
beds in his hotel room. His finger trailed along the waxy paper
surface as he occasionally stopped and lifted his hand to stroke
his moustache in a pensive reflex.

"We're here, the InterContinental Hotel Cascais-Estoril,"
said Jardine, as he pointed on the map.

Felix raised his eyes and smirked. "Well, looks like we got
ourselves an operational genius here."

Jardine frowned and then slowly raised his middle finger
in Felix's direction.

Felix continued. "We'll take the train from the stop down
there." He flicked his arm and pointed over his shoulder
towards the window. "That'll take us to the *Cais do Sodré* near
the centre." He pointed his finger back on the map now.
"Then we'll walk along the foreshore until the *Praça do
Comércio*, before following *Rua Augusta* up until the *Elevator*

de Santa Justa. We can take the elevator up and bingo, we'll be almost on the *Largo do Carmo*. From there, you guys," Felix pointed to the general and Jardine, "will sit at the kiosk and wait for your source."

"Copy that," said the general.

"Got it," replied Veronica.

"Easy peasy," said Jardine.

Felix folded the map up and stuffed it into a leather satchel. "It's not the most direct route, but it will allow us to run a light SDR."

"SDR?" asked Veronica.

"Surveillance Detection Route," replied Felix.

Veronica nodded. "I have experience in that."

"Don't worry; she's an expert at that now," said Jardine, playfully punching Veronica on the arm.

Felix moved towards the door. "Any questions?" The group all shook their heads. "Vamoose time, then."

THE TRAIN INTO LISBON WAS FULL OF COMMUTERS heading into the city for a bout of shopping. A scattering of young tourists was on board talking loudly next to a flock of older Portuguese women who gripped their purses tightly. The train hurtled forward, hugging the coastline as the sun shimmered on the Atlantic to the right. On the left, white facades wedged under terracotta roofs clung to the hillside streaming by like an animated oil painting. It was a perfect day in a beautiful city on the edge of Europe. It was no surprise that Lisbon had rightly regained its popularity as one of Europe's prettiest cities.

Jardine sat watching the buildings flash by, briefly catching his reflection in the window opposite. He wore a pair of light linen pants and a navy-blue shirt, the best that he could find in a local shop between Seville and Lisbon. Next to him was

Veronica who wore a floral-patterned dress with large dark sunglasses and a wide-brimmed black felt fedora she'd bought at the same shop. The whole group had bought new sets of clothes after the tracing chip fiasco. It was better to have a new wardrobe than a death warrant. The general sat opposite them, the ocean shining over his shoulders. He had also purchased new clothes, wearing the same trousers as Jardine, but in a different colour and a short sleeve white linen shirt. His battered Panama hat rested on his knee. Next to him was Felix who wore the same clothes he had been wearing throughout: dark jeans, boots and a light-coloured denim shirt. As usual he wore his New Mexican Stetson with a Pueblo tribal design band.

Arriving at the *Cais do Sodré* station the group exited the metro before pacing along the seaside walk. The Tagus River shimmered beside them as they worked their way along a wide tiled path dotted with small wispy trees swaying slightly in the breeze. Once the pathway finished, they strolled out into the *Praça do Comércio*—a sweeping horseshoe-shaped square on the riverbanks. It spread out in front of them beneath an almost spotless blue sky with only a few wispy clouds drifting above. A group of teenagers with skateboards nestled under their arms mingled around the mounted bronze statue of King José I in the centre of the square as small groups of tourists spun around admiring the canary yellow façades of buildings encircling the plaza. To one side, on the opposite side to the river, stood the *Arco da Rua Augusta*, a large decorative arch of intricate carvings and statues. The group ambled towards it, passing through it and onto *Rua Augusta,* a long pedestrianised street of shops, street performers and with a constant flood of pedestrians.

The street teemed with people as the group made their way over the patterned tiles of large, beige diamonds outlined in dark grey, made up of thousands of small square tiles.

Similar patterns could be seen as far afield as Rio and Macau. Weaving their way through the throng, they eventually reached *Rua da Conceição*. A red tram approached, a sharp bell sound announcing its approach.

"We'll cross just before the tram arrives," said Jardine. "But don't force it, make it look natural."

Just before the tram arrived, the group jogged across the street and peeled off to the side of the wide pedestrian avenue, hoping the small manoeuvre would cut off, even if only momentarily, anyone following. An old-fashioned wine shop housing vintage bottles of port and sweet Madeira wine stood in front of them and Felix suggested they enter. "Let's cool our boots in here a moment, see if anyone's on our tail."

The general became excited and quickly flew into the shop. "A chance to purchase a gift for my source," he said. He and Felix entered the shop while Jardine and Veronica waited in the doorway, holding hands, trying to blend in as an innocent couple of tourists spending the day in Lisbon. Jardine scanned the crowd for familiar faces but found himself not able to concentrate, wishing he could simply enjoy the atmosphere.

"Isn't it great to be travelling again?" said Veronica, squeezing his hand. She smiled at him, and the light reflected in her brown eyes. He smiled back and realised how long it had been since he'd paid attention to details like that. They had been so busy setting up their new business that it had been a while since they were able to spend actual time together, doing things they enjoyed. It felt as if this trip, despite the run-ins with a Cuban assassin, had rejuvenated them both. It had put into perspective how important it was to strike a balance between ambition and not letting life pass you by. For Jardine in particular it had rekindled a fire in him. This new 'operation' had brought perspective and he finally understood the balance of living an ordinary responsible life but sprinkling it with enough adventure and excitement that it didn't kill him with boredom. *Being chased by an assassin will do that to you*, he thought as he smiled back at Veronica.

"I do miss it. Travelling that is," said Jardine as he hugged her, secretly checking the crowds milling by, still wondering if they were being watched. "We should do more of it. It's all too easy to get caught up in the everyday, even when you own a guesthouse in the south of Spain."

Veronica bit her lower lip and spoke in English. "I've been thinking the same thing. I'm happy I'm not in the ... how do you say it, rat races?"

Jardine smiled. "Rat race."

"Yes, that's it, the rat race. But I'm worried what we have now has turned into its own rat race."

Jardine wrapped his arms around her. "Don't worry, we'll change that. We'll have someone come in and look after the place occasionally so that we can get away."

Veronica nodded, resting her head on Jardine's shoulder. Then she froze and her pupils dilated, rapidly turning from caramel-brown to black. "Ollie, don't turn around but look in the reflection of the window. Can you see? Behind the cartoon street artist, next to the newspaper stand."

Jardine twisted his body slightly, naturally, while pulling Veronica in closer for a hug. He lifted his head, peering into the reflection of the shop window. He saw a woman leaning against a newspaper stand, wearing a flat cap with a herringbone pattern and dark sunglasses. After a few seconds, he spoke, trying not to move his lips. "Vero, can you go and tell those two to hurry the fuck up?"

Veronica entered the shop slowly and naturally as Jardine continued to watch in the window's reflection at the woman following their every move. After gazing for several seconds more, he confirmed it was her, the woman known as Alina Calderón. Alias: *Doña Bárbara*. The Cuban assassin.

The woman continued to lean against the newsstand and Jardine noticed she held a cigarette between her fingers occasionally bringing it to her lips and puffing out smoke, as if she were simply killing time or waiting for a bus.

Veronica returned to Jardine's side now. "They're ready," she whispered in his ear.

He reached for her hand and squeezed it. "You go with Felix; I'll follow with the general."

She nodded and stepped out, continuing to walk up *Rua Augusta*. Then Felix appeared at her side as they both strode forward to make some distance between them and the woman.

The general appeared at Jardine's side. "She's as persistent as the real Doña Bárbara," he said. "At least the real fictional character from the book, I mean."

"Nothing seems to faze her," said Jardine, briefly glancing towards the woman. He could see she was still leaning and smoking, not moving.

"She's as cool as a lettuce as one would say in Spanish," said the general. *Más fresco que una lechuga.*

The men moved quickly, power walking in the same direction as Felix and Veronica but drifting to the other side of the pedestrian street.

"How did she find us?" asked the general, striding along. "We're wearing new clothes." He looked down at his shirt and patted himself down.

"I don't know," replied Jardine, his mind whirling as the sun beat down. *We changed our clothes in Seville*, he thought. We replaced the tracker from the Defender to the red BMW in the hotel garage. He glanced across at Veronica and Felix who were hurrying along on the other side of the *Rua Augusta*. Vero had new clothes too. Felix had the same outfit, but he hadn't been tracked from the beginning. Jardine's face felt hot, and he wiped his sweaty brow with his shirt sleeve. The sun wasn't this intense in Seville, he thought, his mind still racing, but he'd had the general's Panama hat there.

He looked at the general walking next to him, who was still patting himself down as if swotting invisible mosquitos under his skin. His face appeared cool, covered in the shade of the Panama hat. Then, Jardine's stomach dropped as realisation hit him. They'd changed their clothes, ditched their mobile phones, but the general's Panama hat had remained with them all the way through. It was the only constant and the only logical explanation as to how they could have traced them all this time.

His mind flashed back to the woman in the restaurant in Granada. She'd knocked the hat off the table and then picked it up. Ever since then, she had been following their location, turning up wherever they were. *It's the Panama hat, that's how she's tracking us!* he thought.

Jardine moved closer to the general. "*El sombrero*, get rid of it."

"Don't you know the risk of a melanoma for a balding man at my age?" responded the general.

"That's how she's tracking us. *Doña Bárbara*."

"Can you stop using that name? It's a blight on Venezuelan literature."

"Alina Calderón, the Cuban assassin. She must have placed a chip in your hat. In the restaurant in Granada."

The men pulled into a small alleyway off the side of *Rua Augusta*. The general took the hat off his head and examined it. Hidden in the stitching where the band was joined to the hat itself, he saw a small flat transparent chip above the size of a fingernail. It had been wedged and stuck on the inside of the band, not visible unless closely examined. He took the chip off and examined it. "*Hijo de...*" Son of a...

Then as if it were a natural reflex, he pulled out a small bottle of port he'd just bought in the shop and wedged the tracking chip under the label on the bottle. He saw a large dumpster bin in the alley and was striding towards it when he saw a homeless man stumbling towards them up the alleyway. The man's wobbly gait suggested he was already on his way to a drunken stupor.

The general, sensing an opportunity, jogged forward and thrust the bottle into the man's hand. The dishevelled man glanced down at the bottle like he'd been handed the Holy Grail from Christ himself. His eyes grew larger and larger, and a smile spread across his face. Then as if acting on instinct, he thrust it under his arm in a protective measure and jumped backwards. His eyes darted from side to side as if his survival instinct had kicked in to protect the bottle and it was fight or flight. Then he let out a laugh, turned quickly, and ran off down the alleyway leading away from *Rua Augusta*. He'd chosen *flight*.

The men turned back to *Rua Augusta* from the alleyway and noticed a figure waving from across the street from a doorway.

It was Felix.

Looking left and right—no sign of the woman—they traipsed through the stream of pedestrians and shuffled inside an old bookshop.

"What was all that about?" asked Felix as they entered the shop.

"Just executing some evasive measures," said Jardine.

"My hat," the general took the Panama hat from his head and held it out. "Our friend had placed a tracking chip in the band."

"No shit?" replied Felix. "Y'all get rid of it?"

Jardine nodded, pointing at the man running wildly down the alleyway. "He's got it. Well, it's attached to the bottle of port he's holding."

Felix smiled. "Shame to waste a bottle of port, but impressive tradecraft. Get away from the window; I don't think she's seen us enter here."

The group shuffled into the bookshop and perched near the window.

"Well, that explains her calm demeanour just now. She's known right where you were all along," said Felix.

"Now we can watch and see if she's taken the bait," said the general.

"Assuming she didn't see us waltz in here," replied Jardine.

"I think we're good," chimed in Veronica now. "I spotted her a way back; don't think she's made an updated visual on us yet." The men's heads swivelled towards her, their faces notably impressed at her skills. She shrugged. "She seems to be more interested in looking down at her phone."

The group crouched, hiding behind a book display near the window. The bookshop was almost opposite the alleyway, providing a perfect vantage point to see if the assassin would follow the now discarded tracking chip. Several minutes passed before they saw her arrive. She strode forward with the confidence of a panther in a jungle. Top of the food chain. Seeing her now amongst the flow of pedestrians, they saw she wore a dark green scarf over a white shirt, with white Converse on her feet. She scanned the crowd, surveying the people passing by from behind her dark sunglasses. She glanced down at her phone again and with a small jolt of surprise, she jumped slightly and jogged to her right, turning into the alleyway. As she turned the corner, the jog turned into a run, gaining speed, as she galloped down the alleyway in pursuit, not of them but the homeless man carrying the port bottle.

CHAPTER 25

LISBON, PORTUGAL

AFTER HAVING STABBED THE HAND OF THE MAN who was helping the general in Seville, Alina Calderón had returned to her hotel and sat watching *The Simpsons* on TV while monitoring her phone. The blue dot had disappeared in the same dense area of hotels in *barrio Santa Cruz*. They must have been in an underground bunker or an underground car park, she had reasoned to herself. Later as they appeared again, she had been astonished to see the two blue dots split, travelling in different directions. Up until then, the two blue dots—the trackers placed in the Panama hat and under the Land Rover Defender—had been in perfect unison, flowing together in the same direction. Now they were separated, she decided to call her handler, again scrolling for the codename JOAQUIN in her phone and dialling.

"*Sí, dígame,*" her handler answered.

"We have a problem."

"*Qué es?*"

"It seems they've split, one heading south for the coast, another west—I'm assuming for Lisbon."

After a few moments of silence, the man replied, "I have a team, Albanians, in Marbella. They can pick up the vehicle heading for the coast. You go to Lisbon."

"*Affimativo*," replied Alina Calderón.

Then she finished watching the episode of *The Simpsons* she was watching before she packed her small bag, took the elevator to the ground floor and checked out. She drove several hours to Lisbon, checking into a small hotel in the *Baixa* district, then rented a scooter and set off in pursuit.

Now she swung in and out of the Lisbon traffic on a green Vespa scooter. Her leather shoulder bag was slung diagonally across her body and the violin case was strung over her left shoulder. With her blue trousers, white shirt, green scarf and flat cap, she looked similar to many of the ubiquitous artists and street performers that roamed the streets of Lisbon and especially *Rua Augusta*. Her mobile phone was perched on the dashboard in front of her as she looked down at the moving blue dot and revved the bike forward. Pulling up and parking the Vespa in a side street near *Rua Augusta*, she dismounted and unlatched the red helmet she wore, stowing it under the seat. She shook her head, letting her long dark hair resettle itself, adjusted her shoulder bag and violin case and strode forward with mobile phone in hand.

After walking to the end of the street and swinging into the pedestrian flow of *Rua Augusta,* she arrived at a small newsstand a distance away from where she could see the blue dot pulsating on the screen—not moving. She didn't know who she expected to see, but as she witnessed a couple hugging and standing in the doorway of a wine shop, as if they were on holiday, a shiver went down her spine like a cold injection into her bones.

She couldn't believe they were still alive, at least not the man, anyway. She thought back to the event in the gardens of the *Alcázar*. Had she withdrawn the poison-tipped mascara case with the retractable syringe as she intended? Or had she taken out the stabbing implement in the lipstick case? I *must have just scratched him with my lipstick case, not the mascara case*, she thought. *Carajo!*

She continued to watch them when another shiver went through her like a jolt of electricity. Her heart started to thump as if she were anxious about something. As if something was not quite right. This was a feeling she'd not had while on assignment. She usually felt nothing, as if it was an everyday, run-of-the-mill job. Like the typing up of a document for an office drone, a carpenter hammering a nail, or a waiter delivering a plate of food. She wasn't sure what it was, but the couple holding hands awoke something within her. She felt as if she were seeing something familiar. Something close to her. A hazy memory bubbled to the surface, seeping into her mind.

She watched as the woman entered the shop while the man remained in the doorway. She decided against immediate action for the moment, preferring to watch and wait until she could work out what she was dealing with. Besides, it was the general she was after; she'd wait until she got a visual on him. She hadn't laid eyes on him since Granada. The area around her heaved with people. Also, this was not the place to make a scene, far too public. Anyway, she could continue to follow them via the tracking chip, the pulsating blue dot on her mobile phone screen that had remained faithful in her pursuit so far. She lit a cigarette and leant against a newsstand, continuing to gaze across at the man who should be dead. But no sign of the general—the traitor. After several puffs of her cigarette, she saw the woman leave the wine shop now with an older man, a man she hadn't seen before. He wore a large Stetson cowboy hat and wore a denim shirt. They walked together up the left side of *Rua Augusta* away from the arch. She was still processing this movement when she saw him: the general. He exited the wine shop accompanied by the younger man who she'd already tried to kill. She watched as they both scurried up *Rua Augusta*.

She was about to follow when another shiver jolted through her. She recalled the couple she had just seen now, hugging in the doorway. A memory flashed through her mind, like a silent movie playing inside her head. In it, her mother, elegantly dressed in a yellow summer dress walked along the *malecón* in Havana, her luscious brown hair blowing messily in the wind. Next to her mother, holding her hand, was her father. Dressed in chinos with a grey short-sleeved shirt tucked in, his slightly tinted round-framed glasses stopping the glare of the tropical sun as the breeze gently ruffled his dark slicked-back hair. It must have been an old home movie she had seen or perhaps just a photo she remembered. She took a drag of her cigarette and realised that it was the couple she had just watched that reminded her of them. They reminded her of her parents. At least what she could remember of them while they were together. Her father was always travelling, and her mother was not much better. It was only recently, now that they were both in Havana, that she could potentially pass the days with them. And now it was *she* that was travelling and working and not having time to spend with them.

A beep on her phone awoke her from her daydream and she threw the cigarette on the ground and stamped on it. She looked down at her phone, tapping the locator app which beamed to life revealing the pulsating blue dot move along *Rua Augusta*. She looked up. A steady flow of people cascaded up and down the street. Her eyes scanned the crowds, but she couldn't see the two pairs of people she had just been watching. Her face burned. The previous feeling of fondness and melancholy brought on by the memory of her parents was replaced by anger as she looked at all the people mindlessly buying tourist trinkets, gorging on pastries, and watching silly street performers like stunned fish. *Capitalism at its worst*, she thought as she pushed ahead.

She walked up *Rua Augusta* with this thought seething in her mind. She saw a small girl beside her lick an ice cream and her mind flashed back to her younger days in Miami. *But hadn't she grown up with all the comforts of capitalism?* she thought. While people in Cuba ate grapefruit rind and whatever they could scrape together during the *período especial*, the Special Period, when the collapse of the Soviet Union left Cuba in an economic tailspin, she had received all the trappings of the decadent West, while her *patriotas* suffered under an autocrat. But *Fidelito* only did that so he could retain their sovereignty, their dignity, *patria o muerte*, she heard herself say softly. Then as if in response, she questioned herself: if it was *patria o muerte* why was she killing in the name of a foreign country?

The uncomfortable contradiction swelled around in her stomach before she said to herself, why not *patria y vida*? That's what the average Cuban citizen had been saying on the streets in Cuba in protest recently. It was whispered among the youth, rapped about in underground concerts, and used as a hashtag on *Facebook* and *Instagram*. At least to those that had ready access to the internet. Sure, the US had always spread its tentacles throughout Latin America from Mexico to Colombia to Chile and Argentina, surpassing, supporting, arming, invading, influencing, and meddling. They were still the imperialist pigs she had been taught about. But wasn't the opposite also true? The control, the arresting of dissidents, the people fleeing, the suppression of expression and limiting of human rights. Was Nicaragua, Cuba, Venezuela really any better? The niggling thought spread through her mind like a slow-moving ooze engulfing a city. She shook her head hard as if to shake out all the negative and contradictory thoughts she was having. Her mind hadn't been the same since the crash. Something had changed.

A round of applause broke her train of thought as she saw a small group of people clapping at a juggling act. She scanned the crowds again when she realised she had completely lost sight of the group. She looked down at her phone again. The blue dot continued forward. It didn't matter if she lost them in the crowd; she could easily monitor them from here. She stepped forward alternating her gaze between the phone and the crowd. She had walked thirty metres when she heard a beep emanating from her mobile phone. Looking down she saw the blue dot speed off down a side alleyway. It increased in velocity away from the busy *Rua Augusta* and then stopped. After a few seconds, it continued again, not as fast as before but leading off into the narrow maze of Lisbon's streets. Further and further away from her reach. *They've spotted me*, she thought. It's time to finish this once and for all. She reached into her bag to ensure she had her mascara and lipstick cases, then made sure the violin case was secure against her body. She ran forward, weaving through the throngs of people and arrived at the alleyway. She glanced down at her phone one last time to ensure she was in the correct place and sped off down the alleyway on foot, her white Converse pounded the tiled pavement as she followed her prey.

CHAPTER 26

Lisbon, Portugal

THE GROUP WATCHED AS ALINA CALDERÓN, THE Cuban assassin, sped off down the alleyway. They all let out a collective sigh of relief as they saw her slowly move further and further away, disappearing around the curve of the alley. It seemed they had finally managed to throw her off their trail and with the tracking chip disposed of, she now had no way of finding them. The looming threat and dread that they had felt over the last few days seemed to slip away in an instant.

The group peered around the old bookshop. It was deep and narrow and contained a second level accessed by a narrow staircase. The aisles towered with books, the rows twisting around like a labyrinth. Although it was bright and hot outside with a bustling crowd, inside the shop it was cool with a musty smell, like a wet dog.

Veronica spoke up first with a request. "I think I'd prefer to go back to the hotel."

Jardine raised his hand to his chin. "Are you sure that's a good idea?"

"I'll be safe there," she said.

"I'll see she gets back safely," offered Felix. "It'll be less conspicuous with just the two of you meeting the source anyway. And now that we've gotten rid of *chica loca*, it should be all smooth sailing. Besides, I've gotta go see a guy about a horse."

Ambrose's words lingered in Jardine's mind. *Don't let Felix near a casino.* Is that why he wanted to head back to the hotel? To get in a round of blackjack or poker at the Estoril Casino? Even if that was his plan, there wasn't much Jardine could do. As long as Veronica was back safe at the hotel, that's all that mattered to him. "Okay. We won't be long," he said. "We'll meet the source and then see you back at the hotel."

Jardine hugged Veronica and patted Felix on the shoulder as he and the general stepped out into the sun once again and continued further up *Rua Augusta*.

As they disappeared from the window, Veronica turned to Felix. "Do you mind if we spend *un momentico* here? I might take a book back to the hotel to read."

"Of course. Be my guest." The edges of Felix's greying moustaches rose, smiling. "I might just pick out something myself." His head swivelled, gazing around the shop.

Veronica turned and ambled down one of the aisles, running her fingers along the books looking for something that might entice her. She passed books by *José Saramago* and *Fernando Pessoa*. One row contained old copies of Portuguese classics by *Eça de Queirós*. Moving towards the centre of the shop she stumbled across a small display—obviously aimed at tourists—of famous books set in Lisbon: *The High Mountains of Portugal* by *Yann Martel* and *Night Train to Lisbon* by *Pascal Mercier*. Next to that she saw a Latin America section with a range of Brazilian authors. She was just about to pick up a copy of *Paulo Coelho*'s latest release when she saw a familiar name: *Gabriel Garcia Márquez*, the Nobel Prize-winning Colombian author. She picked up an old, second-hand hardcover copy of *The General in his Labyrinth*—a fictional account of the *Libertador Simon Bolívar's* last days.

She smiled and picked up the book, noting its weight like the heavy bibles she had seen priests hold at mass as a child in Bogotá. She had seen this particular book growing up: in bookshops, libraries, and in her uncle's house, but she'd never read it. Come to think of it, she hadn't read anything in a long time. She opened the pages to see a map of Colombia and Venezuela showcasing the Rio Magdalena and the once important cities and towns that framed Bolivar's final journey from Bogotá to Santa Marta in an attempt to leave South America for exile in Europe.

She looked at the map and shook her head in disbelief, thinking how in almost two hundred years of independence, things had yet to change a great deal in Latin America. *El Libertador, Simon Bolívar*, had tried to free the people from Spain, a colonial power that projected its demands from abroad. Today, the general was trying to free his country from a tyranny, not imposed by a European colonial power but by the very *revolución* that purported to free its people. She frowned, reflecting that perhaps that was a tad dramatic but true on some level. She closed the book and looked down at the cover. *A small dose of historical fiction might be just what I need at this moment*, she thought. It's about time I got in touch with my own country's history anyway. She strode to the counter and after paying for it at the register, placed it in the fabric book bag she'd also purchased. Happy with herself, she looked around the shop, searching for Felix. She had just twisted her head towards the front window of the shop when she noticed a familiar figure emerge from the other side of the street. A mess of dark hair, blowing in the wind, under a flat cap. She hissed aloud in the shop not wanting to alert attention or disturb the customers. "Felix? Felix? Where are you?"

There was no response. She had to react fast, she whispered again. "Felix, *dónde estás?*"

Still no response.

Gripping the book bag, the heavy book inside, she strode forward and left the shop without him.

JARDINE AND THE GENERAL CONTINUED BRISKLY AT first and then, realising they were early for their meeting and no longer being chased, began to walk more leisurely up the street full of stalls, artists and pedestrians. After the initial scare of the assassin having followed them, they finally felt free and that they could relax knowing that they were not being traced, followed or hunted.

With this feeling in mind, the general took the time while strolling to think of his plan. He would speak at the United Nations in New York and present his findings on the corrupt Madera regime. Not only that, but he hoped the speech would entice the International Criminal Courts to launch a thorough investigation into the treatment of protestors during the attempted power grab by Madera, back when he had stacked the Supreme Court with his supporters and dissolved the National Assembly. He also hoped the UN speech led to some support to open negotiations and stopped the invasion of Guyana. As he walked, he ran through possible snippets of the speech to himself. "Madera and his various ministers were very much aware of these crimes. They gave the orders, coordinated and provided resources to the plans and policies that resulted in the offending acts," he would say as he stood on the podium. "The Madera regime has denied the previous reports and the recent UN report by the ex-president of Chile. It's as if they were living in Narnia! But they cannot deny this, the evidence is indisputable."

He smiled as he walked, pleased with his thoughts. It

would fit with his overall theme that Democracy was in decline around the world. Or perhaps it never had been well entrenched in the first place? Authoritarianism was once again rising its controlling head in an explosion of populism worldwide and Venezuela had written the modern-day populist's playbook, one which was now being tried by authoritarians of the left and the right. Therefore, the world was no longer a battle for left versus right but a matter of democracy versus absolute control. All of this swirled in the general's mind as he and Jardine walked up *Rua Augusta*.

Jardine noticed that the general had been quiet. "Feeling like a weight's been lifted off your shoulders?"

The general nodded but didn't speak.

Jardine asked another question. "Something on your mind?"

The general stroked his chin. "Sánchez and his successor Madera have played out a modern-day version of *Animal Farm*, and we are only just now watching the animals shred their skin to reveal they are pigs, like the swine before." He lowered his hand from his chin and said, "Well? What do you think?"

"A modern version of Orwell's *Animal Farm*?"

The general sighed. "It's for my UN speech. I'm thinking of what to say to spice things up a bit. That's what ex-president *El Comandante* Sánchez did when he took the podium after the US President in 2006. *Everyone* remembers that speech."

Jardine laughed. "The smell of sulphur as if the devil had been there before the US President took the stage?"

The general smiled, nodded, and then continued walking. "That's right. I think I need something like that to ensure my speech is picked up in the nightly news or spread online. Maybe I should drop in the phrase *Orwellian*?"

"I think it's been overused; it doesn't have the same effect it once did."

The general frowned. "Oh, yes, you're probably right." A dark thought suddenly crossed his mind. Perhaps it would be better if he *were* assassinated like the Madera regime wanted? Maybe that would make the news? Maybe becoming a martyr is what Venezuela needed to show the world what was happening there? He pondered this as they arrived at the neo-gothic style tower that housed the *Santa Justa* elevator. It sprang from the ground like a beanstalk among the buildings of the Baixa district. Above was the square where they would meet the source. They waited in line to enter the lift. Once above, it was only a short stroll, and they would be at the rendezvous point.

The doors opened and people shuffled forward. Entering the elevator, Jardine turned to the general. "Ready for the final piece of the puzzle?"

The general adjusted his hat and swivelled his head towards Jardine with a nod. "Ready for life or death, which-ever comes first."

CHAPTER 27

Lisbon, Portugal

Alina Calderón was still breathing heavily as she eyed the familiar battered Panama hat hovering ahead as it entered the *Santa Justa* elevator. The very same hat she had seen in Granada, in Seville, and now here in Lisbon. As she sucked in air, she silently cursed herself, first in Spanish (*coño*) and then in Russian (*blyad*). She had fallen for the group's trick of placing the tracking chip in a bottle of port carried by a bottle-swilling homeless man who had run wildly down a back alley. Quickly realising her mistake, she had returned to the main thoroughfare, *Rua Augusta*, and continued up into the city. Scanning the thronging crowd as she walked swiftly, she had managed to catch a glimpse of the General's hat floating above the crowds. Now, she waited in line, a few rows back from the general and the ex-MI6 analyst. She witnessed them enter the elevator. And then she pushed forward herself, striving to squeeze into the confined space with them.

· · ·

Veronica strolled out into the street as wind swept up from the Tagus River, the buildings on either side channelling it into a wind tunnel. It made her hair sway in all directions covering her face as she reached into her bag, pulled out a hair clip, and twisted it into a small messy bun.

She watched as the assassin strode up the street, her head scanning from side to side. She seemed noticeably more stressed, hurried and rushed this time. She was obviously rattled not being able to track them in her usual way. Veronica pushed forward following behind the woman but kept her distance, trying not to get too close. *If only I had a phone, I could call Ollie and warn him*, she thought, as the assassin darted in and out of the heavy pedestrian crowd, swiftly navigating the throng of people walking around her, like a ballerina pirouetting on stage. At a large inter-section, the assassin stopped and surveyed the crowd, rotating her head like a robot. Then her head stopped, and she took off her sunglasses, squinting into the distance, then rapidly turned, heading towards the *Santa Justa* elevator.

Veronica followed her gaze and could just make out the distant Panama hat floating through the crowd in front of the elevator. She followed the assassin in pursuit, wanting to yell out but she was too far away and didn't want to create a scene nor let the assassin know she was following. She watched as the woman moved steadily toward the elevator, then as she stopped to wait in line to enter. In the queue, the assassin looked sideways at a young mother and a baby; she peered down into the pram and winked and poked out her tongue at the young child. Her head rose to face the mother and her lips moved, but Veronica was too far back to hear what she was saying. The lift doors opened, and she saw Jardine and the general enter the elevator. She thought about jogging forward and trying to also enter the lift, pushing ahead of the people in the line. *But what if she recognises me*, she thought? *And will I make it?* She watched as people surged forward into the open lift. *Should I go?* she asked herself. As she pondered the lift doors slowly shut, and the last entrant, a short, overweight businessman who managed to squeeze in sideways while holding his breath, his body squished against the glass as the elevator ascended.

As it rose, Veronica watched as the assassin remained on ground level. *She didn't make it into the elevator either*, she thought. Then the assassin swung her head from side to side, analysing her surroundings and looking for options. Ten seconds passed and she stepped forward, then darted around the back of the elevator, disappearing.

Veronica followed her and, reaching the area behind the elevator, saw that there were stairs leading upwards behind the tower. *The stairs!* Thought Veronica. *Of course.* She sprang forward, drifting up the stairs trying to take them two at a time but keeping her distance behind the assassin. *Lucky I decided to wear my flats*, she thought as she bound upwards. Like many Colombian women who worked in an office, it was often easier for her to walk in heels rather than flat sole shoes. For climbing stairs, however, a pair of flat sole leather moccasins were far superior. Pumping her legs to propel herself up the stairs, her thighs burned with the lactic acid making its way through her body. She felt an adrenaline surge giving her a feeling of elation which spurred her on. Slightly panting, she reached the top of the stairs and stopped to survey the scene. The lift had already arrived and the small crowd that had disembarked was dispersing, heading off in different directions. She scanned the street, vying for a glimpse of the woman, then saw the familiar herringbone flat cap with dark hair protruding, floating down the walkway beside the ruins of a large convent to the square, *Largo do Carmo*.

Veronica pushed forward and followed the assassin.

. . .

AFTER ASCENDING IN THE ELEVATOR AND THEN exiting, Jardine and the general trailed along a narrow walkway and down a tiled path beside the ruins of the *Covento do Carmo* leading to the *Largo do Carmo* square. The square itself was peaceful and away from the busy shopping district below. It was a relatively unknown but famous location in Portuguese history, a key site of the Carnation Revolution where members of the Portuguese Armed Forces surrounded the authoritarian leader Marcelo Caetano in a former police station that sits on the square, pressuring him to cede power, thus ending fifty years of dictatorship under him and his predecessor António de Oliveira Salazar.

Arriving in the square, the general and Jardine sat at a small table belonging to a kiosk beneath jacaranda trees. A yellow tram with wood-rimmed windows trundled by as the smell of warm sugary pastries filled the air. Nearby, three elderly men sat on a bench, each nursing a glass of red wine while talking animatedly. Two children kicked a football back and forth in the centre of the square next to a large fountain that emanated a faint trickling sound. A cool breeze swept up from the lower parts of the city, breaking up the heat of the day, and the jacarandas dotted around the square provided shade.

Shortly after sitting at their table, a waiter appeared, and the general ordered. "*Um pastel de nata y un café com leite.*"

The waiter turned to Jardine who also spoke in Portuguese. "The same for me, please."

"You speak Portuguese as well?" queried the general.

"I dabble," offered Jardine.

"No doubt useful in your time in South America. Tell me, what exactly is it that you did there?"

Jardine shuffled in his seat as a small group of tourists arrived and congregated beside the convent ruins, sitting on the steps and listening to a tour guide. He watched them cautiously as he replied, as if everyone around him were listening in. "Report, reports, and reports about the reports I'd previously written reports about. And occasionally interviews. Actually, that was the most enjoyable aspect of the job. Getting to know people, visiting different places. It felt more real, like you were involved in something bigger than a piece of paper no one ever reads."

"Ah yes, that's why I joined the military. I couldn't deal with sitting at a desk all day, droning on about who knows what. It's funny, the higher up the chain you get, the more of that type of crap one must deal with."

"I couldn't have put it better myself," said Jardine smiling at the general.

"And now? What of your new venture?

"It's going reasonably well."

"It's different to what you used to do."

"It has its difference and similarities. I think I'll always be changing what I do. I bore easily; I think it's just my temperament."

The general nodded. "Boredom is all in the mind. If I learnt anything while locked up in *Ramo Verde* prison, it's that most pain is caused not by the environment itself, but by the environment that has been created in one's own mind. That is a very difficult environment to change. One does not escape it by simply hopping on a plane, moving to a different city, or changing careers. *No, señor*. It requires much more effort to change the environment of one's mind."

"You seem to be quite knowledgeable in this area."

"Sitting in a prison cell gives you a lot of time to think. It also gives you a good excuse to explore your mind's environment. It's the only option one has when trapped."

The waiter arrived with glasses of water and placed them on the table. Moments later, he returned with warm *pastels de nata* and frothy café lattes.

"Here we are, my friend," said the general, gesturing to the pastries, "the best *pastel de nata* in Portugal, or maybe the world? I've been told they're quite good in Macau, but I've yet to try them there."

The men both grabbed a pastel each and bit into the warm custard, the soft crunch of the flaky pastry the only sound between them. The general leant back in his chair, holding the half-eaten pastel up in front of him. "This," he said as he admired it like a valuable gemstone, "reminds me of old Venezuela. It was never perfect, or fair for that matter, but at least people had a chance to live. The most difficult thing for the old generation of Venezuelans like me is that I remember a more prosperous Venezuela. Yes, there was inequality, but there were also opportunities, something to aspire to. Why else would immigrants from around the world flock there if it wasn't a good place to live? My father left Portugal for Caracas for a better future." He took another bite and chewed thoughtfully. "That's the hard part, looking back and knowing that things could have turned out better." He finished his sentence with a sigh. After a few moments of silence, he straightened his back and asked impatiently, "Where is he?" He tapped his foot on the cold stone ground under the table.

Jardine sipped at his coffee. He knew from his previous life in MI6 that it was often like this. The life of a spy was not action but waiting. Any intelligence operation was planned and organised for days or weeks to meet with a source only for it to fail to materialise at the last moment.

As if on cue, just as the general took another bite of the *pastel de nata*, a man appeared, walking towards them. He was dressed in a charcoal suit with a dark blue knitted tie and black-rimmed glasses. His dark hair was parted to one side and he walked like a mechanical toy but with the confident, self-assured swagger of a businessman. Stopping beside one of the jacaranda trees next to the table, he asked: "General Pereira?"

"*Senhor Silva?*" replied the general.

"At your service." The man extended his hand to shake theirs, then he placed his suitcase on a chair and tried to get the waiter's attention.

Jardine lifted the cup of coffee to his lips and took a sip. Later he would wonder what it was that had caught his eye. A flash? A reflective glint from a window? He couldn't be sure, but he felt a rush of air and in a millisecond the table seemed to give way as he, the banker and the general all hit the ground. The plates and the coffee cups also crashed down, creating a shattering crescendo that echoed throughout the square. Instinctively, as soon as they hit the ground, the general overturned the light metal table to form a shield. He sidled up against it and dragged Jardine in next to him.

Jardine peered sideways at his friend and saw a crimson patch of blood spread over his white linen shirt, soaking the side of his body.

"General, you're ... you're hit?" said Jardine.

The general was still hunched behind the table; he glanced down and dabbed his hand on his soaked shirt, the blood soaking his fingers. He brought his blood-covered fingers up to his face, a look of disbelief spread across it as several thick red drops dripped to the cobblestones below.

"*Sí,*" he replied. "It appears I am."

CHAPTER 28

Alina Calderón watched as the small flow of elevator passengers disembarked and walked along the narrow passageway from the top of the elevator to the square. She saw the familiar sombrero weave through the thinning crowd. As she watched, she considered approaching now. A quick lunge and stab with the mascara case should do the trick, but she'd made that mistake before. Anyway, she might manage to prick the general but how would the man, the ex-MI6 analyst beside him, react? She was still mulling this idea over when two members of the *Polícia de Segurança Pública*, the Portuguese police force, appeared and strolled past stopping outside the exit of the elevator. No, she would need some distance between her and the two men. There were too many witnesses in this area to consider the more up-close-and-personal methods. Any commotion would be caught on camera. She would need to rely on the contents of the violin case.

She ambled forward now, acting as if she were a tourist admiring the convent ruins but really, she was watching the two men as they approached a table in the square and sat down. The brilliant purple of the jacaranda trees set against the blue sky loomed above as she kept her eyes on the general and his accomplice. Then she admired the buildings surrounding the square in an array of pastel pinks, blues, and yellows. It suddenly struck her as the perfect place for an evening drink. A margarita, a mojito, a cool crisp glass of chilled vodka? If only she didn't have to do what she was assigned to do. And with that thought she caught herself, once again, doubting her profession, doubting what she was doing. This had never happened before, she thought. She had always been focussed and dedicated to the task at hand. No doubting or daydreaming. She forced herself to look again at her targets.

A waiter approached the men's table, attending to their order. She glanced back and saw the two police officers still loitering around the exit of the elevator. Still no chance to get close. They would be on to her in an instant, she thought. Her head swivelled around the square again, noting the convent ruins on one side and then a ring of buildings on the other three. Twisting her body in a full three-sixty, her eyes landed back on the passageway between the elevator and the square. Opposite the convent ruins and overlooking the tables and kiosk where the men sat, she noticed a bank of windows and a small balcony facing onto the square. She dropped her eyes lower and watched a small white delivery van offload boxes into the grilled gate of the building. She looked upwards again and then traced her gaze from the windows and balcony down to where the general and the man sat.

I could make that work.

She strode forward with purpose, entered the building, and climbed the stairs before arriving at a corridor with several large wooden doors. The corridor was empty, the muffled voices of the deliverymen below a distance sound now. The writing: '*Escola da Arte*' was written on a plaque on the wall.

An art school with windows out onto the square? A nice place to admire the tranquil setting and paint. Or, in her case, a useful vantage point to 'paint' a dissident general.

She reached into her shoulder bag and withdrew a pair of gloves and slid them on. She turned the door handle on one of the large wooden doors and realised it was locked. She nudged it with her shoulder, but it didn't budge. Taking a step back, she heaved again, this time cracking the small brass lock as it opened with a slight creak. She entered the room. There was a musty smell and a whiff of oil paints. She approached the row of windows, the balcony door between them. She extended her hand to the balcony and twisted the doorknob. Locked. The door this time was heavier with a metal lock and the glass in the door frame meant it was more fragile—and noisier— than the wooden door she had just forced open. There was no heaving this door open. The glass would likely shatter, attracting attention to her position. She moved across to one of the windows and peered out. She could see the square, the lilac jacarandas, the kiosk, a scattering of tables and, most importantly, the two men seated below.

She undid the window latch and opened it slightly. A breeze entered, breaking up the chemical smell of oil paints in the afternoon heat. She peered below again and saw the two men were seated at the outdoor table no more than twenty or thirty metres away, both clear targets. Being only one story up, the angle was not too much of an incline and it was within range. It wasn't the ideal distance or trajectory, especially for her weapon of choice, but with skill, not impossible. Besides, there was not much time left and she might not get another chance like this.

She set the small violin case on the tiled floor and kneeled in front of it. She unlatched the case with two soft clicks which echoed in the large room. From the case, she removed the violin and opened its fake bottom, extracting a leather pouch and laying it on the tiles. The leather pouch itself had been couriered by diplomatic pouch from Havana to Madrid, where she had picked it up from the Cuban consulate.

She slid out the modified pistol and held it in her hand, feeling its weight, its potential power. The older members of Cuban intelligence had preferred a Groza, then a Makarov, the classic standard-issue to Soviet officers and conveniently made under license in Cuba. However, for this assignment, she would use a 9mm PB pistol. It was very similar to the Makarov but modified to accept a lengthened suppressor. It was old school but not *old* old school. She looked at the gun, then peered out the window and bit her lip. The accuracy of a pistol at twenty to twenty-five metres was stretching it. She'd have to hope she could replicate what she had done in training.

She loaded in a box magazine of subsonic ammunition— to further dampen the sound—and then she extracted the suppressor and began to calmly screw it into the barrel. As she did this, she purposely slowed her breathing. In and out, in and out, like a meditating yogi. It was essential she was calm and collected when she took the shot.

With the suppressor attached, she stood and attached a small laser sight which clipped on top. She propped it up on a small slit in the window, noting the added heaviness of the batteries in the laser sight, and aimed downwards to the square below. Resting the pistol on the cold metal of the small rectangular window frame, she peered downwards, aimed, and soon realised that there was a tree partially blocking the table. Nonetheless, both men were still visible. She lined up the general, squinting and looking down the barrel to get a general aim and approximately line up the shot. She didn't want to engage the laser until the last moment to verify her aim.

The general was below talking animatedly with what appeared to be a *pastel de nata* in his hand. She licked her lips, realising she was quite hungry and then shook her head to snap herself out of the thought. She aimed again, focussing on the general's torso and engaged the laser which shone brightly on his chest, like a small dot of fluorescent red pasta sauce wobbling on his shirt. She stopped breathing, and after a second, she squeezed the trigger as the general slightly turned his head and reached out his arm to a mysterious figure stepping out from behind the tree. The shot, barely audible over the background noise of activity in the square, fizzed through the air.

A puff of red blood ignited and sprayed onto the general and splattered across the table. She took in a breath and glanced down to see that the man who had stepped out from behind the tree hand taken the shot before falling to the ground. Blood spilled out of the back of his tailored suit.

Mierda, she thought. *Shit.*

The table came crashing down as the general and his accomplice scrambled to cover themselves behind it. She held her breath and went to take aim again. With the laser sight engaged, the laser dot wobbling over the general's head as he bobbed up and down from behind the table, she was ready to fire a second time. Just as she was about to squeeze the trigger, she heard a footstep on the tiles behind her. For a split second, she realised she was not alone in the room.

She froze.

Before she could turn her head or squeeze the trigger again, she felt a swift movement of air over her right ear, and then she momentarily registered a deafening thud to her right temple before her mind went blank.

Alina Calderón fell to the ground.

CHAPTER 29

THE MUFFLED SHOT SOUNDED LIKE A LOUD CLICK AS Veronica Velasco entered the room on the first floor of the copper red building on the edge of *Carmo do Largo* square. Entering, she saw the woman leaning against the window in the corner of the room. She tiptoed towards her, edging closer and closer. As she approached, she glimpsed the pistol resting on the edge of a small open window. The assassin had lifted her head from the pistol's sight and was peering below to the square. Veronica heard the woman mutter to herself as she was almost upon her. She reached into her fabric book bag and withdrew the hardback version of the novel she had just bought: *The General in His Labyrinth by* Gabriel Garcia Márquez.

As she took it out, the foil gold letters of the title shone briefly against the light entering the window, then Veronica Velasco wound back the heavy tome with both hands and then using all the force her petite frame could manage, she swung the book in an upward sweeping motion into the side of the assassin's head. She connected squarely with the woman's temple. A satisfying thud echoed throughout the room as she collapsed, falling back and dropping the heavy pistol. It made a tinny, clanging noise as it hit the tiled ground.

Veronica stood back, the book still in her hand and looked down at the woman lying unconscious on the floor. Her eyes blinked rapidly, and her breaths came in shallow short bursts, as though she'd been temporarily possessed and was only now regaining consciousness. She stood there for a moment stunned, not knowing what to do next. *Had she killed her? Had she become the assassin?* These were the thoughts running through her mind when she suddenly heard footsteps behind her.

She gripped the book tightly and swung around, her eyes wide open like a rabbit caught in the hunter's spotlight. She was ready to take another swing, the adrenaline of the encounter now pouring through her veins.

A man stood in the doorway. He held up his hands to reveal he was empty-handed, then his gaze shifted between Veronica and the woman lying on the ground.

"I think you just saved the day, *señorita*," said Felix Aguilar, stepping forward.

"*Al menos por ahora*," replied Veronica. *At least for now.*

Felix moved forward, kneeling down beside the body and picking up the 9mm PB pistol before lifting his shirt slightly and sliding it into the back of his jeans. Still crouching, he checked the woman's pulse and then looked up at Veronica. "She's alive."

"Thank God," said Veronica, relieved.

"We'll leave her here."

Veronica nodded. Still holding the heavy book in her hand, she looked down again at the body, still not quite computing what she had just done.

"Those boys still down there?" asked Felix, indicating towards the window.

"Oh no! I didn't think of that..." replied Veronica as she lunged towards the window and looked down desperately. In the movement, she dropped the book. It landed with a heavy thud. Outside, a small group had gathered around a body lying on the ground. Veronica held her breath as she stared out the window, waiting to get a glimpse. Then one of the waiters cleared people away and attempted to resuscitate the man lying there. Then she saw it. A man lying in a pool of his own blood but dressed in a suit. "It's not him," she whispered as she finally sucked in a breath.

"Not Jardine?" asked Felix. "What about the general?"

"Not him either," replied Veronica. "It's a man in a suit."

"Must be the banker then," said Felix. "Any sign of them?"

Veronica turned now and shook her head.

"Well," said Felix, standing. "I should probably call it in. See if I can't get someone down here to make sure the *señorita* here is locked up for good this time. But in the meantime, we should probably get the fuck out of here, *pronto*."

"Let's go," replied Veronica as they both made for the door and strode out into the corridor, jogged down the stairs, and out of the building into the waning light of the day.

OLIVER JARDINE WASN'T SURE IF IT WAS FEAR OR adrenaline that coursed through his veins as he sat in a blood-stained shirt in *Largo do Carmo* square in Lisbon. Around him, people ran for cover and the waiters looked on with a mix of annoyance and disbelief. They were probably used to dishevelled Englishmen on stag weekends fronting up in a much worse state, but he doubted they'd seen anyone shot before. He glanced at the general, who in turn was staring at his confidential source, the Portuguese banker, who now lay in a pool of his own blood on the ground. The suited man had barely placed the documents on the table, ordered, and was about to take a seat when he seemed to fall in slow motion. His blood spurted out and splattered onto the general's white shirt like a macabre Jackson Pollock painting and it now flowed along the grooves of cobblestones like a red river through a stony canyon.

The general, having patted himself down, his hands covered in blood, responded again to Jardine: "No, on second thought, I'm not hit. I thought I was; it must be *his* blood." He nodded towards the banker lying on the other side of the table.

"I barely heard anything, a loud click, like an air rifle."

"It must have been a suppressor," said the general, as he poked his head above the overturned table. "But it seems like they've stopped."

A short while passed and they heard sirens in the distance. Around them, people ran and a small group of people had gathered nearby. Jardine made eye contact with the general and spoke with a resolute calmness: "Time to go?"

"Time to go," he replied. "We don't know if there'll be more shots coming." They both stood up, immediately clinging to the tree next to their table. Then, calmly and with confidence Jardine motioned to the waiter. "We need an *ambulância*," he said in Portuguese, pointing at the banker lying on the ground. "*Agora, rápidamente.*"

The waiter, still watching on in shock, snapped out of it and ran into the kiosk and picked up a phone.

Their backs against the tree, Jardine whispered, "Back to the hotel?"

"Let's regroup," the general said.

Jardine looked out into the square, thinking. Then he turned towards the general. "We'll need to get the Defender and get you straight to the airport."

The general looked down to his right as if thinking hard. "Yeah, you're right. We'll regroup at the hotel and then get out of there as quickly as we can."

The waiter returned and asked them if they were okay. The sirens became louder now as people gathered around, staring down at the body.

"We need to get to a hospital," said Jardine, lying.

"But your friend?" asked the waiter.

"We didn't know him," replied the general quickly. "We must go."

In the chaos, they slipped away and down the hill towards the Tagus River.

CHAPTER 30

TWENTY MINUTES AFTER THE BULLET HAD STRUCK the Portuguese banker, a group of police were swarming the area around the crime scene in *Carmo do Largo* square. João Neves, the lead investigator and expert in ballistics from the *Polícia Judiciária*, Portugal's investigative police agency, knelt next to the body. Lifting the man's suit jacket and shirt he examined the entry wound—there was a hole in the man's back as he lay face down on the cobblestones. Next, he carefully lifted the head, examining the forehead which revealed a large gash from where he'd obviously hit his head as he fell. Blood still oozed along the grooves of paved ground pooling under the tree.

Neves replaced the head carefully back on the ground, and then he again examined the man's back. After twenty-seconds, he turned and peered up, following the likely trajectory of the bullet. His gaze landed on the window overlooking the square, and then, lowering his eyes, he looked back at the sprawled body under the Jacaranda tree to confirm.

He turned to a group of officers. "Check that window." He pointed at the first-storey window with a gloved hand. "I estimate the bullet came from there."

Immediately a small team of police officers shuffled towards the entrance and made their way to the first floor of the Escola do Arte. Reaching the top of the stairs, they entered through the open door with a broken brass lock, noticing the room was empty apart from a scattering of art supplies in the corner. Closer to the window, a hardback copy of *The General in his Labyrinth* by Gabriel Garcia Márquez lay on the ground. One of the officers picked it up and turned it over in his hands, a quizzical look across his face. Later as they examined the room further, they would find gunpowder residue around the window frame but no fingerprints and no weapon. The large hardback book was placed in a large plastic ziplock bag and taken back to the police station for forensic analysis. It would later be released and returned to a small second-hand bookshop on *Rua Augusta*.

Had the investigator and police officers arrived ten minutes earlier, they would have witnessed a black Porsche SUV arriving outside the building. Two men descended from the vehicle while two remained inside. The men who had exited the vehicle had looked down at a mobile phone to verify they were in the correct location and then had swiftly scaled the stairs to the first floor and entered the room with the broken lock. One of them had picked up the body of the woman who lay unconscious on the floor while the other collected a leather pouch. This man placed the pouch inside a cheap violin case which also lay on the floor and snapped it closed and fastened the latches. He picked up the mobile phone the assassin had used to track the general and his accomplices and then glanced down at the floor with a confused look and then asked in Albanian: *"Po libri?" And the book?*

The man carrying the woman, who was almost at the door, had looked back at him, replying also in Albanian, "There are no instructions for a book. Leave it." The men then exited the room and trotted down the stairs.

It was while she was being carried down the stairs that Alina Calderón began to come to, feeling her body, light and airy, as if floating through the air on a soft bed of duck feathers. The rage and anger and blood lust had dissipated, and she felt peaceful as cool air rushed over her face. Her mind still felt groggy and it took several moments for her to realise that she was not floating and most definitely not on a bed of duck feathers. She froze; she must be in the arms of one of the thugs that had been hired to finish the job that she had failed to execute.

The man placed her body in the trunk of the SUV and closed the door. She felt the vehicle hum as its engine idled. As she lay there, she heard voices in a language she didn't understand. It wasn't a romance language or Slavic. It didn't sound Greek or Middle Eastern. Every now and then she heard a word and thought it was Italian.

A mobile phone rang. A voice answered and spoke in Italian-accented Spanish. She couldn't hear every word but managed to hear two phrases: one phrase in Italian: "L'operazione è fallita." The operation failed. A phrase in Spanish followed, "Ella esta aquí." She's here. The 'ella' was pronounced in the Italian way, an 'L' sound instead of a 'Y' sound. The man said, "Ciao" and the phone conversation stopped, and the vehicle's occupants spoke to each other again in their unfamiliar language.

She lay there still as the last sun rays of the day erratically burst through and washed over her as the SUV cruised through the streets of Lisbon. She drifted in and out of consciousness as she continued to hear the voices in the strange language, then she heard an eruption of laughter followed by an accented voice that said in English, "Never send a woman to do a man's job." Another bout of laughter followed, then the same voice spoke again, closer now, as if coming from above her. It was a voice in Italian that continued that earlier comment and said, "Especially not a woman as beautiful as this."

The voice seemed very close, as if hovering above her. She felt a hand touch her side and then grab her, moving its way along her body, feeling and groping as she weakly tried to push it away. She arched her head up and vaguely saw the man's face, but it was a blur. She tried to sit up but still felt dizzy and her strength was waning as she tried to stop the man's hand.

She looked up again and saw a silver metal bracelet with an inscription which she couldn't read. Eventually, as she felt her mind slipping, she muttered to herself, "Bastards..." as she drifted back into unconsciousness.

CHAPTER 31

THERE WAS A SHARP KNOCK ON THE DOOR TO THE presidential suite in Caracas. Before the president could respond, the door burst open and Sindios Calvo, otherwise known as *El Pulpo* (The Octopus), entered the room accompanied by the Cuban Military Attaché, *Comandante* Lazo, by his side. *El Pulpo* strode forward with the confidence of a world leader and stopped before the president's desk.

The president's temper quietly simmered but he didn't want to say anything. Not to *El Pulpo, no señor*. He was the only person in Venezuela that the president feared, the only one that could potentially usurp his position and take power. Because everyone knew that as a current serving captain in the Armed Forces and Speaker in the National Assembly of Venezuela, as well as being the Vice President of the Venezuelan Socialist Party, it was *El Pulpo* who pulled the underground operational strings in the Bolivarian Republic of Venezuela.

"Ah, Calvo, always a pleasure," said the president.

"*Comandante* Lazo, good to see you. I was wondering where you'd gotten to. Please, both of you, take a seat." The president stood and indicated with his hand outreached.

"Thank you," replied *El Pulpo*, sitting on a chair opposite the president.

Comandante Lazo smiled and sat down also but did not speak.

The president nodded and now also sat.

Sindios Calvo leant back in his chair and put his feet up onto the president's desk. "We have an update, *Presidente*, from Lisbon," he said, crossing his arms in front of him.

The president looked forward with a steely gaze, trying not to convey any emotion, but underneath he was seething. *How dare this chamo put his feet on my desk*, he thought. However, the president didn't want to challenge or upset *El Pulpo*; he had many allies and there was a wisp of a rumour that he was waiting to take the reins from the president should he slip up. Some even thought he was actively undermining the president. The fact that *El Pulpo* had his own national TV show, which was growing in popularity, also scared him.

Comandante Lazo spoke next. "Unfortunately, our operative, codename: *Doña Bárbara*, was not able to fulfil her duties, but fortunately, *El Pulpo* here was able to come to our rescue with some contacts out of Marbella. They were able to locate our agent and have now picked her up."

The president nodded but didn't smile. "Thank you, *Pulpo*."

In return, *El Pulpo* smiled. "*De nada, mi presidente*. It's not wise for you to know too much, but it's important to note the Cuban's method did not go as planned. However, we were able to rectify the situation." Sindios Calvo had originally welcomed the Cubans, especially for their help following the failed coup against ex-president Sánchez of 2002, but now he despised them. He felt they were getting too close to the president and strengthening his position, although he wasn't one to let anyone know it.

Comandante Lazo looked menacingly at Calvo. "However, we *were* able to neutralise a contact of the general's. A banker out of Lisbon."

"Which bank?" asked the president.

"I believe you know which bank," said Calvo.

The president stroked his moustache. "Well, at least that is good news. No documents were exchanged then?"

"Unfortunately, yes," said *Comandante* Lazo.

The president frowned. In that moment, one of his employees entered carrying a tray with a platter of pastries. "Thank you, Marta," he said. "You can leave them on my desk here." He patted a space between himself and *El Pulpo* and *Comandante* Lazo.

The woman placed the tray on the desk and left the room.

The men each chose a pastry and ate enthusiastically nodded their approval as they chewed.

"One hundred percent Venezuelan ingredients, *Comandante* Lazo!" said the president. "As you know we are very capable here in the Bolivarian Republic. Independent and capable. We don't need Yankee or imported products here; Venezuela can finally stand on its own two feet without foreign interference!"

Comandante Lazo nodded his approval. "*Delicioso, Presidente.*"

In that moment, a presidential aide interrupted and entered the room, scurrying to the president's side. "Sorry, *Presidente*, I just wanted to confirm that the meeting with the Turkish supermarket chain will need to be changed because the Russian economic advisors have had to reschedule."

"Excellent, thank you, Manolo. Just as long as it doesn't interfere with the petroleum technical support meeting with the Iranians?"

"No, that's confirmed for tomorrow, right after the Chinese investment seminar in the morning."

"*Muy bien*," replied the president. *Very well*.

The president's aide retreated slightly and began writing in the president's diary and then left the room.

"Now, where was I? Ah, yes, this operative of yours, Lazo. *Doña Bárbara*, was it?"

"*Correcto, señor*," replied *Comandante* Lazo.

"And she failed us?"

Comandante Lazo nodded but stayed silent.

"We have a team of Albanians to finish the job," replied Sindios Calvo.

"Under your command, Calvo?"

"Not on paper; that will officially fall to the defence minister, but unofficially, I'll be in charge."

"Excellent. Thank you for taking responsibility for this operation."

"Yes, sir." *He wants me second on the list behind the Godfather, the defence minister. If it goes pear-shaped, he'll throw me to the dogs*, thought Sindios Calvo, before adding, "It's vital I am involved with such operations, but let's not forget it'll be *The Godfather*, as minister of defence, on the documents."

The president slapped his thighs. "That's settled it then. I really do hope we find that general before he gets on the plane. Isn't that right, *Comandante* Lazo?"

"*Claro que sí*," said *Comandante* Lazo, as he stood and saluted the president, adding, "Everything will work out just fine, *Presidente*." He left the room.

El Pulpo also stood and made for the door but stopped, turned, and spoke to the president. "Just how much longer will the Cuban advisors be with us?"

"As long as is needed. Even since the 2002 coup attempt, we can't take any more chances. The revolution's enemies are all around us. You remember that time, you were vice president in that period, no?"

El Pulpo nodded. "Yes, that's right. But they were only here as advisors then; they are now integrated."

"That's for me to worry about, Calvo. *Buen dia, ministro,*" replied the president rising to his feet, his hand outstretched.

"And a good day to you too," came the reply. Sindios Calvo, *El Pulpo*—The Octopus—made for the door without shaking the president's hand. As he was just about at the exit, he threw a half-eaten croissant over his right shoulder. The pastry flew and landed on the presidential carpet with a slight thud.

CHAPTER 32

InterContinental Hostel Cascais-Estoril —
Lisbon, Portugal

Felix Aguilar and Veronica Velasco rolled
past the valets at the entrance to the InterContinental Hotel
Cascais-Estoril, waving politely and descending from a taxi at
the hotel lobby. In the chaos after the assassination attempt,
they had fled the scene and jumped into the first taxi they
came across.

Fifteen minutes after they had returned to their hotel
rooms, Jardine and the general arrived at the *Monte Estoril*
train station behind the hotel. After climbing a chicane-like set
of stairs they entered the hotel and limped through the reception area. Their blood-splattered shirts and dishevelled appearance had caused a few strange looks while on the train, but
none of the front desk staff at the hotel noticed as they passed
through the lobby. Moments later, they were both slumped on
the beds in their respective hotel rooms.

After all that had happened in the hills outside Granada,
at the *Royal Alcázar* in Seville, and now at a *Carmo do Largo*

square in Lisbon, it finally appeared as if the general would actually make his flight to New York to appear at the UN, taking with him the cache of documents he needed to prove that the government of the Bolivarian Republic of Venezuela was siphoning off state funds to enrich themselves and the rest of the 'boligarchy' that Sánchez's Bolivarian 'Revolution' had produced. Not only that, but proof of a spate of extrajudicial killings, the exodus of close to six million Venezuelans, numerous human rights violations and a serious descent into authoritarianism. To top it all off, there was also evidence of a planned invasion of a neighbouring country. It was almost the general's time for an urgent call to action. Something would have to be done by the international community. He hoped it would be the beginning of the end so that fresh, free and fair elections could be called to bring about a new government and end the misery that the country had suffered.

Jardine entered his room and slumped onto the bed. His heartbeat was like a wasp caught in a coke can. He tried to slow his breathing and only concentrate on his breath as he had learned on a meditation app. As he lay, Veronica came out of the bathroom and hugged him tightly, then she began to explain the details from her side. Her pursuit of the assassin, running up the stairs, following her to the window above the square, and then the thumping swing of the hardback book to the assassin's head. After five minutes of her animated explanation, he sat up and smiled at her. "Remind me next time to take you along when I need some muscle." He hugged her again.

Veronica pushed him back slightly, looking down at his body. "What about you, *cariño*? Are you sure it's not your blood on your shirt?"

"No, it's the blood of a Portuguese banker. That was the man the assassin shot before you put her on the floor."

"The poor man," said Veronica, shaking her head. "I mean, he was a banker, but he was only trying to help."

Jardine stood. "I'm going to take a quick shower and then I told the general we'd meet in his room with Felix. We need to get out of here. After all that's happened, we can't take any more chances." He turned to face her and smiled. "Fingers crossed it's smooth sailing from here."

AFTER CLEANING THEMSELVES UP, THE GROUP convened in the general's bedroom. He sat on his bed with Felix in an armchair by the balcony; Jardine and Veronica sat next to each other on the bed. The general spoke. "Team, I think the worst is behind us, but let's ready ourselves and get to the airport as soon as we can. Once we pass through security, we can finally rest. There's no harm if we get there early. I'm sure there's a bar there we can spend time in."

"Sounds like a plan to me," said Felix. "I've been thirsty since we purchased that bottle of port we never got to drink."

Jardine stood, moving towards the balcony and looking out at the sea. He was about to speak when there was a knock at the door.

Felix instinctively reached for this recently commandeered pistol he had, still wedged in the back of his jeans. He withdrew it and pointed it towards the ceiling and then approached the door. He pressed his eye against the peephole. After five seconds looking, he turned quickly and hissed at the group. "Looks like the Portuguese National Guard!"

They stood frozen and exhausted.

Another knock followed. Felix shrugged, the pistol still pointed at the ceiling in his right hand, as he pressed his eye again up to the peephole.

Jardine stepped forward, his index finger over his lips, indicating silence. *The police must have tracked them*, he thought. *If they were caught, who knows what would happen to the general, let alone themselves. They were wanted in Spain for supposedly killing the farmer who was run off the road by the assassin and now they could be blamed for the killing of a banking executive.*

Felix still peered into the peephole again. He withdrew his face and turned to the group, indicating a walking motion with his index and middle finger and then pointing to the balcony. He had just finished pointing when the door burst open, knocking Felix to the ground. A team of four Portuguese National Guards entered surrounding them, the cascading click of their guns ricocheting around the room. They wore navy blue uniforms with berets and two of them held HK MP5 submachine guns.

The group froze and raised their hands.

Felix lay flat on his back on the ground. He slowly lowered the pistol and then held his hands up. The guards peered frantically around the room before setting eyes on the general. One of the guards barked a question. "General Angel Fernando Pereira Gallegos?"

The general, his hands still in the air, sighed. "*Sí.*"

One of the officers stepped forward and spoke in Portuguese. "We've just spoken with our counterparts in Madrid, and they have explained the situation. You'll be coming with us."

Jardine interjected. "There's a mistake, we weren't involved in killing a farmer. We're innocent, we've just been trying to escort the general to the airport so he can catch a plane and speak at the UN."

The guard frowned and then nodded as if weighing up the information.

Jardine continued. "If we don't get him on the plane, his life is in danger and—"

The guard held up his hand in a stop gesture. "We know that. You've been followed by a trained, international hitman."

"Hit-woman," added Veronica. "In fact, I guess I'm now a hit-woman hitter?" Her tone rose as if asking a question.

The guard looked at her confused and then continued. "Our counterparts in Spain, after liaising with British Intelligence, have made us aware of a woman driving a black Audi who ran an Andalusian farmer off the road before escaping from hospital and disappearing. An internal arrest warrant was lodged through Interpol and so when we received a report of a shooting incident occurring this afternoon, we were open to the possibilities that there might be a connection."

Jardine began to speak. "How did you know...?" He stopped himself as he realised what the guard had said. *British Intelligence*. Ambrose must have finally gotten through to his MI6 and *Guardia Civil* contacts and relayed the message that we weren't involved in the car crash. Changing track, he asked: "Did you arrest the woman for shooting the banker?"

"He was a banker?" one of the guards asked. A serious look spread across his face. He straightened his uniform and then smiled, saying to his subordinates, "*Ele era apenas um banqueiro.*" *He was only a banker.*

The group of National Guardsmen let out a collective sigh of relief.

The leader looked seriously at Jardine: "We are still searching for the assailant." Then he turned to the general. "General, we believe you are on a flight to New York this evening?"

"That's correct."

"We have been ordered to escort you to the airport. We have a vehicle downstairs, outside the lobby."

"You don't want to use the underground parking lot, *amigo*?" asked Felix.

"No, we know what we are doing. We are professionals."

The National Guardsmen leader looked at Jardine, then Veronica, and then Felix. "Can anyone tell me why the general doesn't have a proper security team anyway?"

"A retired CIA technical officer and an ex-MI6 analyst isn't enough for you?" asked Jardine.

The National Guard rolled his eyes. "Amateurs..." he muttered in Portuguese.

The general frowned. "My team has worked well thus far, besides," he gestured to Veronica, "we also have a highly qualified lawyer and book assassin."

Veronica smiled innocently and nodded. "Sometimes surprise and secrecy is much more valuable than force and weapons."

The guard leader shook his head. "Anyway, it doesn't matter, *agora* we have the situation under control." He turned to Felix. "Our car is at the lobby entrance; it will enable us to get onto the road as quickly as possible."

Felix nodded. "If you say so, Captain."

The Guard returned his gaze to the general. "Can you ready yourself in ten minutes?"

"Team?" the general asked, opening his hands wide.

Jardine, Veronica, and Felix all nodded and signalled their approval.

Twelve minutes later, the group was ready and descended in the lift to the ground floor. Felix checked them all out at reception while the National Guardsmen loaded their gear into a military green Mercedes Sprinter van. Felix strode across the lobby and was about to hand back the group's forged ID documents when a gut-rumbling boom reverberated through the lobby. An ear-piercing screech of tumbling glass followed as the hotel's front doors shattered like thin ice on a frozen lake. The group were knocked to the ground as two of the National Guardsmen were struck with flying debris, appearing to absorb most of the blast's impact. Their bodies crumpled to the ground and they lay bleeding on the floor without moving. Screams and yells came next as hotel guests and staff wriggled on the ground in pain or tried to crawl to safety.

It was Jardine who first stumbled to his feet, helping up Veronica and then Felix who in turn aided the general who was limping with a small shard of glass in his right leg. Their ears rang, making the surrounding sounds seem muffled and distant. They glanced quickly down at the two guards who still lay lifeless on the ground, having taken the full impact of the blast. Looking toward the hotel entrance, they could see a mangled mess of twisted metal, enshrouded in smoke with small shards of glass that glistened like glitter on the floor. A hazy dust still hung in the air like a dirty mist, clouding the outside view.

Jardine squinted. Could he see a large SUV? Shadows moving behind the dust? He heard shouts and then several gunshots rang out. He felt a rough tap on his shoulder as Felix whispered in his ear, "The underground car park."

The four of them stumbled backwards towards the lifts before taking the emergency exit stairs down to the underground car park. Throwing the door open at the bottom of the stairs, they managed to jog towards Felix's vehicle.

"We'll need to split up," said Felix. "You take the general, in your—" Felix stopped as he watched Jardine rummaging through his old Defender. "That's you?"

Jardine looked up and tapped the roof of his car. "This is me."

Felix shook his head and continued. "You take the general; I'll go with Veronica."

"Vero, I'll call Felix's phone from my burner. Put it on

speaker as you're driving so we can communicate," said Jardine.

Veronica nodded seriously and then climbed into the passenger seat of Felix's jeep.

Jardine and the general jumped into the Defender and fastened their seat belts.

Felix reversed out of his parking space with a screech of tyres.

Then Jardine did the same as both vehicles weaved through the underground car park eventually speeding up the exit ramp and out into the Lisbon night.

CHAPTER 33

LISBON, PORTUGAL

THE TYRES OF THE JEEP SCREECHED AS FELIX swerved onto the coastal *Avenida Marginal* with Jardine close behind in the Land Rover Defender. Night had fallen and the lights of Lisbon twinkled along the hills as they accelerated away from the hotel.

The general took Jardine's burner phone and called Felix's number, putting it on speaker phone.

Jardine glanced back at the front of the hotel and saw a large SUV surrounded by three men. He watched as another man came running out of the hotel's entrance and after scanning the horizon pointed towards his and Felix's vehicles.

The general looked back too and saw the other three black-clad men turn their heads in their direction and then scramble to get into the SUV.

"*Hola*," said Veronica, answering Felix's phone in the passenger seat.

"Think they're Russians?" asked Jardine his hands tense on the steering wheel.

Felix weaved in and out of the night-time traffic. "The Russians aren't so brazen; they wouldn't blow up a hotel lobby. Not their style."

"Albanians," the general chimed in. "The Sun Corporation, the front company that Madera and his cronies use, have an alliance with Albanians to distribute narcotics in Europe. It's only natural they would use them for other purposes. And unlike the Russians, the Albanians don't give a *carajo*. When they mean business, they mean it."

It made sense. Jardine briefly remembered filing a few minor CX intelligence reports on the Albanians growing footprint in narcotics distribution, first out of Ecuador running banana trading companies and then acting as distributors for the BACRIMS of Colombia, the Mexican cartels, and now the Sun Corporation out of Venezuela.

Both vehicles continued speeding down *Avenida Marginal*, flying past the *Torre de Belém* and then under the 25th of April Bridge—Lisbon's answer to the Golden Gate Bridge. To their right, a large, illuminated statue of Jesus Christ, his hands outstretched, sat on the hill on the opposite side of the Tagus as if watching them speed along the river-hugging road. They flashed past the *Praça de Comércio* watching the large arch of the *Rua Augusta* pass by as Felix swung left up into the narrow streets of the *Alfama* district, with Jardine just behind. It wasn't the most direct or efficient route, but he had considered it would be easier to lose the SUV in the winding, hilly streets of old Lisbon than the open highway to the airport. As they began to wind their way through the narrow cobblestone streets, Felix turned his head slightly and spoke to Veronica: "In case we get into some close quarters, we might need a little something." He tapped his hand on the centre console between the two front passenger seats. "Veronica, push in the two AC control knobs back there and lift up the console."

She leaned backwards from the front passenger seat and pushed in the two temperature control knobs, hearing a clicking sound. Then she lifted the lid of the console to reveal a hidden cache of small handguns. She reached in and pulled out two Glock pistols.

"Aren't you full of surprises," she said. "Only two?"

"Afraid so."

"Why do you have this compartment?" she asked.

"This is a decommissioned CIA vehicle for Euro operations. Looks like a piece of shit on the outside, but it's fine-tuned on the inside."

Espionage movies would have you believe spies drive flashy Aston Martins, but the opposite was true. A vehicle needed to slip under the radar, to look run-of-the-mill, unremarkable, designed to blend in with its surroundings, but engineered for high performance underneath. The results were a fleet of ordinary-looking vehicles with high-powered engines and hidden compartments.

"What have we got there?" Jardine asked over the phone.

"*Dos pistolas*," came the reply from Veronica as she examined the handguns closely.

"Only two?" asked the general.

"Yeah, sorry about that," said Felix. "Handguns are as rare as rocking horse shit, especially in Europe. If we were stateside, they'd be a little easier to come by. We practically come out of the womb brandishing a firearm."

Veronica held up one of the Glocks, examining it further.

"You know how to use it?" asked Felix.

She shook her head.

"How about you, Analyst?" Felix asked Jardine over the phone, smiling as he said it. "Know how to use a gun?"

Jardine looked straight ahead, his eyes on the road. "I didn't for a long time, but a small incident in Colombia changed that."

"Just make sure you protect yourself. This isn't an intel report. There's no *Control Alt Delete* if you fuck up in the field."

"Is there a *Control Z*?" asked Jardine.

"What's that?"

"Undo."

"Do or not do, there is no undo," said Felix, looking down at the mobile phone in Veronica's hand.

"Thanks, Master Yoda," replied Jardine.

"That's the spirit; you're learning."

The vehicles convoyed up *Rua da Madalena*. Rose and magenta-coloured buildings with dark wrought-iron balconies flashed by. Ahead, a yellow tram slowed and then stopped at a small square to let passengers board, momentarily stopping the flow of traffic.

Felix brought the jeep to a stop behind the tram and Jardine halted behind them. The general glanced nervously back down the street. It was empty; just a small string of pedestrians walking along the footpath and a string of cars parked on one side. He looked sideways at Jardine and grinned, a wave of relief evident on his face. Then a flash in the corner of his eye caused him to turn and look again. There it was. The black Porsche SUV. It revved up the street towards them, accelerating fast and gaining ground. The closer it got, the louder the revving of the engine sounded, like an angry bee buzzing towards them.

Jardine turned back towards the road in front of them. "Looks like they're on to us," he said desperately. "There must be another way around that tram."

In the jeep, Veronica pointed to a narrow street before the tram stop. "Take a left here?"

Felix looked to the left and swung the jeep down the small alleyway leading them in a circular motion around the block through a maze of one-way streets—a common feature of

Lisbon's hilly warren of *ruas* and *avenidas*. After turning and weaving for several minutes, they burst out onto the *Praça de Rossio*—a large tree-lined plaza with two prominent fountains and a large column statue in the centre. Felix slammed the brakes, stopping metres from entering the pedestrian square, just outside the *Teatro Nacional Dona Maria II*. The plaza buzzed with people out for a nightly stroll. The cafés surrounding the square were filled with customers. A large group congregated around the fountain, drinking, chatting, and whiling away the evening.

"Which way?" Felix asked Veronica.

Veronica had opened Google Maps and was now pinching the screen, zooming in and out, looking for an alternate route. She looked up and pointed. "Loop around there and we should be able to take one of those side roads to get back on track."

Felix nodded and moved the jeep forward.

Veronica relayed the instructions over the phone to the men in the other car.

"Copy that," she heard the general reply down the line.

Rounding the square, the jeep had just rounded the first corner of the square and was running alongside it when they heard a screech of tyres and a metallic bang. Felix glanced in the revision mirror to see that the SUV had launched out in front of the *Teatro Nacional Dona Maria II* and clipped Jardine and the general in the Land Rover Defender. The Defender now careered off into the large square, narrowly missing the fountain and spinning out of control, eventually coming to a halt near the column statue at the centre of the square.

Both Felix and Veronica watched as the SUV screeched to a halt after the collision. Then it turned sharply and entered the square. It revved and accelerated, heading straight for the parked Defender.

CHAPTER 34

Praça do Rossio — Lisbon, Portugal

Felix peered left as the SUV burst forward towards the Defender which sat idling in front of the large column at the centre of *Praça de Rossio*. A trickle of smoke seeped out from under its bonnet and the bumper was crumpled from the collision.

He reacted immediately, pulling hard on the steering wheel and jerking the jeep into the square as people dived for cover, desperate to avoid his abrupt change in direction. He sped forward heading for the left side of the parked Defender as the SUV propelled forward coming in at a right angle to his left. He planted his foot to the floor and then, after only a few seconds, slammed on the brakes bringing the jeep to a screeching halt in front of the battered Defender.

The men in the SUV slammed on the brakes, skidded and eventually stopped twenty-five metres away, facing directly towards the left side of the jeep. Veronica looked out of the right front passenger window and saw Jardine in the driver's seat of the Defender. His head was back against the headrest and a small stream of blood trickled down his forehead. She jumped out and ran around to his driver's door and flung it open. She reached her hands up to his face, trying to examine where the blood was coming from.

Meanwhile, Felix looked to his left, out of the jeep's driver's window. He could see the Albanians' SUV was still facing them, not twenty-five metres away, its black tinted windshield dull and lifeless like a still, dark sea. He continued to watch, not sure whether to run or stay put. He chanced a glance to his right and saw Jardine still wasn't moving, but at least his jeep was covering the Defender while Veronica attended to him.

Then the SUV's doors swung open in unison and the four Albanians dressed in black descended from the vehicle, stationing themselves behind the cover of the two opened front doors. He could see they held automatic weapons, AK47s, the barrels of which were being propped up in gaps between the SUV's door and chassis.

Along the fountain, groups of people began to shriek and scream and run, realising what was unfolding. A scattering of people hit the ground, lying face down with hands on their heads as if it were a children's game.

Felix sat in the jeep, frantically wondering what he should do. The general appeared at the front passenger door, opening it.

"It's me they want, let me deliver myself to them," he said.

"No, General," replied Felix, his eyes darting. "We're in this together. Don't give up just yet."

"Is this thing bulletproof?" asked the general, tapping the glass. "In Venezuela they are."

Felix nodded. "Up to a point."

"What's that mean?" In that moment, a barrage of shots sprayed over the jeep pelting against the left side windows, thwacking against the side like large hailstones.

Felix flinched and when the shooting stopped, he said, "It means we can't just sit here like fat geese. We need to return fire or we're cooked." He shuffled across the front console, exiting the front passenger door and then crouched down behind the body of the jeep. He reached up onto the passenger seat, extracting the two Glocks that Veronica had left. He handed one to the general. "How long since you've fired one of these?"

"A while, but one never forgets."

Felix shuffled forward and then popped his arms up on the car bonnet and returned a flurry of shots towards the SUV.

The general went to the back of the vehicle and did the same. He pointed the pistol around the back of the jeep and peppered off a few shots. He glanced back to see Veronica appear next to Felix.

"How is he?" Felix asked.

"He's fine. It's just a small cut."

"Is he planning on helping us?"

"He just needs a minute."

Felix reached behind, pulling out the assassin's pistol he'd picked up earlier. "Know how to use it?"

Veronica shook her head.

Felix handed her the gun and whispered. "Just point at them and shoot when they're not shooting at us."

She shrugged. "Seems easy enough."

A flurry of shots flew overhead as passers-by clambered for cover behind café tables and chairs or lay flat against the ground.

Veronica leant her hands on the front of the jeep and let off a round of shots towards the SUV with the assassin's weapon. The general sprang up next to her and released a barrage of bullets towards the SUV before popping down again. In return, another spray of bullets pelted the jeep, hitting its left side. They ducked down as the volley of bullets blasted towards them.

Felix rested his back against the jeep turned and looked at the general and Veronica. "Where I come from we call this a 'Mexican standoff.' Not sure that's an appropriate way to describe it anymore."

"How about a clusterfuck?" said Jardine, appearing from the other side of the Defender.

Felix grinned. "Yeah, that seems better."

"That's also an appropriate word for the state of Venezuela at the moment," said the general as another rain of bullets thudded into the side of the jeep.

CHAPTER 35

Alina Calderón woke to loud cracks of gunfire. She lifted her head momentarily, listening as more shots rang out. She felt dizzy and so laid her head down again and peered at the ceiling. She felt for her caiman tooth necklace and held it in her right hand. She held it for ten seconds as if it emitted a special power and would cure her dizziness.

She popped her head above the back seat again, looking around and then quickly realised what was happening. Two of the men crouched behind the open front doors of the SUV. They took it in turns to pop up, like jack-in-the-boxes, letting off a barrage of shots towards a jeep parked lengthways in the distance at the foot of a large column. On the other side, one man crouched behind the front passenger door, playing the same game as the two men on the other side. She arched her head forward, straining to see into the distance. She could make out figures but couldn't see who was behind the jeep.

She lay down again, trying to remember what had happened earlier. She looked around where she lay and saw the leather pouch, the violin case, and her small shoulder bag. Then everything clicked into place. The square. The failed shot. The general. His accomplice. Her mission. She had been interrupted before she could let off a second shot.

She placed her hands on the side of her head. Her temples throbbed. Had she been hit? Knocked unconscious? That must have been what happened. But by whom? All she could remember was firing one shot at the general, missing, and the next thing she knew she was being carried downstairs and put in the back of an SUV. She recalled hearing a strange language being spoken in the car. What was it? After a few moments, it came to her. They must be Albanians. That must have been the language she had heard. It wasn't familiar to her. She also vaguely remembered they were sometimes used by the Venezuelans in Europe.

She peered over the backseat again to watch the Albanians. Were they the ones who had collected her after the failed assassination attempt on the general? *No doubt, henchmen for The Sun Corporation*, she thought. Perhaps part of Madera's network of European 'distributers' of cocaine and illegal gold. As she watched the men firing sporadically, an electric current-like river shivered through her body as she remembered. A hand. One of *those* men. The creep who had run his hand along her body, grabbing at her as she slipped in and out of consciousness in the back of the SUV. She remembered seeing his face as he smiled and reached over from the backseat, touching her, groping her as she lay there. She remembered glancing at his hand and seeing a silver bracelet with an inscription.

Her face became hot and her heart began to beat faster as her breathing increased in short rapid breaths. She felt a flow of energy crack through her body, giving her strength.

Surreptitiously she slid her leather shoulder bag diagonally over her body, then slowly pushed herself up. She glanced at the back door of the SUV and saw a small panel on the bottom right. She waited for more gunshots, then punched the panel several times. On the fourth punch, it came loose. A yellow emergency pull was behind the panel; she reached forward and yanked it. There was a metallic click as the back door of the SUV released.

A rush of cool night air streamed over her body, further revving her and making her more alert. She looked around behind the SUV, people were still clambering for cover, ducking and crouching under outdoor furniture at cafés nearby. Some pressed their bodies behind stone ballasts and behind rubbish bins, anywhere they could get some cover. Others lay flat on the ground face down, as if attempting to push their bodies into the ground. She could hear babies screaming, men shouting, and car horns blasting, but nobody approached the SUV.

She swivelled her legs around and slid out onto the cobblestones of the square, instinctively crouching onto one knee. She shuffled half a metre from behind the SUV and peered around the left side to see a man crouching behind the open front door. He held an AK47.

She still didn't know who they were shooting at. All she had been able to see was a jeep. *The police, perhaps?* The only thing she knew for sure was that *they*—these men—had surely come to finish the job she was unable to. In this moment, something stirred inside her as she remembered the strange mixed feelings and flashbacks she had been having since her car crash in the mountains outside Granada and the questioning of the orthodoxy she'd been fed since she was young. Since that moment, a strange cognitive dissonance seeped through her as if her subconscious was telling her she had had enough of the killing and the supposed '*revolución*' she was fighting for. She thought of Cuba, *la patria*. What if it was no longer *patria o muerte*? *Fatherland or death.* That repeated mantra

241

she was spoonfed until it became as ubiquitous as a nursery rhyme. What if it were *patria y vida* instead? *Fatherland and life*. It sounded corny and silly, naive even, but perhaps it was true?

A flurry of gunshots snapped her out of her musings. She peered around to the left side again. The solitary man was still there, shooting from behind the open SUV's door. She watched the back of his head hovering in front of her, and then her mind flung back to the hand reaching over and touching her from the backseat. The hand that touched her, had taken advantage of her as she lay there in semi-consciousness. She felt her temperature rising again, and the vein in her neck pulsated.

Then in the distance, she saw a figure appear from behind a jeep at the foot of a large column. It was *him*. The dissident general, her target, the sole reason for her being here. It was him they were firing at.

This was her chance to finish the mission, return to Cuba and relax, regain her strength and faith in her country. Her mind switched back to kill mode.

She reached down to her caiman tooth necklace and held it, mulling over her decision, and then as if a bolt of lightning had struck her, it came to her. She knew exactly what she was going to do. She crouched, then crept forward like a panther, reaching with both hands.

CHAPTER 36

THE GENERAL CROUCHED AGAIN AFTER LETTING OFF a blast of shots until the Glock 19 was empty. "How much longer can we hold out?" he asked. "Looks like I'm out." He released the magazine and examined it.

Felix stood, still crouching slightly, and leaned into the jeep through the back right door. He opened the hidden compartment Veronica had earlier taken out the Glocks. He grabbed four magazines of 9mm bullets and distributed two to the general and kept the other two for himself. "Not long," he said.

"How many shots have you fired, *señorita*?" Felix asked Veronica.

She shrugged. "Maybe three?"

"You're almost out then."

Felix looked at the general. "Well, that means between you and me, we've got a little more than thirty shots left apiece."

The general nodded as he moved again to the back of the

vehicle and shot towards the SUV while Felix popped up on the front of the jeep again and fired at the Albanians.

It was after firing a fourth shot in succession that Felix fell backwards, landing with his hands outstretched behind him. A red mist exploding in the night air above him. "Jesus H. Christ," he yelled as he reached for his shoulder, wincing in pain. The Glock rattled to the ground metres away.

Veronica scurried forward and grabbed a pashmina from the jeep, then bent down and applied pressure on Felix's wound.

Jardine crawled to pick up Felix's dropped Glock and crouched near the jeep's bonnet.

Incoming fire from the Albanians flew overhead, also peppering the side of the jeep. The bulletproof panelling and windows still held out, keeping the bullets from passing through the jeep.

Felix dragged his body closer to the jeep, leaning against it. He raised his good hand and took over applying pressure with the pashmina on his shoulder.

"You got anything left in the box of tricks of yours?" asked Jardine.

"The hidden compartment? Nope," replied Felix. "That's it. We might need to get behind that column and see if we can disappear down one of these side streets." He tried to look Jardine in the eye, but he groaned and moved his body back to its original position.

"You're not going anywhere with that shoulder."

"I can run," said Felix. "It'll hurt like hell, but I can run."

Jardine shook his head. "No, not an option." He popped up and let rip several shots with the retrieved Glock.

The general did likewise from the back of the jeep.

Jardine crouched again, looking down at the wavy pattern of black and white tiles under his feet causing him to feel dizzy, his mind still swirling from the crash. "I'm not so crash-hot myself," he said.

"We've got to do something," said Veronica, biting her lip and looking up at the starry sky as if looking for an answer.

Jardine reached up again and let off more shots until the Glock clicked empty. He slumped back down beside Veronica and Felix. "Are you sure there's no more?" he asked, holding the gun up to Felix.

"*Nada.*"

A few moments later, the same clicking sound came from the back of the jeep as the general swung around and faced the group. "I'm out, too."

Another assault pelted the jeep as the group slumped down and glanced at each other.

"What do we do?" asked Jardine.

CHAPTER 37

Praça de Rossio — Lisbon, Portugal

Alina Calderón sprang forward, crouching and peering around one side of the SUV. She was about to approach one of the Albanians holding an AK47 when she heard a yell coming from the jeep opposite the SUV. The Albanian in front of her cackled an evil twisted laugh as he ducked down again behind the open front door. It appeared he'd hit one of them, she reasoned.

She crept forward so she was directly behind the man who had just laughed. She could see the hairs on the back of his neck and a fine gold chain as she reached forward. She firmly grasped his head, holding tight and then violently twisted it sideways, pulling through with her arms and shoulders and throwing all her body weight behind it. She heard a cracking sound as his neck broke and his body slumped to the ground like a large sack of coffee beans.

She sat still for a second or two, breathing heavily as the gunshots continued, then she picked up the man's AK47 and scurried around to the back of the SUV. From there, she peered around the other side of the SUV where she could see two men in similar positions to the man she had just killed. Both hunkered behind the open front door, taking it in turns to pop up and release a flurry of rounds.

She lifted the AK47 and briefly peered down the barrel and then with two quick squeezes of the trigger the man on the left dropped. Without a moment's hesitation, she then focussed her attention to the man on the right and with another squeeze on the trigger, he too dropped.

She moved forward still holding the AK47 towards the front of the SUV. Now was her last chance to get the general, she thought. It would be messy and unprofessional, but at least it would likely be blamed on these Albanians, not her. She moved towards the open door which shielded her from any incoming fire and would give her a vantage point to aim at the general. She moved forward silently, almost to the front door of the SUV when she saw a glint of silver from the passenger seat of the SUV. She froze. There was still one man left? A man was crouched in the front passenger seat. She hadn't seen him earlier. But now, as she approached the open door, she stood face to face with him.

The shooting coming from the jeep had stopped and the man turned now and looked at her. His eyes trailed downwards to the two men lying dead. His mouth opened slightly, and his eyes seemed big and wet. Then he looked back at her and a glint of recognition appeared in his eyes as a smile spread across his face.

Alina Calderón peered back at him, her mind immediately screaming to herself, '*Shoot him*!' But the glint of silver caught her eye again and she looked down to see it came from a metal band on the man's wrist. *It was him*, she thought. *He was the one that violated me.* The man still smiled at her and arched his body slightly out of the SUV, pointing his AK47 towards her.

Shoot him, she screamed internally.

The man had the AK47 raised and pointed at her.

He didn't deserve to be shot. It needed to be slower, she thought. She continued to stare straight into his eyes.

He smirked now and pressed his finger on the trigger of the AK47.

Alina Calderón continued looking the man in the eye as she heard the empty click of an AK47 that had run out of ammunition.

It took a few seconds for them both to realise what had occurred but when it became apparent, Calderón dropped the AK47 she held and launched herself towards him.

Caught by surprise the man attempted to defend himself with the empty weapon, swinging the gun at her and trying to knock her out with the butt, but she pummelled him in a flurry of punches to the face and gut. He managed to block some of the punches and recovered, then lunged and pushed her until she fell backwards.

As she fell, she flicked her left leg upwards and connected her foot to his chin.

He stood, wobbling slightly, dazed from the kick to the jaw. He stepped forward out of the SUV, his head bobbing above the open door. He bent down and attempted to pick up one of the dropped AK47s from his fallen partners but failed to grasp it. The kick to the jaw had obviously shocked him, putting him off balance.

"Never touch a woman like that again," hissed Alina Calderón, looking up at him as she reached into her leather shoulder bag. She clutched the mascara case, ready to withdraw it. It was the weapon best suited to poisoning someone. But, in that moment, it didn't matter. For what she had in mind, she could use a sharp pencil.

He swayed in front of her, courting and clumsily trying to pick up one of the AK47s on the ground.

She gripped the mascara case, withdrew it, and took off the lid. She held it firmly as she rose to her knees.

The man had finally managed to pick up an AK47 and stood up straight.

She arched her legs and was ready to launch forward and plunge the needle into his neck, but he slung the butt of the gun into his armpit and pointed it down at her.

I'm too late, she thought, as she crouched on the balls of her feet ready to lunge.

The man smirked and peered down the barrel.

Too late, she thought.

In that moment, before he could pull the trigger, a solitary bullet whistled through the air, colliding with the man's head with a juicy thud. His eyes froze and his body became limp; he seemed to fall in slow motion as he slumped forward onto the ground, narrowly missing Alina Calderón as she crouched on the cobblestones. After his lifeless body hit the ground, another single shot rang out overhead followed by the distant sound of sirens. Calderón crawled towards the SUV, resting her back against it, breathing heavily.

The night air tasted metallic, a mix of dust and gunpowder hung like a mist. The sirens still rang in the distance and then a shout came from the parked jeep twenty-five metres away.

CHAPTER 38

Praça de Rossio — Lisbon, Portugal

Jardine lowered the hunting rifle, having watched the Albanian drop to the ground and disappear behind the SUV's door. He shouted out in Spanish, *"Ya basta."* That's enough. "The police are on their way. Give yourself up." In the commotion they'd seen a flash of Alina Calderón.

He raised the old rifle again, gripping it firmly as he pointed it towards the SUV. He glanced sideways at the general, speaking out the side of his mouth. "I told you it would be useful."

The general nodded his approval. "Didn't doubt you for a second, *amigo*."

Then suddenly, the assassin, Alina Calderón, rose from behind the front door an AK47 in her hands pointed directly at them.

Jardine tensed and held the rifle steady, not taking his eyes off her. *"Ya no más,"* he said in Spanish. "It's over."

The assassin didn't move, she stood her ground, eyes

250

fixated forward like lasers.

The general spoke now. "Ya," *Enough*. "*Váyase! Nadie más tiene que morir.*" *Go! No one else has to die.*

The assassin looked down the barrel of the gun. "I have orders," she yelled in reply.

"Orders from who?" asked the general.

Calderón twitched uncomfortably. "You know who."

"Ah so, you must be Venezuelan then?" the general asked.

Calderón cocked her head. Doubt crept back into her mind. Then she shook her head and held the weapon tighter. "It doesn't matter where I'm from."

"It does matter if you're taking orders from the government of Venezuela to assassinate a dissident general."

"I'm a patriot, a revolutionary," she shouted in reply.

"You're a mercenary," responded the general.

Silence followed, and then the sirens drew closer.

He said, "*Mira, señorita*, I know you mean well, you're doing this for a cause you believe in, but it's an illusion."

"And your side is better?"

"No, the other side isn't any better."

"*Entonces?*" So?

"Both sides together can find a way to make it work. The best of both worlds. That's what we need in the world. Not this ideological division into two cut-throat tribes."

Calderón clicked her tongue and peered down the barrel, squinting. Her mind swirled, she couldn't focus. She was questioning all that she'd been trained to do.

"Lower your weapon and I'll lower mine," said Jardine.

"Save yourself, Calderón," said the general. "Go and live your life."

She raised her head from the barrel and looked across at the two men. They knew who she was.

"Look, I'm lowering it slowly," said Jardine.

She watched as Jardine carefully lowered the old hunting

rifle and placed it on the bonnet of the jeep. Once it was down, he held his hands up and walked slowly back. The general did the same.

She loosened her grip and relaxed her shoulders. She lowered the AK47 and stared ahead at the two men. *Patria y vida*, she said to herself. Finally finding some clarity.

Jardine and the general exhaled forcefully, sucking in deep breaths. They'd been holding their breath this whole time.

The sirens whirred loudly now as if almost to the square. Calderón placed the weapon in the passenger seat of the SUV and then turned back to face the jeep. She saw the younger man, the ex-MI6 analyst with his hand on the general's shoulder before they hugged and slapped each other on the back. She stared at them for a moment longer and then moved to the back of the SUV and collected her violin case and the leather pouch, then she turned and surveyed the scene around her and sprinted behind the fountain, across the square, and down a side street off into the night.

THE SOUND OF THE POLICE SIRENS BOUNCED OFF THE surrounding buildings as two police cars roared around the corner and entered the square in front of the theatre. Moments later, they pulled up between the SUV and the jeep. Jardine, Veronica, the general, and Felix watched as the police officers got out and began to case the scene. Jardine discreetly slid the rifle off the bonnet of the jeep and placed it under the front passenger seat of the Land Rover Defender. He looked back as a group of police officers swarmed around the SUV, staring at the four dead Albanians. He approached the jeep again and saw Felix lying across the back seats, blood still leaking from his shoulder.

"How you holding up?" Jardine asked.

"I've seen better days." Felix lifted his head slightly. "But

I'll live. At least it wasn't novichok," he added with a smirk and a wink.

Police officers from the second of the two cars jogged over and minutes later, an ambulance arrived and the paramedics carefully lifted Felix from the jeep to a stretcher and then into the ambulance.

The general sighed and slumped into the front passenger seat of the jeep. Jardine approached him. "There's still time to make that flight."

The general nodded but didn't speak.

Jardine continued. "I think it's now more important than ever that we get you there."

CHAPTER 39

Humberto Delgado International Airport —
Lisbon, Portugal

THE GENERAL, VERONICA, AND JARDINE WERE
exhausted by the time the khaki green Mercedes sprinter van
pulled up outside Lisbon's Humberto Delgado International
airport. Before leaving the square, they'd managed to rescue
their mobile phones from the metal box in the back of the
Defender. Jardine had arranged for the vehicle to be repaired
and then sent down to Granada. The coast was clear and
finally they felt as if their lives had returned to normal. En
route, they'd each called their loved ones to let them know
they were fine.

After exiting the police van, the general checked in for his
flight to New York. Jardine and Veronica had a flight back to
Granada a little later and decided to accompany him to his
gate. He clutched his boarding pass and all three of them were
shuffled through the diplomat's line at customs and immigration and then escorted to Gate 1A. Once there, they sat in a
cordoned off waiting area in the smaller private aviation

section of the airport. The two police officers that accompanied them remained for ten minutes to finish off their questioning of what had occurred in the plaza earlier and a small group of National Guardsmen—who provided airport security—remained to ensure the general got on his flight safely.

In a corner of the waiting area, a flatscreen TV showed footage of the aftermath of the scene in *Praça de Rossio*. The news reporter spoke, mentioning the general, the blast at the hotel, the crisis in Venezuela, and all they could reveal to the audience so far. The footage was a shaky montage of on-the-scene filming from bystanders. As the news report was finishing, a small group of people entered the cordoned-off area. Jardine turned his head and did a double take as a short stocky man, the spitting image of the general, waltzed into the room followed by a large man in a dark green shirt with two breast pockets, a woman in a smart pantsuit, and a woman who looked like a stereotypical librarian.

The general stood and smiled warmly as he pulled Jardine and Veronica over towards the entourage. "May I present my team." He introduced his bodyguard, his assistant—the librarian lookalike—and his PR Manager in the suit.

"Why does a dissident general need a PR Manager?" asked Jardine.

"It's the twenty-first century; it's all about your personal brand," replied the PR Manager with a smirk.

"And this," said the general, "is my alter ego. Or my decoy if you will." The man who looked like him stepped forward with his hand outstretched.

Jardine smiled and shook hands with the decoy. On closer inspection, the two men were by no means identical but were similar enough to fool from a distance.

The decoy general laughed. "I've been cooped up in a Madrid hotel while this one has had all the fun!"

As laughter trickled around the group, Jardine added: "It

wasn't all fun and games, though; we had a few hairy moments there. He's lucky to be alive." He patted the real general on the back. After a few more pleasantries, the decoy and the bodyguard retreated slightly and sat down on a group of armchairs in the centre of the room, while the PR Manager and the assistant sat next to each other, opened their laptops and started to type furiously.

Jardine and the general approached a large window looking out over the runway. A lady approached and offered them a complimentary glass of red wine. They both accepted, raised their glasses to each other and simultaneously took a sip.

"This is where it began," said the general.

Jardine furrowed his brow in confusion.

"The two of us chatting over a glass of wine before we were followed by that wo..." the general stopped and corrected himself, "by Alina Calderón."

Jardine took a sip of wine. "It turned out all right in the end." He smiled. "Looks like I'll go back to being a guesthouse owner."

"I'm sure you'll find yourself in trouble again."

They both peered out the window for a few moments, lost in thought. Below them were two small aircraft parked on either side of the same air bridge.

"Which one are you travelling in?" asked Jardine.

The general looked cagey and mumbled a response, "I'll be in one of those two jets. My assistant is organising it."

"A private jet?"

He nodded sheepishly. "Due to security reasons, of course. All paid for via private donations."

A sly grin spread across Jardine's face. "Remind me to become a dissident one day. The royal treatment."

"*Pues*, it's not every day I fly like this. Only under such extreme circumstances."

"They're serving champagne and caviar I suppose?"

"*Dios mío!* I hope not. Rum and *arepas rellenas* will be fine by me." The general let out a loud laugh and patted Jardine on the back before taking another sip of wine.

The waiting room speaker crackled, and an announcement began. "Ladies and gentlemen, we will be boarding in ten minutes. Although these are private flights, your identification will still need to be shown. Please have your passports ready for our staff to..."

"Almost time to board," said the general. "It's time I should say thank you for all your help. I know you didn't want to undertake this endeavour."

"You're a very convincing man," said Jardine. "The fact I was wanted by the *Guardia Civil* and chased by a Cuban assassin helped your case too."

Veronica approached now and leant in to hug the general. "Take care, Don Angel; you're always welcome to stay with us in Spain any time."

"Thank you, Veronica. I'm sure it will happen in the future. Hopefully next time it will not be so eventful." He turned to Jardine again. "Take my number. I already have yours, it's how I found you, remember? I'll call from New York to let you know how I get on."

Jardine nodded and smiled. "We'll be watching online. They stream the UN speeches now."

A second announcement sounded asking for the passengers to come forward. The decoy general and the bodyguard stepped forward as the PR Manager and the assistant snapped their laptops shut and approached the gate for boarding. Following behind, the general—the real one—waved as he took out his passport and moved toward the gate. Moments later, he turned for a last wave, and then entered the air bridge. Jardine and Veronica watched as he disappeared down the long air bridge, losing sight of him towards the end.

Jardine put his arm around Veronica. "Let's get a hot chocolate and watch the planes take off?"

She nodded, then frowned. "Do we have time?"

He looked at his watch. "Yeah, we can see them off and still get to the domestic terminal for our flight."

They strolled back into the main terminal area and bought two cups of hot chocolate at a café before moving and sitting on a bank of seats in front of a big window. Outside they could see an aircraft taxiing out to the runway, waiting, and then accelerating forward before launching up into the night sky. There was something therapeutic about watching planes take off, thought Jardine as he sipped his drink. He looked down at the seat beside him and saw a copy of the day's newspaper. He reached to pick it up when he felt his phone vibrate in his pocket. Withdrawing it, he juggled it in his left hand, the hot cup of chocolate in his right, before he tapped the green phone symbol and answered.

CHAPTER 40

*Humberto Delgado International Airport —
Lisbon, Portugal*

Alina Calderón stepped back from the counter
with her ticket in her hand.

The desk attendant smiled and gave her instructions on
how to reach the gate: "Your flight to Miami will depart from
Gate 7A which is to your left, past the coffee shop." He
glanced again down at her passport. "You have a diplomatic
passport? You have access to a small waiting area for VIP
guests and other members of the diplomatic corps like yourself. If you go to gates 1A to 3A, you'll see the area I'm talking
about."

The assassin nodded. "*Obrigada*," she said and strode
away towards customs and immigration.

Since the shootout in the square Calderón had managed
to make her way back to her hotel room, clean up, collect her
belongings, and make it back to the airport. Once there, she
immediately bought a one-way ticket to Miami. She was
exhausted, her head throbbed, and she felt a migraine coming

on. She briefly stopped by the small airport pharmacy and bought a packet of aspirin and a bottle of water, also purchasing a copy of *The Economist* which she rolled up and placed under her arm. Outside the pharmacy, she extracted three pills, popped them in her mouth, and took several large gulps of water.

She took a deep breath and reflected on her task, her current assignment. She had failed for the first time. It was the first time she had been unable to eliminate a target. Before the mere thought of failure would leave her feeling deflated and depressed, endlessly questioning her professionalism. But now, that she had *actually* failed, there were no such feelings. She was tired, yes. But sad? No. And the more she thought about it, the more she realised that she didn't care. It didn't bother her in the slightest. In some ways she felt free, like she had finally concluded that she didn't relish working for ideological zealots whose only plan was to gather more and more power while claiming to be the good guys.

She continued down the main passageway of the airport before reaching the end of the terminal, then looked up at the gate numbers to see 1A on one side and 2A on the other. *I've gone too far*, she thought. Her daydreams had made her miss her gate. *But at least I can wait in the area that the desk attendant mentioned*. She turned to check where she should go when she saw him standing looking out of the window, no more than twenty metres away from her.

His back was to her and she was glad she'd seen him before he saw her. He wore a dark business suit and just below the cuff on his left wrist she saw a flash of silver. When he placed his travel bag down beside him, an inscribed silver bracelet slid down his wrist. She held her breath, unable to take her eyes off him.

It's him. I know it's him.

An electric current seemed to pass through her and she felt

her blood coursing through her body, becoming hot. She had decided she didn't want to kill for a particular ideology, but it didn't mean that she didn't still have her personal vendettas to avenge. And he's right there for the taking. She could easily sidle up to him and poison him with aconitine. No one would realise it was her; she could be out of there and striding towards her gate to make her flight on time.

She walked towards the man, quickening her pace as she got closer. She reached inside her leather shoulder bag for the mascara case. Finally, she would get to use it. Her hand slid out of her shoulder bag with the smooth, cylindrical mascara case firmly in her hand. This time there would be no mistake. Three metres, two metres, and now she was directly behind him.

She grabbed his shoulder with her left hand, swivelling him around softly. She wanted to look him in the eyes as she killed him but didn't want to arouse any attention. The man turned and she moved her right arm towards him, hoping to puncture an area just above the belt line. The needle protruding from the mascara case was centimetres from his skin. And then...

As he faced her, his face revealed a mix of surprise and shock. If she could've looked into a mirror in that moment, her face would likely have registered a similar expression as she saw a stranger staring back at her. She'd never seen him before in her life. He was completely unknown. His shocked face turned to a smile, and he put his hand forward as if offering a handshake, his silver bracelet visible on his wrist as he asked, "Do I know you?" in Portuguese.

She couldn't speak.

He cocked his head sideways in a curious gesture.

Alina Calderón stepped back abruptly and shook her head, muttering, "*No, disculpe, disculpe.*"

Her thoughts were pounding in her head. *I already killed*

him, outside the SUV in the square, several hours ago. He's already dead. The man with the silver bracelet is already dead. Now face to face with the stranger, she realised it was only from behind he bore a striking resemblance to the Albanian mafia man that had groped her earlier that evening.

The man, eyes opened wide and with a worried look on his face now, spoke again in Portuguese. "*Sem problemas*. Are you okay?"

"*Sí, perdónme,*" replied Alina Calderón in Spanish as she shook her head, trying to dislodge the memory.

He smiled still and nodded in a slightly awkward manner. "There really is no issue at all."

Alina Calderón, the assassin, alias *Doña Bárbara*, managed to smile back. She looked up at him confidently and managed a slight smile, "It's just that you remind me of someone. He's no longer with us."

"Oh, I'm sorry," said the man, frowning slowly and looking sympathetic.

"Not to worry. It's better that way," replied Calderón as she turned and strolled to Gate 7A for her flight to Miami.

CHAPTER 41

*Humberto Delgado International Airport —
Lisbon, Portugal*

JARDINE ANSWERED THE CALL AND IMMEDIATELY
heard Felix's voice boom down the line. "Howdy."

"Hi," Jardine replied.

"I'm at the airport; where are y'all at?" Felix's unmistak-
able New Mexican drawl seemed to bounce through the
speaker and jump into Jardine's ear.

"Near Gate 3—big window with a view of the runway.
Want to make sure that plane gets off the ground. I can't relax
until I know it's in the sky and off into the night."

"Gotcha. I'll be there in two mins."

Jardine ended the call as he watched a plane barrelled
down the runway, lifting and disappearing into the dark night
sky. Only the red and green flashing lights on the wings were
visible until they too disappeared. A few moments later, Felix
arrived and sat down next to Veronica and Jardine. He was
carrying a small roller case and his arm was in a sling. He held a
takeaway cup of coffee in his sling hand.

"They fix you up?" asked Jardine.

"Yeah, they fixed me up real good. Just had to take the bullet out, patch 'er up and I gotta keep it in a sling for a week and then I'll be good to go. Lucky it hit all flesh, no artery or bone."

Felix sat down next to Jardine, and all three looked out at the runway.

"Where are you headed, Felix?" asked Veronica.

"*Estados Unidos*. Decided I'll return to New Mexico. This whole adventure made me realise I gotta sort these issues out. It's time I took back control of the ranch and sorted things out with the cartels." Felix smiled and sipped his coffee. "How about you two? How did it feel to be 'back in the saddle' so to speak?"

"It feels better that I'm now out of the saddle, actually," said Jardine. "I think the key is to *occasionally* get in the saddle and then get off when you've had enough adventure and want to return to normal. But that was one hell of a ride."

Felix again sipped his coffee. "It's in a man's nature, hell, maybe a woman's too,"—he looked at Veronica, smiled and continued—"to want excitement, something to strive for. That's what we're all looking for. Either that or you wind up disillusioned and start lashing out at the world and everyone in it. Then you start sending bombs in the mail, flying planes into skyscrapers or storming the Capitol building."

"Maybe there's a way to do both? Excitement and something to strive for as part of a normal life?" offered Jardine.

Felix nodded wisely and then looked down at the other man's hand. "I see you've got your phone back."

"Yeah, not sure if it's a good thing or if I'll fall into my bad habits."

"Is that the plane?" asked Veronica, pointing out to the runway now.

"That's it," replied Jardine. "At least it looks like one of the two I saw."

The three of them watched as the small private jet taxied out and lined up on the runway, preparing for take-off. They could just about hear the revving of the engine as it warmed up, gathering enough power to propel itself forward when Jardine felt his phone vibrate in his hand.

He glanced down quickly to see a *WhatsApp* message from Ambrose, quickly followed by another.

GOOD YOU'RE SAFE. USED OLD MI6 CONTACTS TO GET MESSAGES THROUGH TO PORTUGUESE AND SPANISH SECURITY FORCES.

AMBROSE

Jardine smiled. So, it *had* been Ambrose who'd arranged for the Portuguese authorities to help them. The smile slowly turned to a frown as he read the second message.

FYI — 2 VENEZ GOV OFFICIALS ARRIVED LISBON THIS MORN. ONE USED AN ALIAS PREVIOUSLY USED BY ALBERTO CASTILLAS, THE BASQUE BOMBER — WANTED BY SPANISH AUTHORITIES — WHO HAS BEEN WORKING SECURITY FOR THE VENEZUELAN MINISTRY OF AGRICULTURE.

AMBROSE

Jardine's heart sank and his stomach started to churn with acid. He looked to the runway as the private jet continued to rev its engine, about to take off. He opened his mouth to speak but nothing came out. The plane started moving now, gathering speed down the runway before finally launching and taking off into the sky.

"Safe at last," said Felix. Turning to both Jardine and Veronica and smiling, his moustache rising and his eyes twinkling. However, his smile disappeared when he saw Jardine's face, drained of colour, looking up from his phone.

"Everyone alright?" asked Felix.

Jardine didn't respond but peered out the window.

The plane rose higher and higher until only the red and green flashing lights of the wings were still visible, like a small Christmas tree. The lights continued to blink then stopped abruptly. A giant orange fireball erupted in the sky, engulfing the plane and lighting up the dark night with a flash of white followed by fiery bursts of orange and red.

"What the..." said Felix, standing and moving towards the large glass window, his mouth agape.

Other passengers sitting nearby jumped to their feet and ran to the window as screams of shock reverberated around the terminal. Some slid out their mobile phones and filmed as the giant fireball seemed to break into pieces, then dropped in large flaming chunks, smoking and smouldering as they fell.

"What the fuck? The general, he's... he's..." said Jardine, now managing to find some words.

"I don't believe it," said Veronica, tears forming in her eyes. "It can't be true."

Jardine stood still, his heart heavy and his throat itching. His whole body began to ache as they watched the carnage unfold.

A minute passed; nobody spoke. Jardine felt his phone vibrate in his hand. Another message from Ambrose, he assumed, only this time it kept vibrating. He glanced down at the screen. It was an incoming call from an unknown number.

He pressed the green answer button and lifted the receiver to his ear. He was silent at first and then answered cautiously. "Hello?"

CHAPTER 42

THE LINE CRACKLED AS A VOICE BROKE THROUGH the static. "Did you see what they did?"

Jardine stood still looking out the window. "General?"

"*Affirmativo.*"

A curious mix of relief washed over Jardine but tinged still with slight disbelief. "But we just watched your plane explode!"

The general sighed. "It was the decoy's plane, unfortunately. And those *hijueputas* blew it up!" His voice distorted as he yelled into the phone. Then more calmly he said, "You remember there were two planes attached to the air bridge."

"Yes," replied Jardine.

"My decoy and bodyguard went in the first plane, myself in the second. It's like when they say the president and the vice president should never travel together in case something happens."

Jardine stood silent still in disbelief, his hands shaking. He didn't know how to respond. "The decoy, he's...?'

"*Muerto*," said the general. "It's a tragedy; I never thought it would come to this. My bodyguard was on that plane also."

Jardine could hear rapid-fire Spanish in the background as the general's team—what was left of them—made calls, trying to find out what had happened.

The man continued. "It is now more important than ever that I speak at the UN. They will be the martyrs of the new free and fair Venezuela. Of course, Madera was behind this. We know that much."

Jardine continued gazing out the window. "I think I know specifically who it was. I have some information via Ambrose; I'll send it through to you. You should probably focus on your task, your speech at the UN."

"What is the information?"

"Alberto Castillas."

"*El Vasco*? I know him. He worked in security for the Bolivarian government. He's wanted in Spain on terrorism charges."

"I know, ex-members of ETA."

"*Un momento*," said the general.

Jardine could hear more conversation in the background, muffled voices speaking in Spanish. Then after a few moments, the general's voice returned.

"Our aircraft is now being checked that there is no explosive device and then we will take off ourselves. Do me a favour, will you?"

"Yes?"

"Take that information from Ambrose and leak it to the media. Let the Spanish media know it was Castillas and he was working for Madera. It's important the world knows who is responsible for this. I know it will be using their deaths for our agenda, but I don't want their deaths to be for nothing."

"Leave it with me. I'll work out something," replied

Jardine.

More muffled and panicked voices in Spanish burst down the line. Then the general's voice again. "I must go now. *Hasta pronto, amigo*. I'm sure our paths will cross again."

"*Hasta luego*, general," replied Jardine.

Thirty minutes later, Jardine, Veronica, and Felix watched as the second private jet taxied out onto the runway, powered up, and then took off into the right sky. This time there was no fireball or explosion only the flashing red wing lights becoming more distant until they faded into the night sky.

Alina Calderón saw a commotion of passengers running towards the large windows overlooking the airport runway. She heard screams and heard, "Explosion!" and "Oh my God!" being yelled in Portuguese, English, German and Spanish. She looked across as she saw various fiery flashes in the sky. She considered walking over to see what had happened, but she didn't care. She was over her previous life. Over killing for ideologues. Over political dramas. Over violence for violence's sake.

She remained slumped in her seat, staring at the ground. After a few moments, she rummaged in her backpack and took out a pair of noise-cancelling headphones. She lifted them to her ears and then withdrew her mobile phone. Instinctively her thumb hovered over the tracking app. I won't be needing that anymore, she thought as she pressed down and held the icon until it began to shake. Then she hit the small cross in the corner and deleted it.

She opened a music playlist of tracks she had liked from her university days and began to blast a song from Nirvana's *In Utero* album. As the song began, she closed her eyes and laid her head back against the headrest, while the commotion of the exploding aeroplane played out around her.

CHAPTER 43

PALACIO MIRAFLORES — CARACAS, VENEZUELA

SINDIOS CALVO, THE MAN KNOWN AS *EL PULPO*—THE Octopus—stormed into the president's office, appearing red-faced. It made his almost bald head look like a large bright tomato. "You mounted an operation without telling me?"

President Tomás Madera Toros lay back in his gold-leaf chair and smiled. "It seems your Albanians were not up to the task in the end. That's why *Comandante* Lazo and I," he motioned to the corner to the smiling, cigar smoking *Comandante* Lazo, who nodded and tipped his military cap, "launched Operation CIENFUEGOS. We mentioned it to the defence minister earlier in the week."

"Why wasn't I informed about this 'Operation CIENFUEGOS'?"

"It's what we did to Camilo C—" said *Comandante* Lazo.

"Well, you blew up the wrong fucking plane!" *El Pulpo* interrupted.

The president thrust his body forward from his slouched position, standing abruptly. "*Coño tu*—! What do you mean?"

"It's all over the news, the general's still alive. He's arrived in New York. *Los Yankees* are providing security for him from now on. There's no way we'll stop him!"

The president slammed his fist on the desk and slumped into his chair once again. "Lazo?"

The Cuban hurried towards the president.

"Is there nothing we can do? Exploding pen? Poison dart from a cigar? Novichok in his toothpaste?" asked President Tomás Madera Toros.

Comandante Lazo frowned and shook his head. "Too late, *mi presidente*. We no longer have the reach we did in *Gringolandia*."

The president fumbled on his desk for a remote control, eventually finding it. He switched on a large flatscreen TV on the wall and shouted for his assistant. Still holding the control, he waved it frantically in front of *El Pulpo*. "This is all your fault, Octopus. I'll be making some readjustments to my cabinet, and you might find yourself out in the cold."

"My fault? *Qué rayos...*" The Octopus abruptly stopped speaking and stared down at the floor, shuffling his feet before saying, "I'm sorry, *Presidente*."

The president still fumbled with the remote control to the flatscreen. "I thought this was a bloody smart TV. How do we watch a fucking speech at the UN?" He hit several buttons on the control and the flatscreen flashed and changed to *CNN En Español*.

On-screen, a journalist stood on a rooftop, the outline of Lisbon behind her as she spoke. "We have reports just in that wanted ETA terrorist Alberto Castillas has been apprehended in Lisbon and is being charged with planting a bomb on a private jet which exploded overnight in the Portuguese capital. A source from British Intelligence confirmed that Castillas, working with a Venezuelan national, and under direction from the president, Tomás Madera Toros, planted the bomb while attempting the assassinate the dissident, General Angel Fernando Pereira Gallegos. Now in custody, it is likely that Castillas' testimony will be added to a string of human rights violations committed under the Madera regime and along with a constitutional crisis, it will call into question the legitimacy of the current government and its standing in the international community."

"Mierda," said the president, as he looked down at the remote control again. "The fucking UN speeches! I want to watch the livestream of the U-fucking-N, *carajo!*"

An assistant finally appeared and scurried forward with his hand outstretched. Once he received the remote control, he tapped a series of buttons arriving at the UN *YouTube* channel broadcasting all the UN speeches. The candidate for Uzbekistan was finishing his speech while a banner across the bottom of the screen read: *The next speech will be from the member for the exiled Venezuelan Community*.

"*Que coño pasa?*" screamed President Madera, slamming his fist again on the desk like a spoiled child.

Comandante Lazo took off his military cap and scrunched it up in his hands, seething with rage. He took the large cigar from his mouth and thought about throwing it on the ground to show his dismay but decided instead to take a long, thoughtful drag.

On the screen, a UN employee strode on stage and adjusted a microphone at the podium, and then the cameras cut to a side door opening as the dissident General Angel Fernando Pereira Gallegos stepped out to a roaring applause from the delegations. He stepped up to the podium and smiled and waved to the cheering assembly, then shuffled several pieces of A4 paper, took a sip of water and cleared his throat, ready to speak.

CHAPTER 44

United Nations General Assembly — New York, the United States of America

"Your Excellency, General Secretary Antonio Guterres, honourable representatives, *queridos compatriotas* from Venezuela, a good day to you all." The general's eyes cast around the room, taking a moment to lock eyes with individual audience members.

"I address you today, not as a president of Venezuela, not as a politician, and not as a member of the Venezuelan Armed Forces. Yes, I *was* a general. Now I am retired, an ex-general of the *República de Venezuela*. Now a civilian, a regular citizen. A dissident citizen, in fact, of a country that I love dearly. Although I may not hold authority in any official capacity, it is hoped that my words will speak for those millions of Venezuelans that have been forced to leave their country as it crumbles economically, politically, and lastly, socially. It is estimated that five to six million such citizens, *los compatriotas mios*, as I will call them, have fled.

As much as I'm speaking *for* those exiled Venezuelans who

can no longer live in their *patria*, I am also speaking out *against* a dictatorial regime with links to drug trafficking. A regime that has committed serious violations of human rights, with 18,093 extrajudicial executions, 15,501 cases of arrest and arbitrary detention, 724 forced disappearances, and 653 documented cases of torture. All of this under the regime led by the current President Tomás Madera Toros, has corrupted and manipulated the judicial, executive, and legislative branches of government to fulfil and continue their illegitimate hold on power. An illegitimate hold on power that has been perpetuated and consolidated with foreign influence from Cuba, Russia, and Iran, among others. Countries, who have sought to influence and project their own power onto the sovereignty of Venezuela, through the illegal siphoning of government funds and the exploitation of the valuable natural resources of our great nation. Here," he raised his hand holding a manila folder, "is proof of this corruption and the illegal network of not only natural resources but also illegal narcotics which have been financing this regime and their international support. Not only that, but I can prove that the current cabinet of the Madera regime, even members of his own family, are involved in this scheme, in direct contradiction to UN sanctions."

In this moment, the whole UN caucus let out a gasp of shock followed by a rumbling murmur which radiated through the auditorium. The general waited for the noise to die down before continuing.

"It is not my place to judge this information and be the judge, jury, and executioner. No, *señores*. It is simply my duty to present this information to the world and let the correct and proper authorities deal with its contents and repercussions. However, *it is* my duty to bring light to the situation that is now occurring in Venezuela. It is a situation that first began when..."

He continued, systemically conveying the events that had

led to his country's downfall, focussing on his experience in the military and how it had been integrated into Madera's power structure before leading into the second revealing piece of information he held.

"It is this integration of the military into the government that has led to a particular nationalistic fervour which has been escalating year on year. In fact, it has escalated so much that here," he held up another folder, "I hold plans for an invasion of the Essequibo region of Guyana. For hundreds of years, successive Venezuelan governments have wanted to take control of this province considered to be lost Venezuelan territory. Now I have proof that the Madera government and its *Fuerzas Armadas* are planning to take it back by force. This aggression and lack of care for due process is well known by the people of Venezuela with regard to this regime and I believe it is vital the world is made aware of these intentions."

There was no cheer this time but a rumbling of chatter amongst the delegates as the general stopped briefly, taking a deep breath before his final words.

"I will reiterate. I am here not as a general, not as a military man, but as a concerned and patriotic citizen of my country. A dissident, if you will. I call on the international community to listen to me, to examine the evidence I have collected and, if judged correctly, to condemn the corrupt dictatorial regime of Tomás Madera Toros. I call for United Nations intervention in the state of Venezuela so that free and fair elections can be held. This, I hope, will lead to a sustainable form of democratic government which it is hoped, will bring lasting peace to our country, our *patria querida*. I am happy and content—as are my family—that it did not take my death to bring about this change. As many of you here today are aware that there were several attempts on my life since I escaped Venezuela. And we should also remember the names of Diego Pérez Zamora, my bodyguard, and Eduardo Orozco, my decoy. They sacrificed their lives, putting themselves in harm's way for the future of Venezuela. So, I dedicate this speech to their lives and sacrifice. I am very grateful and honoured to have had the opportunity to speak here today in front of you. And in that vein, let my words be heard around the world so that you, the intentional community, can help to restore democracy and rule of law in Venezuela. Your Excellency, General Secretary Antonio Guterres, honourable representatives, *queridos compatriotas* from Venezuela, I thank you for your time and hope you will see the evidence for what it is and bring about just change in Venezuela. Thank you and *gracias*."

The room burst into applause with a standing ovation as the general bowed slightly before being escorted off the stage and into a secure room.

CHAPTER 45

HOTEL CASA BOSQUE — GRANADA, SPAIN

THE APPLAUSE CONTINUED TO ERUPT OUT OF THE tinny speaker of the iPad that Oliver Jardine held in front of him while lying in a hammock outside on his terrace. On the screen, the general bowed slightly and then held his hands together up in front of him in a gesture of peace. He hovered there for thirty seconds before the clapping died down and he slid off to the side and the next speaker approached the podium. Jardine put the iPad down under the hammock and lay back looking up through a gap in the vines above his terrace and into the blue sky. Veronica leant over and kissed his cheek.

"He finally got there," she said.

"That he did," he replied, still staring up at the sky.

"Would you like a drink?" she asked, rising to her feet.

"Yes, a coffee would be great, thanks, Vero."

Veronica Velasco retreated and strolled to the kitchen.

He continued staring up into the sky and then sat up in the hammock and looked around him. He smiled to himself and then reached for the acoustic guitar he had laid down next to the hammock. He strummed a few chords with no particular pattern or structure in mind while looking out over the Sierra Nevada mountains. A soft squeak of car brakes sounded, and Jardine strained his neck trying to look at the driveway. He half expected it to be Lieutenant Muñoz poking his head in and blaming them for the latest crime wave. But he was surprised when he saw Ronald Ambrose, former head of station for MI6 in Colombia, now an amateur olive grower and part-time arranger for wrongly accused fugitives, scramble out of his SEAT Leon and wave.

"Do you always turn up unannounced?" he shouted as Ambrose approached, his feet crunching under the gravel before he arrived at the paved terrace and sat on a wooden deck chair.

He leaned forward, resting his elbows on his knees. "Isn't this a delightful hippy scene. You, in a hammock with a guitar. Thought I was the one who experienced the seventies."

Jardine raised his middle finger to Ambrose and then asked, "Business or pleasure?"

"A little of both," he said.

"I thought you were retired?"

"I told you back in Colombia that I'd try to be involved in a small project or two, if I could. Besides, I helped you out, didn't I?"

"That you did. Thanks for that," said Jardine, imitating a soldier's salute.

"So, what is it?"

Ambrose turned his head out and looked at the view of the hills before them. "I think it's best to tell you over a glass of red."

"Yeah, all right. Stay for dinner?"

"That'd be great."

"But you can't leave me hanging like that! I can't hold out if you've got some juicy information for me."

Ambrose sighed. "The impatience of youth."

"So?" said Jardine, glancing at the guitar's fretboard as he strummed.

"You remember the defector Jin Hong-Soo?"

"Yeah," he stopped strumming and looked at Ambrose now. "Low-level bureaucrat with the North Korean government gave us, the Yanks, and the South Koreans some intel about the inner workings of the government there."

"Yes, well turns out he wasn't so low-level."

"How so?"

"I can't really divulge too much information here, but I've been asked to see if you wouldn't mind popping over to South Korea to help them out."

"Don't they know I'm no longer in the Service?"

"Oh, they know, all right."

"Then?"

"Well, this chap, Hong-Soo. He's asked specifically for you."

"For *me*?" said Jardine, trying to sit up in the hammock.

"That's right. Says he has some intel that'll change the course of history and only wants to speak to you."

"Why me?"

Ambrose shrugged. "How the bloody hell should I know?! I'm just the messenger. I guess he just likes you, that's all."

ACKNOWLEDGMENTS

The germ of an idea for this book occurred to me back in 2011 while crossing the border from Colombia into Venezuela. I wasn't going far into the country, just to the nearest town (San Antonio) to have my Colombian work visa approved. Speaking to locals around the empanada cart in the town square, many told stories of relatives that had already left the country. In Bogotá at the time, I knew many Venezuelans who had fled for brighter opportunities abroad. Some were my students at the university where I taught. Later, as the situation in the country worsened, millions more would flee, turning it into the largest recorded refugee crisis in the Americas. Then, in 2017, large protests erupted onto the streets of Caracas as a constitutional crisis engulfed the country. Key members of the government, the military, the police, and other prominent state institutions began to voice their concern about the current regime in power, leading to a further crackdown on dissent, forcing many to flee abroad, often secretly. It was at this moment that I thought back to that border region as I read stories of dissidents crossing the border by foot at night or bouncing across the seas in speedboats to Aruba or Trinidad. Stories that, while covered in some news outlets, were largely unknown to the wider population. This led me to begin the story: *The General of Caracas*. And while I don't speak for Venezuelans or have any skin in the game, so to speak, I hope that in some small way, this story might draw attention to what has happened in Venezuela since the early 2000s.

With that in mind, I'd like to thank all of those Venezuelans who have helped me, guided me, and been the recipients of random questions thrown at them. For one reason or another, they won't be named (many requested not to be named), but you know who you are. *Muchísimas gracias por su ayuda y apoyo.*

On the writing side, thanks to Mary Torjussen, the wonderful editor, who was patient and made the book sparkle. Likewise, thanks to Jericho Writers for your support and guidance and wealth of knowledge. Thanks also to Kate Noble of Noble Owl Proofreading for your thorough final check.

Thanks to my parents for reading (and proofreading) an early draft. Also thanks to a small sling of beta readers who gave their thoughts and advice. In particular, thanks to Richard McColl, FE Beyer, and Lance Karlson for reading an early version of the manuscript.

And finally, thanks to my wife, Mónica, for all your love and support. (Also thanks for laughing at the funny parts in the book, even when you didn't know I was listening.)

L.P. 2022

ABOUT THE AUTHOR

Lachlan Page has lived in Colombia, South Korea, Europe, and Nicaragua. He has worked as: a volcano hiking guide, a red cross volunteer, a marketing analyst, a language teacher, a university lecturer, and an extra in a Russian TV series (in Panama).

THE GENERAL OF CARACAS is his second novel. His first was *MAGICAL DISINFORMATION*.

Visit www.LachlanPageAuthor.com to sign up for news, my blog, and much more.

facebook.com/LachlanPageAuthor

twitter.com/donlachlan

instagram.com/donlachlan

ALSO BY LACHLAN PAGE

Oliver Jardine Series

Magical Disinformation (Book 1)

———

Praise for '*Magical Disinformation*'

"Our Man in Havana meets A Clear and Present Danger" — ***ARC Book Reviewer***

"A slyly comedic thriller with a good amount of action, suspense and fantastical story on events in Colombia." — ***ARC Book Reviewer***

"Imagine a work of fiction set in Colombia where the line between real and unreal, fact and fiction no longer exists...Think Waugh, think Greene and then a smattering of de Bernieres and you know what you're in for, a romp of a read which brings a smile to your lips as you enjoy this fast moving tragicomedy." — ***Richard McColl, Colombia Calling Podcast***

"Forced to choose between a career transfer and love, a spy attempts both by adding imagination to his intelligence reports. With satire and Marquez-esque imagery, Page evokes the colourful experiences of expats in Colombia, bureaucratic hypocrisy and the ease of deception in the age of fake news." — ***Lance Karlson, Author of THE NORIEGA TAPES***